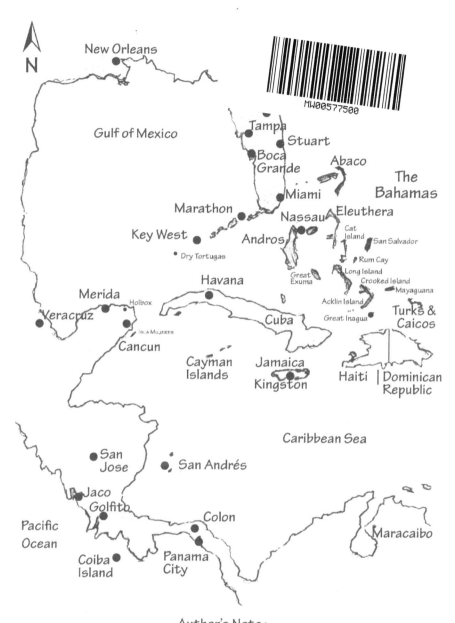

Author's Note :
You might consider tracking the plot with
Google Earth to enhance your reading experience.

Providenciales

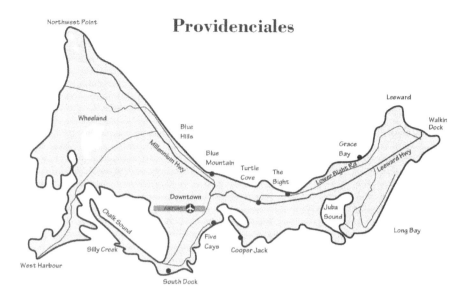

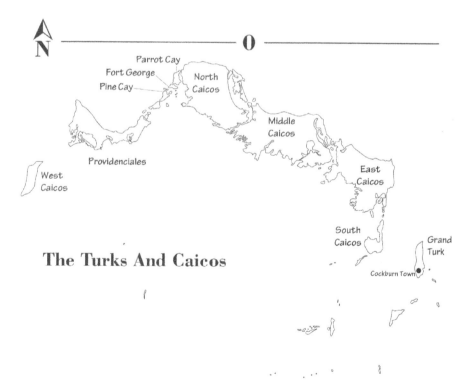

The Turks And Caicos

CAICOS CONSPIRACY

BY

National Award Winning Author

WILLIAM VALENTINE

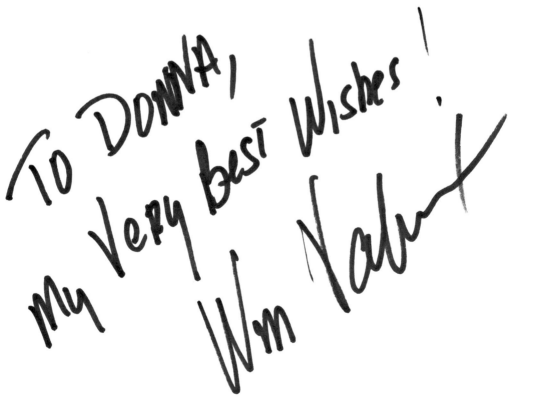

To Donna,
My Very best Wishes!
Wm Valentine

Cover Design by Kat Klingerman
Cover Photo under Shutterstock license

ISBN: 978-09894754-4-0

OTHER NOVELS — by William Valentine

SALT CREEK JUSTICE ......

Winner - 2014 - NEXT GENERATION INDIE BOOK AWARDS — **First Place** — REGIONAL FICTION

Winner - 2014 - INDIE EXCELLENCE BOOK AWARDS — **First Place** — CRIME FICTION

INDIE BOOK OF THE DAY — MARCH 13th, 2014

COSTA RICAN REPRISE ......

Finalist -2016 - NEXT GENERATION INDIE BOOK AWARDS — ACTION-ADVENTURE

Finalist - 2016 - INDIE EXCELLENCE BOOK AWARDS — CRIME FICTION

DEDICATION

To the good people of the Turks and Caicos Islands who toil every day to make it what it is: The dive boat owners, the rental car operators, the restauranteurs, the charter fishing captains and mates, the bartenders, the waiters and waitresses, the hotel and resort owners, the bellmen and maids, the musicians, the croupiers, the real estate and rental agents, the marina crews, the bar entrepreneurs, the cab drivers, the service suppliers and technicians, the watersport hosts, the gift shop and boutique staffs, the IGA's, the contractors and their suppliers, the car dealers, the Junkanoo dancers, the bonefish guides, the spa teams, the airport personnel, Customs and Immigration, the power and water companies, the hospital doctors and staff, the Wine Cellar, the Port Authority, the Police, the massage therapists, and last - but certainly not least — the lawyers and politicians.

And, of course ...... *Slim!*

THANK-YOU

TO my crack crew of eagle-eyed editors who kept me on track: Andy Arnold, Bob Astley, James Byrne, Marshall Craig, Frank Cooper, Debbie Hayden, Dean Karikas, Lee and Page Obenshain, Harvey and Pat Partridge, and G. Louise ...... **Also** to all my fishing and hunting buddies *(you know who you are),* who I have traveled with half-way around the world in small planes and boats. **And** to all my readers and reviewers.

Foreword

Potcake dogs are referred to throughout this novel. Wikipedia defines them as, "A mixed-breed dog found on several Caribbean islands". Their name comes from the congealed peas and rice mixture at the bottom of the family cooking pot that local residents traditionally fed dogs. In Nassau alone, there are an estimated 5,000 – 8,000 stray potcakes. The Turks and Caicos Islands have spay-and-neuter programs, adoption agencies, and unfortunately, have euthanized the resilient potcakes to reduce their numbers. Rescue programs featuring free air delivery exist in TCI, the Bahamas, Puerto Rico, and St. Croix.

CHAPTER ONE

Morton "Jock" Baffert sat on the veranda of his Blue Mountain house looking east over Turtle Cove and Grace Bay. Outside the reef, the persistent trade winds swept the dark blue Atlantic Ocean with whitecaps and streaks of foam. Jock chilled over his second ice cold Turk's Head Lager and wondered which of the island's watering holes his wife was patronizing that night. The girls on this island were known to tip a few toddies after their committee meetings, and Providenciales had a wide array of choices. Many of those bars overlooked the reef-ringed oceanfront, some were on the secluded back bays, and others viewed the picturesque interior lagoons. Jock never begrudged "Kat" her time with her charitable friends. She was always rushing to this event or that, but still managed to run Provo's most successful construction equipment rental business. He had been home since 6:00 p.m. after a busy two-trip day at his dive business. All three of his boats had been full, and he was booked up well into next month. They were busy with the early summer kids and families, just out of school from the States. Kat usually left him a text message or gave him a call if she was going to miss dinner. Jock checked his recent calls and messages again, but there was nothing from her. It wasn't like her not to give him a heads-up. He made himself a sandwich, popped open another cold one, and settled back in on the veranda. The weather forecast predicted the brisk trade winds would knock down from 20 knots to about 15 tomorrow. The constant breeze cooled the temperatures down, but the island's dive operators would welcome a respite from the wind. Jock phoned the rental business just in case she was tied up there but only got the recorded business hours message. He thought fleetingly about his son Jordan who was somewhere in the Atlantic, sailing from Brazil to Miami with Paul Cayard on the third leg of the Volvo Challenge … and his daughter Megan, who was finishing up her psychology master's degree at Florida State this summer. He looked at his watch again and thought *if I don't hear from her by 8:30 … I'll call a couple of her girlfriends.*

CAICOS CONSPIRACY

Jock watched the sun set in the west at 7:30. He paced back and forth on the veranda as darkness fell. At 8:15 his cellphone vibrated and rang.

"There's the old girl now," said a smiling Jock to no one … as he pulled his brand new iPhone from his pocket. He tapped answer, but there was no caller I.D. on the screen. He frowned and said, "Kat?"

A computer generated voice quickly said, "Mr. Baffert, don't panic, your wife Katherine is OK. She is in our custody, and we have not harmed her in any way. I represent a group of businessmen who are interested in your Grace Bay beach property. We have a client who is interested in buying the six residential acres you own down in The Bight area. My client has made you three different offers over the past two years through different agents. He came to me to make a fourth offer, and I told him I could get you to sell. He does not know that we have your wife, and there's no reason he ever has to know. I have guaranteed him you will take his offer of eight million dollars for the six acres. I will earn a generous commission from this client. You will be eight million dollars richer and get your wife back unharmed when the deal is closed."

"Whoa …wait one minute, whoever you are. Put Kat on the phone right now before you go any further, I want to hear her voice."

"Of course, but remember … I am running this show. She can live or disappear in eight thousand feet of water. It's your choice."

Jock heard some rustling at the other end of the line and then Kat said unsteadily, "I'm all right Jock. They have a woman looking after me, but I'm scared. Do what they say, it's only money."

The computer voice returned, "My client is prepared to pay cash so we can close in three days with just a title search and survey. He will be back in Provo in five days. I will contact you directly in a day or two, to tell you where and when on Tuesday. Until then, you are to tell anyone who needs to know that your wife is in Miami to greet your son's sailboat when he arrives there at the end of the Volvo Challenge Race from Rio."

"You know about the race?" asked Jock warily.

"I know a lot about your family, Mr. Baffert, and it's not like we're stealing from you. Eight million dollars, with no realtor commission, is more than a fair price for that piece of property."

2

"I wanted to wait until I could get it zoned commercial. It would be worth two or three times what it is now."

"Who knows what the future will bring, Mr. Baffert," said the annoying computer voice. "I can only guarantee you millions and a healthy family. Now listen carefully — if you contact the authorities or anyone else — or decide not to go through with this deal legitimately — your wife will disappear, and you will be next, right away or any time after the fact. Rest assured, I will be the second person to know if you choose to reveal our bargain to anyone. Do you understand?"

"I do … I don't see where I have any choice. I will act normally, but I do have some friends on the way down here in their sportfish to fish in the Caicos Classic Billfish Tournament. They're coming all the way from Florida. I'll have to socialize with them a bit."

"Just act normally and stick to the Miami story."

"I'll do it, but if my wife's harmed in any way, I promise I will hunt you down!"

"I'll keep my part of the bargain. Don't bother to try and trace my calls; I'm speaking on a stolen prepaid cell phone. My people are watching you right now. Your wife's Land Rover is in the Las Brisas restaurant's parking lot, the keys are behind the sun visor, the coil wire is off the cap, and her purse and cell phone are under the back seat. Your lawyer will hear from my client's property lawyers next, so call him and make it happen. Good night, Jock."

Jock sat down and stared out into the darkness and caught his breath. *Well … Fuck Me! My wife's kidnapped, and I seem to be shit out of luck. I can't call the cops, tell my lawyer or anybody. My lawyer is going to wonder why I'm selling now … It's a good thing it's still in my name only — I've got to get Kat back, but it frosts my ass to give the beach property away after all these years. I don't dare call this person's bluff … hell, the crooked government here might be behind the whole thing. This joker could have connections all the way to the top.*

He thought through the pros and cons and finally decided to call his old friend Seth Stone on his sat-phone. Jock had made plans to fly up to San Salvador in a day or two, whenever Seth got there in his Hatteras 46,

TAR BABY, and fish with Seth and his crew in San Sal and Rum Cay. Then they'd fish down past Samana Cay, the Plana Cays, and Mayaguana before heading for Provo. He rooted around in the top drawer of his home office desk, found Seth's sat-phone number in his address book and dialed it on his iPhone.

"Hello."

"Hey Seth, it's Jock."

"Are you checking up on me, buddy? We left Nassau running 24 knots this morning and came through the ship's channel into Exuma Sound. We saw a nuclear submarine surface and go over the underwater rock bridge between Eleuthera and Little San Sal Island. The water is 4000-feet deep on both sides of the mile-wide by eleven-mile long bridge, but it's only 25 to 60-feet deep over the top. You don't realize how big one of those fuckers really is until you're near one of them. The sub was over 500 feet long, had a 42-foot beam, and a 35-foot draft. We're slowly moving past Cat Island right now. We came off of a plane at dusk and started chugging. The wind has laid down up here so we'll stand watches, monitor the AIS, and chug all night. We should be close to San Salvador in the morning. We're looking forward to seeing you."

"Are you steering right now, Seth?"

"I've got her on autopilot."

"Well, give her to Gene or somebody and sit down someplace private. I've had a change of plans."

Seth came back on the phone, and Jock proceeded to fill him in on the whole situation, blow by blow. Ten minutes later Seth had a pretty good handle on Jock's predicament, but he had loads of questions.

"Do you want us just to go into San Sal, and come in after you've sold the property and gotten Kat back safely, or do you want us to run down to Provo tomorrow and try to help you? You did say you told the kidnapper you were expecting us, right?"

"Yeah, even if we can't find a way to thwart this whole thing, I would feel better if you were here with me, Seth. I might crack up and do something stupid if I'm alone."

"Well, you already know Gene Johnson, my retired St. Petersburg detective buddy, and John Harvey, my dermatologist friend … they're aboard. I also brought Dino Vinocelli and Fred Buckley along. "Dino Vino" is especially anxious to meet you. He's got a dive business in Key Largo and wants to run a trip to Provo every year. He also has a Black Belt in karate and saved my ass down in Key West a few years ago. Freddy's hobbies are Judo and survival sailing."

"Sounds like a lot of brain and manpower. I can use all the help I can get, as long as you guys can keep a low profile. I'm not going to get any help here."

"People have a hard time believing what these harmless-looking old guys can accomplish. We'll be discreet and see if we can figure something out. I'll prep them up tonight if you want."

"Bring it on! Call me when you get to Turtle Cove Marina."

"I'll call and change my reservations while I'm fueling up tomorrow morning. If the wind continues to lay down and I can run 24 knots, we should get in sometime late tomorrow. Hang in there, Jock."

"I will … I'm going to call a cab and go pick up Kat's Land Rover at Las Brisas when we're finished talking; then I'll try and get some rest."

"Put it in your garage and touch as little inside or outside as possible. We'll let Gene go over it when we get there. You never know what he might see that we don't. See you tomorrow."

"Thanks, Seth."

Jock had told Seth the whole story so far. How buyers had approached him for years. The Bight property was to be Jock's big hit. He had put his pro football signing money into it many years ago and felt he could enjoy the money it could bring and still leave a 20 or 30 million dollar legacy for his family. Losing Kat was not an option, but it had never been in his nature to let someone beat him down or give up anything easily. His dive business was thriving, and Kat's rental equipment operation had tripled over the past ten years. Sometime in the next five years, he figured the zoning at the east end of Grace Bay would change from residential to commercial, especially if a politician bought any beach property in The Bight area. Jock figured he would check the property records, when he had Kat back, just to see who might be behind all this. Americans, Russians, Europeans, British, Canadians, and even Chinese investors were pouring investment money into the Turks and Caicos. The absence of income and property taxes had made it a financial haven.

Seth gathered his crew together on the flybridge and explained the situation. All four agreed they would help Jock in any way they could.

"We'll have to be careful when we get there. I know the high dollar real estate business is cut-throat, but this outfit must call itself, "**Take No Prisoners Realty Inc.**"... This takes negotiating to a new level. Seriously, we can't let on in any manner that we know anything about Kat's kidnapping. I mean, these guys are playing for keeps. Gene, will you review all I've just told you, and apply your police training to possible ways of locating Kat? If they haven't moved her off the island, we're only dealing with 37 square miles. It's our only upside — that, and Jock hearing her voice, so we know she's still alive."

"The fact is, a group of small isolated islands is definitely a plus," said Gene. "It limits the possibilities."

"The biggest downside, according to Jock, is the political situation which has developed on the island. There is a climate of fear perpetuated by the government, along with corruption and patronage from top to bottom. We can't trust the police."

"When we get there, we'll put together what we know. Like we know they took her from the parking lot at a restaurant. Maybe we can ask some questions there about that period of time from a different perspective and find some useful information," said Gene.

Seth refigured his course and fuel usage, then steered a more southerly heading. They would skip San Salvador, and motor past Conception Island and Rum Cay. Then make the run down Long Island to the Flying Fish Marina in Clarence Town to fuel up. From there they'd pass by Mayaguana Island, then head over to Providenciales.

Seth and Gene handed *TAR BABY* over to Freddy and John and went below to get some sleep. Seth tossed and turned in his bunk and thought about the change of events. Jock Baffert played football at the University of Virginia with Seth and Bobby Thompson. Jock was a Florida boy, an all-state tackle out of Edison High School in Miami. Jock was six foot five and played at 250 pounds. The three of them became fast friends during those four years. After graduation, Jock was drafted and played for three years with the Baltimore Colts before a shoulder injury cut his career short. Jock went back to Miami and joined his father's residential construction company. He worked in every facet of the home building business while building subdivisions in Miami, Homestead, and the Upper Keys. Jock's passion became scuba diving and spearfishing. During the building recession in the early 80's, his dad bid and won a contract to build an upscale subdivision on Providenciales. Provo was starting into its second phase of development. At that time, there was little civilization in the Turks and Caicos beyond Cockburn Town on Grand Turk Island, where the government is located. The original developer built an airstrip on Provo and used the beachhead and natural harbor at South Beach to offload building materials from barges. There were a few small hotels in Turtle Cove and Grace Bay, and a Club Med opened on the eastern end of the island. Seth reconnected with Jock three years before at their 35th class reunion at Virginia honoring the seniors on the team that won the Liberty Bowl. It was a big deal in those days when there were only ten bowl games. Seth flew down the next summer to fish with Jock and Bobby Thompson in the Caicos Classic. Jock still weighed about 250 pounds, and the daily dives had kept him in good shape. Seth liked the island immediately. Each year there was more demand for retirement homes from Americans and Europeans. What fueled the demand was the British protectorate's ideal climate, unspoiled beaches, and tax advantages. The Turks and Caicos were finally shedding its stepchild existence as a part-time salt source for the new world and was blossoming into a vacation paradise attracting millionaires, entertainers, movie stars, and wealthy vacationers from all over the world.

Jock was sent off to manage the project, bringing a couple of Baffert Construction foremen and craftsmen with him. They headquartered down in Turtle Cove at the west end of Grace Bay. With some difficulty and through perseverance, Baffert Construction mastered the logistics, local labor issues, political nuances, and countless other hurdles. They survived a couple of hurricanes and finished the project in four years. Jock made the company a tidy profit. The bad news for his father was — Jock had fallen in love with the island and the unparalleled diving on the West Caicos' wall, French Cay, Northwest Point, and actually anywhere around the islands' extensive barrier reef. He also caught marlin fever fishing the 1000 foot drop-off, less than a mile offshore, on the leeward side of Provo. The marlin migrated past the islands in the spring and summer. The lee of the island provided about 40 square miles of comfortable fishing in 20-25 knots of wind within five miles of the lee shore. There wasn't anything like it in the entire Caribbean.

Jock ceded his share of the family's construction business to his younger brother Roscoe and turned his work boots in for a pair of flip-flops. He saw the tourist potential for Provo and invested his NFL signing bonus in a parcel of waterfront land along the western end of Grace Bay and Turtle Cove. His father gave him the waterfront construction yard and office on Turtle Cove as a bonus. He built a house on Blue Mountain and started a scuba-diving business, called Turtle Divers. Jock met a vivacious English girl the year before, who swept him off his feet. Her family owned the island's equipment rental business. Kat loved to fish and dive and was the lusty companion Jock had always envisioned. She was close to six feet tall, voluptuously built, with an appetite for everything that Jock liked. They married a couple of years later. In the meantime, a marina had been dredged out in Turtle Cove, and a few more luxury hotels went up along Grace Bay. A new tourist-friendly downtown sprang up in the Grace Bay area. Provo now had a championship 18 hole golf course, lined with vacation houses and townhomes. Two casinos sprung up near the hotels. The Provo airport had been upgraded from a few regularly scheduled flights to and from Freeport, Nassau, and Puerto Rico, to 737's bringing planeloads of tourists in daily from Canada and the United States. There was talk of extending both ends of the runway to accommodate the jumbo jets that were servicing other popular tourist destinations in the Caribbean. A ferry service and a jumper flight ran daily from Provo to Grand Turk Island, where a cruise ship dock now existed. There were plans for a mega-yacht marina at the east end of Grace Bay in the Leeward-Going-Through passage between Provo and Little Water Cay. Next to it was Walkin Dock, a second container port that was busy unloading gourmet food and drink, cars, trucks, and building supplies. Now there were scores of upscale four and five-star restaurants, bistros, beach bars, quaint watering holes, and native conch eateries. There seemed to be no end in sight for Provo's tourist explosion.

***

When Jock returned from retrieving Kat's SUV, he looked for her calendar in the kitchen office alcove and found it in the top desk drawer. He noted some upcoming meetings and jotted down the chairwomen's names and numbers. He would call them tomorrow morning, but his first call would be to Cecil Goforth, Kat's office manager at the rental business. None of them would be surprised by the sudden Miami trip because she was the kind of mother who put her kids first. Jock did not look through Kat's purse or touch anything but the steering wheel and keys. He had taken a pair of latex gloves from his workshop in the garage and put them on after the cab driver left him at Las Brisas. The car and purse were ready for Gene Johnson's inspection. He would go into work tomorrow and run one of the dive trips just to try and keep his mind occupied. Otherwise, he might go nuts. He hoped Seth and his crew would make it to Provo before dark tomorrow. He knew if they didn't, Seth would radio "Crazy George", Provo's answer to Boat U.S., to come out in his skiff and lead him through the treacherous reef opening and poorly marked Turtle Cove channel. Jock threw back two shot glasses full of brandy and headed for the bedroom. His last thought, as he fell into bed mentally exhausted, was his love for Kat.

***

9

CAICOS CONSPIRACY

Kat found herself confined in an air conditioned room, lying on a soft bed that smelled of laundry soap. She thanked God she was still alive and for the clean bed. They cuffed her hands behind her back and her ankles with a foot of chain between them. She was blindfolded and had a cloth gag in her mouth. The woman who was tending her came close and asked, in a thick Spanish accent, if she needed to use the *baños* or was thirsty. Kat shook her head *no*, and murmured through the gag, "But, *gracias*". The woman reeked of the cheap orange blossom perfume the island's Dominican hookers and strippers seemed to favor. Kat couldn't hear any conversations outside the room, but she could hear people coming and going through doors, and the sounds of cars coming and going. She could hear the surf breaking close by and the wind whistling through palm trees. Her abductors must have her purse.

Everything had happened so fast after she left her lunch with Marissa and Margaret at Las Brisas. Her two friends arrived in Marissa's two-seater and valet parked. They waved when they left while Kat walked further out in the crowded parking lot to her new Land Rover. Paying $10 to park anywhere on this little island was against her principals. She got in and turned the key. The big SUV's engine turned over but would not start. Kat started to perspire so she got out, pulled her business cell phone from her purse, and started to look for Mac Motor's number. They could come and get the Rover and drop her off at her office. She heard the door to the white van parked next to her slide open. As she started to turn her head, everything went dark. Two strong men grabbed her after pulling a burlap sack over her head. She was startled and tried to scream, but nothing came out. They wrestled her into the back of their van, and the door slid shut with a bang. One of her attackers said in a thick Spanish accent, "If you scream or keep struggling, I'll hurt you right now! If you stop, I won't."

The whole thing took about ten seconds. She had no chance to pull out the pepper spray or the Cobra Derringer she kept in her purse. They cuffed her and gagged her through the burlap. She heard the doors to the Rover slam and then they started out of the parking lot in the van. She remembered that both her kidnappers smelled of body odor and cigarette smoke. They listened to a Spanish-speaking radio station on the short ride

10

to her present destination. The music was mariachi sounding. She was sure she was still in the Chalk Sound area, as they were on the road no more than ten minutes.

Kat really did have to pee, but she was sure when the matron pulled down her stretch jeans that she'd find the iPhone in her back pocket. The smelly kidnapper named José, who patted her down, had missed it. She guessed they got careless because they got her business flip-phone right off. More probable, it was because he'd spent more time feeling her up than patting her down. When they first brought her into the house, the boss said in guttural English, "Freesk her, José."

"*Gracias, Jefe*!" said the one called José with a laugh.

Kat was wearing stretch jeans with an overblouse, a bra, and t-back thong panties. Her long blond hair hung to her shoulders. Jock had bought Kat, Jordon, and Megan iPhones in Miami when they first came out in January.

They stood Kat up, turned her towards the wall and took the gag and the burlap bag off her head. They retied the gag and added a sleep-aid type blindfold. José slowly turned her around and checked her perspiring underarms. Next, he ran his hands down her sides to her waist and worked slowly up under her overblouse. He felt under each of her size C bra cups. Then he crossed his hands, slipping them inside her bra one at a time, and felt each of her breasts from the top down. Kat exhaled sharply and tears trickled down her cheeks from under the blindfold. She could smell his putrid, garlic-tinged, cigarette breath and gagged a little. José stepped backward and ran his hands down the outside of Kat's legs. He dropped to his knees, turned his hands, and slowly ran them up the inside of her long legs towards her crotch. He didn't stop until they rested on her pudenda. As José lingered there, Kat stiffened, and the Boss finally said, "That's enough, José."

"She's clean, *Jefe*," said José as he rose quickly and stepped away.

The matron took Kat and laid her on a bed in another room. Kat rolled on her side and started working on pulling the thin iPhone out of her pocket with her fingers. The matron had turned on a Spanish-language TV show, and Kat figured her attention was on the show. She didn't worry about a sudden call or text from Jock because it was still early and the iPhone was always kept just on vibrate. She kept it in her back pocket, because it was only for family or close friends' calls, and she didn't want to chance someone stealing it from her purse. She slowly pulled it out and worked the phone under the padded mattress cover, close to the wall. Once she got it hidden where she wanted, she made some noise through the gag and alerted the matron she needed to use the *baños*. The woman took her into the bathroom and turned her around in front of the commode. She unfastened Kat's jeans and pulled them down around her ankles. Next, she pulled her t-back panties down and helped Kat find the toilet seat. Relief at last. Kat hoped Jock would remember this iPhone had a little GPS in it, making it trackable if lost or stolen. At least now she felt she had a sliver of hope of getting out of whatever was happening. Later that night, *El Jefe* put her on the phone with Jock after letting her hear the entire conversation about the property deal. She knew Jock would do the deal and secure her safety, but she still hoped in her heart he would find a way to thwart these crooked bastards.

***

The kidnapper ended the call with Jock and left Kat in her room with the matron. He walked out on the terrace of the palatial island residence that Alistair Hixon, the Turks and Caicos Minister of the Interior, was leasing and lit an Arturo Fuentes cigar from the Dominican Republic. "El Bomba" was a large, powerful man with glistening dark brown skin, long curly black hair, a *pistole* mustache, and pale blue eyes. His real name was Rodrigo Moreno, and he had become a "belonger", the island's name for a voting citizen, just two years before. A feat engineered by his lofty political connections. His spooky eyes showed no remorse for the evil things he had perpetuated during his forty years on earth. The wind settled down, and he could hear a couple of potcake dogs barking somewhere along Chalk Sound. The call to Jock Baffert had gone as well as expected. Jock's wife's reaction was exactly what he anticipated, *sell the fucking land — it's only money.*

12

Eight million dollars with no real estate commission was nothing to sneeze at. Based on what the land would be worth with the zoning change, Rodrigo's commission from the buyer was a cool one million dollars. Add that to the payoff he would receive from Alistair, who stood to gain two million on the deal, and he would net another $500,000. El Bomba liked making this kind of easy money; it was huge *dinero* for such a little effort. It would take him five years of running hookers, strippers, and illegal gambling night after night to even get close to that figure. The minister was absolutely right when he told Rodrigo, "I can steal more money with my pen in ten seconds than you can make in five years with your muscle and gun."

They had forged a lucrative partnership. The minister granted him immunity in Provo so El Bomba could apply a different kind of pressure for the minister when political pressure was ineffective. The minister's nickname in the real estate world was *"The Bartador"*, given to him by a Spanish developer who had bribed him some years before. Alistair had spent most of the week in the Dominican Republic, along with his family, at a Caribbean political conference. But, he would send back his private helicopter on the day of the real estate closing to collect Rodrigo and his bribe for the forthcoming property zoning change. Alistair would take his share of the cash to a Dominican Bank and give El Bomba his share after the helicopter landed in Santo Domingo. Vacating the island would complete their alibis that they both had been out of the country the whole time. El Bomba wanted to use the minister's residence because of its remoteness and the ease of escape by boat or helicopter afforded by the mechanical swing bridge that created a moat when it was open. He would move Mrs. Baffert to one of his safe houses in the Dominican Five Cays neighborhood the night before the closing in case any shit hit the fan. He wanted the Silly Creek property vacated when the helicopter came in for him.

CHAPTER TWO

It was the first Monday in March and Peter Petcock had been in the closet with her for about three minutes. His pants and jockey shorts were around his ankles, and he was doing his best to lift the doctor off the floor with each stroke. He looked down and could see her sagging breasts and bulging hips in the uneven light of the naked light bulb above and thought it might be better in the dark. But she liked to see his well-muscled chest, and she always dug her nails into his bare back as they performed this twice a week ritual in her office coat closet. He stifled her moaning with one hand clamped over her mouth. They had to finish in another two minutes, or the guard might come in to see why no one was visible on the security camera in the office. By law, their conversations were not allowed to be recorded, but prison security visually monitored the office. She would climax like clockwork in another 30 seconds, but it had been taking him longer and longer. They discussed switching to oral sex, but that was difficult to perform simultaneously in a small closet. They finally finished, pulled their clothes back in place, and quickly returned to the office setting.

Peter's incarceration started almost three years ago, after his arrest on drug smuggling, grand theft, attempted murder and several other related charges in Key West. He spent the first six months in the Coleman Federal Prison Hospital, in Coleman, Florida, recovering from a gunshot wound to his right shoulder inflicted in a shootout with the Monroe County Sheriff's Department. During the same arrest, Peter also suffered broken ribs and fractured neck and back vertebrae from a bone-jarring tackle executed by Seth Stone as he fled the scene. His recovery was slow and arduous, and Peter protested when he was released from the hospital, assigned a cell, and forced to join the general population in the maximum-security section of the prison. Peter had been quite an athlete in high school winning All-State honors in football and swimming. At 6'3" and 230 pounds he still was an imposing figure, but he was a shell of himself when he left the prison hospital. He had a run-in almost immediately with five black gang members in the shower. The group of Crips beat a weakened Peter senseless and then sexually violated him. The shower guard made himself scarce and later found Peter, unconscious and covered in blood, lying on the shower floor. He was readmitted to the prison hospital and put in solitary confinement for his own safety when he was released from the hospital three months later. Peter's assault and rape scarred him both physically and mentally. He started working out incessantly in his cell and used his 60 minutes of solitary yard time to run on the yard track. After six months he had rounded himself into the best shape he'd been in since high school. His physique looked chiseled, and his stamina was formidable. Mentally, he concocted a self-deluding, psychotic scenario blaming others for his bad life decisions. At the top of his list was Seth Stone. When Peter was a senior at Boca Ciega High, he was offered a full ride football scholarship to the University of Miami. In the last game of the season, Boca Ciega vs. St. Petersburg High, Seth had tackled him on the sideline late in the fourth quarter of the St. Petersburg City League championship game. Peter sustained a career-ending knee injury. The truth of the situation was that Peter's pulling guard missed his block on Seth and fell on Peter's knee as all three rolled out of bounds.

Peter wasted the next ten years commercial fishing and pursuing beach bunnies. Then he, and his partner Randy Garrett, finally got serious and started a successful boat bottom cleaning and maintenance company. But they never took the time to learn the commercial diver's regulations. When OHSA shut them down, they felt it was the government's fault, not theirs. Facing bankruptcy, they resorted to stealing and disguising their best customer's yacht, a Huckins 62 high-speed jet drive cruiser, to enter the international drug-smuggling business. Predictably, it was Seth's fault for finding the disguised Huckins and setting the authorities on them. Once again, it was Seth who tackled Peter and knocked him unconscious, just as he was about to elude the arresting task force. Peter rationalized all this and became consumed by revenge. He didn't just want to kill Seth. He wanted to make Seth suffer, like he had, before killing him. More importantly, Peter wanted Seth to know exactly why he was killing him.

Out of solitary, Peter was transferred to the medium-security section of Coleman and joined up with a skinhead faction for protection. He dreamed each night of escaping and going after Seth Stone.

One of his swastika-tattooed skinhead friends, "Lefty", mentioned that the prison psychiatrist had asked about Peter.

"Where did she see me?"

"Runnin' around the track with ya shirt off. She can see the yard from her office winda."

"What are ya goin' to see her for?"

"We talks about anger management."

"What does she look like?"

"She's bout 40 … I'd pork her if she'd let me."

"How didja' get in?"

"My lawyer said might could get me some time off my sentence."

"Who didja' ask?"

"Doc Hobbs at the infirmary."

"Thanks, Lefty."

Peter knew he had no chance of getting out of prison for at least 35 years because of his attempted murder of the Monroe County Deputy. He got a referral the next week for an interview with the Psychiatrist, Doctor Fickert. They talked about his anger problems and his depression caused by his sexual violation by the Crips. She thought he should come twice a week. He never let on about his sociopathic view of Seth Stone, or his failure to take responsibility for his many bad decisions. They just dealt with his depression related to the Crip's shower incident and his anger issues. Six months later, after playing footsie under her desk and exchanging love notes, Peter told her he loved her, and their closet romance ensued. Six months later they started to plan Peter's escape.

Peter had thought of every way he might escape from Coleman. He didn't want to enlist another inmate because he already knew there was no honor among thieves. His partner, Randy, turned state's evidence on him and was doing one-third of Peter's time up at Eglin, the federal prison for white collar criminals. Lefty had given him the edge he needed, and Peter used every trick in the book to romance Dr. Rhonda Fickert. He spent time asking her questions about herself. She was accustomed to only discussing questions about her patients because they were only interested in their own problems. She was flattered to have some attention focused on her for a change. Peter learned she had no family in the area; only a brother in Seattle whom she never saw. Her parents were both dead and buried. She was plain looking, a neatnik, and overweight. But he sensed she craved the attention he was giving her and was sure she would be a ticking, pent up, time bomb when they started into the physical side of their relationship. Peter never pressed her and gave her the right amount of time to ease into the relationship. He played her like a six-pound bonefish on three-pound test line.

When they finally became intimate, and he knew she had totally fallen for him, he told her about the escape stash he'd left behind. He didn't tell her it was buried on his gravesite at the Gamble Mansion, in Ellenton, Florida. Peter's grandfather purchased plots there for the whole family. His family was from Ellenton, but his father moved to St. Petersburg in the 60's where he went to work for Charley Morgan at Morgan Yacht. Peter figured, when the Keys' drug running started to get really profitable, there was a chance they might get caught. He had a plan "B" if he could escape the bust. He hid $350,000; a second new identity bought in Miami complete with a birth certificate, a passport, a brown wig, a Glock 9mm pistol, four clips of ammo, and a driver's license all ready to go. He put it all in a 48 quart Coleman cooler which he completely fiberglassed. Then he buried it, on a moonlit night, in the Ellenton Cemetery on his gravesite. He figured if he died before he got to it, the gravediggers would find it, and what the fuck would he care then.

He told her his plan. If she helped him escape from Coleman, he would retrieve the money and documents, and both of them would travel to Miami where he knew the people to buy her a new identity. Then the two of them would fly to Australia, and travel to Queensland, the northernmost province on the Great Barrier Reef. It was lightly populated and would be a good place for them to settle and become Australian citizens. Peter could support them being a sportfishing captain or a river tour guide. They could spend the rest of their lives there, loving each other.

She bought it, hook, line, and sinker. Peter had finally figured a way to escape from Coleman. Peter settled on the Coleman Prison Hospital, where he had spent so much time, as his avenue of escape. The federal prison was too well staffed, with a dedicated mix of former police personnel and retired national guardsman who double dipped their pensions. There were too many checks and double checks. He knew that anything more than regular emergency room medicine was contracted out to specialists from Shands Hospital in Gainesville and various Orlando specialists. There were a lot of doctors coming and going every day. Peter's idea was to have Rhonda prescribe him a prescription for Ritalin for his depression. Then he would go to the prison pill line twice a day to receive it. Once the pill regimen was established, they would plan an escape date. Rhonda would slip Peter some extra Ritalin during their bi-weekly office visits, a pill at a time, and also supply him with a package of Ex-Lax. Peter would take a triple dose of Ritalin and the whole package of Ex-Lax on the appointed day and would soon develop a high fever, high blood pressure, breathing problems, and diarrhea. He would be admitted to the prison hospital and would slowly improve over the next two days. Peter knew the overdose could be fatal, but this was his only chance, and he had to take the risk. On the second day, Rhonda would visit him during her regular rounds at the hospital. She'd drop off a stolen set of green scrubs complete with a green surgery cap, mask, stethoscope, and a stolen hospital I.D. badge with a headshot of Peter taken in her office on her phone and printed on her home PC.

On the prescribed day it all went off like clockwork. Rhonda signed herself in at the gate and added another doctor's name on the line above her own. She signed in every day, so the guard didn't even look. Rhonda did her rounds, delivered the scrubs to Peter, then walked out through the security gate to the parking lot and waited in a rental car for Peter. Twenty minutes later Dr. Steven Russell, a gastroenterologist from Shands Hospital, walked through security, out to the parking lot, and got in the passenger seat next to Rhonda. They headed for Ellenton.

It would be a couple of hours before anyone missed Peter at the hospital. He left a note on his pillow; **Patient is downstairs for x-rays**. By that time, Rhonda and Peter would have traveled south on I-75, turned the rental car in at the Tampa International Airport, taken a cab to South St. Petersburg, and bought a used Explorer SUV for $4500.00 cash. Peter knew it would take weeks before the Florida DMV got the paperwork into their computers. They headed south to check into a run-down motel on Route 41 in Bradenton, where they could pay in cash. That's where they would have their first sexual experience with each other in a bed.

The next day the lovebirds laid low as Peter recovered from his overdose, and the couple made love between eating takeout food, and sleeping.

"I never dreamed I'd end up with a man like you, Peter. I don't mean a convict or anything, I mean a handsome, viral man who takes care of my wants, and talks to me."

"Sometimes things work out for the best, Honey. Falling in love with my psychiatrist is the best thing that ever happened to me. If it hadn't been for you, I'd have probably killed myself after what happened to me in prison."

He reached for her, pulled her close, and kissed her deeply. Then he rolled her over and slapped her playfully on the butt.

"Let's try something you might not have ever thought about," as he positioned himself over her. "We'll just take it slow and see if you like it."

That afternoon Rhonda wore a baseball cap and sunglasses while shopping at a local Ace Hardware store for a shovel, a chisel, a hammer, and a couple of flashlights. Later that night they checked out of the motel, traveled north to Ellenton, and turned east on Route 301. Peter turned left on Franklin Road and eased left into the cemetery. Groves of 100-year-old live oaks hung with Spanish moss dotted the grounds. It was a clear night with a half moon, but it was still hard to see with the mossy trees blocking most of the moonlight. Peter doused the car lights and twisted off the interior lights as he coasted to a stop.

"Stay here. If you see anybody come in this drive, blink the lights twice."

He got out of the darkened SUV, retrieved the shovel and a flashlight out of the rear and was gone.

Fifteen minutes later he was back toting a large rectangular object, which he put in the rear space with some effort. He went back into the darkness and returned a few minutes later with the shovel.

Peter drove back out to Route 301, turned east, then went south on I-75 across the Manatee River and turned east on Route 70.

"Where are we headed?" asked Rhonda.

"To Okeechobee, then Stuart on the other coast. We should get there about daybreak."

They drove all night, and Peter pulled up a desolate country road on the east side of Arcadia. He worked for about ten minutes with the chisel and hammer and finally opened the fiberglass covered cooler lid. He slid back into the driver's seat, and Rhonda noticed a pistol in his waistband.

"What are you doing with that?"

"It's just in case we're pulled over. The money is in good shape, along with my passport and other documents. With what I've got in the cooler and the $40,000 you brought along we have almost four hundred thousand. But, wait until you see this."

He reached into the back seat and pulled a wavy brown hairpiece out of a plastic bag and plopped it on his shaved head. They laughed as Rhonda matched it up with his picture on the new passport and driver's license.

"I thought I was going to see some of the blond hair that I see on your chin, on your head," laughed Rhonda. "I guess I'll have to get a new hair color when we get to Miami."

"We're headed that way, Babe."

Peter worked the hairpiece on in case the police stopped him for a traffic offense, and he had to show his new license. They drove silently through the night except for a coffee stop in Okeechobee in the wee hours.

After breakfast at a Waffle House on Okeechobee Road, they checked into a Motel Six in Fort Pierce near I-95 about 7:00 a.m. They slept most of the day and watched newscasts on all the TV stations that were carrying stories, along with both their photographs, about Peter Petcock's escape and Dr. Fickert's disappearance from the Federal Prison in Coleman. The police had no clues but related that Dr. Rhonda Fickert was missing from her undisturbed apartment where her vehicle was still parked. The authorities didn't know if Petcock had abducted her from work that morning. She was a person of interest at this point. Peter felt safe in Fort Pierce since he checked in as brown-haired Grant T. Morris of Miami, Florida. He prepaid, as the plan was to drive down I-95 to Miami in the morning. The desk clerk had not seen Rhonda, and he was going to suggest a hair color change later in the afternoon.

Rhonda dyed her mousy brown hair black after having Peter cut about three inches of it off. He thought it was an improvement. They made love in the late afternoon, Peter being spurred on by Rhonda's new look. Peter went out and brought back a takeout dinner from Tillman's Famous Barbeque on Route 1. He hadn't eaten decent BBQ for quite a while. After dinner, he suggested they take a hot bath together, something he also hadn't been able to do for three years or more. Rhonda drew a hot tub for him, and Peter got in. It was soothing, and his tired muscles started to relax.

"Can I get in there with you?" said Rhonda walking through the bathroom door stark naked.

"I was hoping you'd ask," said Peter looking up at her sagging breasts and paunchy middle, while smiling.

Rhonda got into the tub as gracefully as possible and positioned herself between Peter's legs. She found his flaccid penis under the hot, soapy water and said, "I think I can improve that with a little work."

"Slide up here and give me a kiss," said Peter huskily.

Rhonda moved toward him, and Peter reached out and grabbed her by the throat. He turned her under him and laid all his body weight on top of her while pushing her head under the water. She struggled briefly, but it was over quickly with hardly a sound. Peter got out of the tub and toweled off. He pulled the tub plug and ran more water in, washing death's inevitable debris down the drain. When Rhonda and the tub were clean, he lifted her out and dried her. He laid her on the bed and dressed her in clean clothes. Next, he got dressed, wiped both rooms of all their fingerprints, and laid down next to her.

Peter watched television until 2:30 a.m., then went outside and backed the SUV up to their motel room's door. After turning the interior lights out, he opened the Explorer's back hatch and looked both ways; there was no sign of movement anywhere in the half empty motel. He went back into the darkened room and carried Rhonda out and laid her in the rear cargo space with the empty cooler. Rigor mortis had set in which made her body easier to carry. The luggage was loaded next to her, along with her carry-on bag where he'd stashed the money; along with the shirts, pants, and toilet articles she'd bought for him. He took a blanket off the bed to cover her and left twenty dollars for it with the maid's tip. He would drive back to Lake Okeechobee through Indiantown on Route 76 and then drive the rim route to Okeechobee. Before dawn, he would stop along the lake and put her in the water. The lake's massive alligator population would find her before anyone else would. Before getting to the lake, he planned to drop her clothes, the empty Coleman cooler, and her unmarked suitcase in three separate dumpsters. Peter felt no remorse for Rhonda's murder. She'd been a necessary step, actually his only possible way, of getting out of prison so he could enact revenge on Seth Stone for ruining his life. He was on his way to St. Petersburg.

***

Peter abandoned the Explorer at the Tampa airport in long term parking. Its location would further throw off the authorities if it became a factor. He took a cab to downtown St. Petersburg and decided on the Hampton Inn behind the St. Petersburg Yacht Club on First Street North and Beach Drive. Next, he rented a car from Enterprise for a month with his new identity and paid cash. Realizing he needed a credit card, he established an address at the UPS mailbox location on Second Avenue South. After opening a checking account with $9500 at the SunTrust Bank up on Third Street, he applied for an expedited credit/debit Visa.

As he walked around downtown St. Pete, Peter hardly recognized it. During the five years he'd been gone, the city had gotten trendy with several new high-rise condos and apartments, sidewalk cafes, and restaurants. The new amenities complimented the blocks of waterfront parks that had been there forever. He explored uptown Central Avenue and found many new avant-garde eateries and hip bars. Frequenting those establishments would lessen the risk of running into someone who might recognize him. He did some clothes shopping and settled in.

Peter researched the banking world and realized he could not travel abroad with $400,000 in cash. His research turned up SunTrust's International Division. He learned he could move his money offshore and still comply with U.S. reporting, interest income, and capital gain/losses law. His international personal banker opened three overseas accounts for him in three different countries and reported them to the IRS. Peter then opened two additional domestic accounts at Wachovia and Wells Fargo. He moved $358,200 overseas by depositing and wiring non-reportable installments of $9950 into each account every day over 12 consecutive business days. The rest he kept in cash. He had complied with the law and would be liable for only the interest income on those accounts. After he killed Seth, Peter never intended to return to the United States. Once established in Australia, he would transfer his overseas accounts into their banking system and simply ignore the IRS.

Peter checked the airlines and found a 27-hour flight out of Miami that landed in Sydney for $1500. Once there, he would book a jumper flight to Queensland. With his exit strategy planned, he began his surveillance of Seth Stone.

***

First, Peter took a ride over the Sunshine Skyway Bridge to check out his old hog hunting camp, south of Fort Lonesome and Buggerman's Corner, on Route 39. He wasn't surprised there was a faded **Wells Fargo-For Sale** sign on the driveway's rusting bull gate. The gate was unlocked, so he pushed it open and drove in. He plowed thru the waist high weeds that covered the trail he had cut through the palmetto and live oak forest years ago. Two hundred yards down the trail was the camp clearing which was also overgrown with weeds. Peter got out of the rental Chevy and walked over to the pole barn that he and his partner Randy built. The door was ajar, and as he pulled it open a couple of pigeons flew out. The interior was dusty, full of cobwebs, and as hot as a furnace. The bunk beds were still in the corner, and the iron cook stove still stood in the middle of the small barn. Beer cans littered the floor, probably from some high school kids partying. The generator and fridge were gone, and all four windows were busted out. Obviously, no one had been there for quite a while. It reminded him, for a moment, of happier times. He brushed off any nostalgia and looked to the future. The old barn was the perfect place to hold Seth in solitary confinement, before dispatching him to his deserved fate. Fort Lonesome was truly in the middle of nowhere.

**

Peter started watching Stone's Boatworks, located on Salt Creek, just 16 blocks south of downtown. Besides the brown wig, he also grew a mustache which he dyed brown. The yard was as busy as it had always been, but Seth was not in attendance. He only showed up once in the first four days to take his son, Jeb, to lunch.

Peter mused about Salt Creek as he sat on 17th Avenue South in his car watching the Boatworks parking lot and front entrance. Salt Creek flowed from freshwater Lake Maggiore about 12 blocks east into Bayboro Harbor, which emptied into Tampa Bay. The area had grown over the last 30 years from one fish plant, two boatyards, a fuel depot, and a small Coast Guard facility into a busy marine district. Bayboro Harbor now housed a large Coast Guard Base, The Florida State Marine Biologists and Department of Natural Resources, and the 300 boat Harborage Marina. Salt Creek now had five boat repair facilities, a 400 boat high and dry, and a waterfront restaurant.

Once Peter found that Seth didn't spend much time at the Boatworks, he started staking out his Treasure Island townhouse on the Gulf of Mexico. In three days, Seth only showed up there one time. During that visit, he put about ten fishing rods in the back of his Yukon, along with some tackle, and headed towards downtown. Peter followed him to the Yacht Club docks located on Bayshore Drive across from the Club, and a block from Peter's hotel. Peter parked in the hotel parking garage and quickly walked into the park north of the Yacht Club just in time to see Seth take the rods out to his Hatteras sportfish *TAR BABY*. Peter sat on a park bench and watched Seth unload the rods from a push cart and put them on the boat. Seth still looked in good shape for an old guy, but Peter thought he was in way better shape than him. Seth retrieved another cart load of gear from his SUV and stowed it inside the Hatteras. It was obvious to Peter that Seth was getting ready to go somewhere in his boat.

Seth got into the Yukon and drove around to Beach Drive, then two blocks north, before disappearing into a condo parking garage with a roll-up steel gate. Peter walked down to the condo and crossed the street from the park. He went into a coffee shop, bought a cup of coffee, a newspaper, and a chocolate chip cookie. He went back to the park, sat on a bench, and waited. Just before dark Seth walked out of the condo with an attractive, slim brunette with a smile on her face. They walked north hand in hand. Peter shadowed them from behind on the park side of the street. They walked two blocks and went into the Parkshore Grill Restaurant at the base of another high rise condo. Peter passed the Museum of Fine Arts across the street and found a bench. An hour and a half later Seth and the woman came out laughing. They walked hand and hand back to the condo and disappeared inside.

Peter sat outside mulling it all over. It would be hard to snatch Seth downtown as there were always crowds of people at all hours. Coming out of his beach townhouse at night, while walking to the dumpster, was a possibility. Coming and going to his cars from the townhouse wouldn't happen because they were both in the garage. He noticed Seth had also driven his car into the downtown condo garage and used an opener for the automatic roll gate. Maybe he'd gotten married again. Peter had known Seth since high school, and they'd been rivals on the playing field. They were never friends, but for years, he or his partner Randy cleaned Seth's boat bottom every month, at the Boatworks, his townhouse, or at the Yacht

Club docks. Peter waited until 2:00 a.m. and Seth never appeared, so he was certain Seth was living there. Seth was obviously getting ready to go fishing, but not around here. The rods he put on the boat were 50 and 80-pound bent-butts, meant to be used in his fighting chair for big marlin and tuna. He needed to find out Seth's destination. Peter walked back to his room at the Hampton and got a few hours' sleep.

At dawn, he was back on a different bench in the park. Seth drove out of the condo parking garage about 8:30 a.m. and headed west on First Avenue North. Peter walked up First to Starbucks and bought a coffee, a newspaper, and a breakfast sandwich then headed back down to Pioneer's Park on the south side of the Yacht Club. It gave him a clearer view of the *TAR BABY'S* cockpit out on the docks. He sat on a bench and thumbed through the paper. In the State section of the *St. Petersburg Times,* there was a report stating there were still no leads in the escape of Peter Petcock from the Federal Penitentiary in Coleman, even though a massive manhunt had taken place in that area. There was also no sign of Dr. Rhonda Fickert, but investigators reported she had withdrawn a large sum of money from her bank recently, and a rental car in her name had been turned in at the Tampa International Airport. She was now being sought as a possible accomplice.

At 10:30 a.m., Seth's Yukon pulled up in front of the Yacht Club dock on Bayshore. A sturdy looking older man, six feet tall, with gray hair, and an easy gait, got out of the car in front of Seth's. They unloaded groceries into two big push carts and went out to the boat. Peter stood up and trained a pair of pocket binoculars on the Hatteras. Seth got down in the cockpit and pulled open the bottom drawer of his tackle center and removed a yellow bobber with a key on it. He unlocked the salon door and started loading the groceries on the boat. Peter laughed to himself; *that's where they all hide it, either there or in the propane locker.* After they unloaded all the groceries, they closed the salon door and stayed awhile. Peter hoped they weren't leaving that afternoon. That would set his timetable back for who knows how long. He wanted to punish Seth for what he had done to him, then fly out of Miami to Australia to safety, before the FBI or the police found him.

Finally, the salon door opened, and Seth and his friend left. Seth drove off south in the direction of the Boatworks, and his friend walked across the street and disappeared into the Yacht Club. Peter went back to the Hampton and drove his rental car out to West Marine on US 19. If Seth didn't leave on his fishing trip this afternoon, he needed some supplies for tonight's activities. He bought a dive mask, snorkel, a pair of Mares X-Stream fins, and a lightweight neoprene rash guard top; along with black swim trunks, a small waterproof bag, an all-purpose serrated dive knife, and two underwater flashlights. He added a couple of Guy Harvey beach towels and a mesh duffle bag to his cart and checked out. After stashing the dive equipment in the car's trunk, he drove back downtown and took a nap.

At 6:00 p.m. Peter was on a park bench across from Seth and his lady friend's condo on Beach Drive. At 7:30, Seth and his squeeze walked south to the Z-Grille and had dinner. He tailed them and sat outside across Second Street and had a fish sandwich at the Pacific Rim Restaurant. It was right next to his official St. Pete address, the UPS store. Peter was nursing a second ice tea when they finally came out of Z-Grille and walked back down towards the waterfront. He left cash for his check and ambled down behind them. They ducked into the Yacht Club, and Peter continued to his park bench. About 10:30 the two of them walked by on the other side of the street and went into the condo's front entrance. Peter stayed on the bench until midnight then retrieved his car and headed for Demen's Landing Park. He drove around to the public ramp by the Ship's Store and fuel dock and parked next to the seawall. There was a dock along the seawall with a sewage pump-out station on it. The dock was 100 yards from the Yacht Club's docks.

Peter climbed over the seat of his darkened car and donned his dive gear in the backseat. He checked the dimly lit area in all directions, exited the car, put the keys on top of the front tire, and silently slipped into the water. A few minutes later he located *TAR BABY'S* transom and eased up to the emergency ladder at the end of the finger pier. He knew the Yacht Club did not have a security guard patrolling the docks; the club depended on the handful of members who lived on their boats inside the locked gate

27

entrance. Prismatic yellow lights on the top of each electric supply pedestal lit the dock walkways. Seth's boat was dark, as was the end of each finger pier. Peter took off his fins and mask and slipped them up on the dock, then quietly ascended to the finger pier. Quickly, he climbed down into the Hatteras's cockpit and retrieved the key from the tackle center. After checking the main dock for any movement, he put the key in the door lock, held his breath, and opened the door. No alarm started beeping, so he closed the door behind him. There was a nightlight plugged in at the galley. First, he closed all the blinds, then swept the carpeted salon with his flashlight. There were stacks of charts and a notebook on the salon dining table. Peter went down the companionway steps to the guest head and retrieved a towel. After drying himself off, he returned the towel to the head. He shuffled through the charts and recognized the Keys and the Bahamas. The notebook yielded a list of waypoints leading south to Marathon, across the stream to Orange Cay, then to the Northwest Channel and past Chub Cay, to Nassau. From Nassau, he continued to Little San Sal, the southern tip of Cat Island, past Rum Cay, then to San Salvador, circled in red pencil. There were more waypoints south past Samana Cay, the Plana Keys, to Mayaguana Island, then to Providenciales, in the Turks and Caicos Islands, also circled in red. As Peter paged through the notebook, he found a confirmation number and date for a slip on or about June 16th at Riding Rock Marina in San Salvador. Below that entry was another confirmation. This one at Turtle Cove Marina, in Providenciales, tentatively starting on June 22nd. On the next page were some paper-clipped printed sheets outlining the 2007 Caicos Classic Billfish Tournament dates of June 29th thru July 3rd, along with sheets with the rules, and all the different tournament activities and events. There were also some penciled in phone numbers for Art, Belinda, and Jock, but no last names. Peter removed a blank page from Seth's notebook and wrote down all the pertinent information including the tournament headquarters location, the cocktail party and dinner venues, and all the phone numbers.

Peter put everything back the way it was. The salon carpet was a little damp, but it would dry before morning. He was careful to wipe down any footprints on the teak and holly sole in the head below and the galley above.

After putting his notes in the waterproof pouch, he doused the light and opened all the salon blinds. He slipped out, locked the door, and returned the key to the tackle center. Peter sat in the dark for a couple of minutes making sure there was no one walking or sitting in the area, then slithered out of the cockpit and slipped into the water. He reached up, retrieved his mask and fins, donned them, and swam silently back to his car.

Once safely back in his hotel room, he sifted through all of his notes. Seth would leave for the Keys tomorrow, probably at dawn. Then he would travel over the next four or five days to San Salvador. Peter would know in the morning how many crew members would be traveling with Seth. He would leave San Salvador, depending on the weather, a couple of days before June 22nd to motor to Provo. Peter had been almost every place in the Caribbean during his commercial fishing days. He remembered San Salvador as a small sparsely populated island with a couple of restaurants, a Club Med, a small beach resort, and a small hotel at the marina. He would be conspicuous in that setting, and getting on and off San Sal by air was not easy.

Providenciales was a different story, as it had scores of hotels and restaurants and a resident population of 23,000. A thousand tourists traveled in and out of Provo every day, and it had a large airport with five or six major airlines flying in and out to many locations every day. He recalled the crowded downtown areas and beaches, but also the large undeveloped tracts of land at both ends of the island that were pitch black at night. There were rental cars, boats for hire, and secluded cottage rentals. The island was user-friendly with supermarkets, hardware, and automotive stores.

It was obvious to Peter that it would not be possible to snatch Seth before he left on his lengthy voyage tomorrow. San Salvador would offer only a small four-day window and logistical problems. Peter would hatch a plan B in Providenciales, where he had ten or twelve days to get settled and two weeks to snatch Seth. He would drive down to Miami as soon as Seth left St. Petersburg tomorrow, and would leave Miami as soon as he could book a flight to Provo. It would give him time to become very familiar with the 37 square mile island, get the right rental house, and put together a plan to punish Seth before he killed him. He was also looking forward to sampling some of the island's grade-A pussy, ending a drought which started when Seth put him in jail.

CHAPTER THREE

Awakening just before dawn, Seth climbed out of his bunk. The phone call from Jock had not been a dream, and he had a full day of travel ahead of him. *TAR BABY* was moving through the seas easily, and Seth hoped the wind would continue to lay down. He went up to the galley, made some coffee, woke Gene up, and got ready to take the helm back from Freddy.

"Good morning Fred, what kind of night was it?"

"Not bad, I got a couple hours sleep when Dino relieved me, and John went down when I came back up. We saw three ships on the AIS (Automatic Identification System) at the same time about 3:00 a.m., a cruise ship, and two fuel tankers. It would have freaked me out in the old days, but your AIS is worth its weight in gold in those situations. One of the tankers was bookin' it at 20 knots."

"How far are we from Clarence Town?"

"About an hour ... if we get up and run."

'That's what I'm planning on doing," said Seth as he took back the helm. "Get some rest Fred. I'm planning on running hard all day."

Seth put the Hatteras up on plane as they headed down Long Island in the morning light. An hour later he radioed the Flying Fish Marina to alert their fuel dock.

"Come right in *TAR BABY* ... back in starboard side to the pumps and we'll fill you up."

"I know it's early, but could you call up to the Rowdy Boys restaurant and order me five cracked conch lunches with black beans and yellow rice to go? I want to give my crew a treat. I'll walk up there and pick'em up while we're refueling."

"Consider it done, Captain."

Five years ago, Seth stopped in quaint Clarence Town with his friend, Captain Toby Warner, on their way to fish Crooked Island and Samana Cay.

31

They doubled back twice for fuel staying overnight each time. The crew ate dinner both times at Rowdy Boys Bar and Grill. The cracked conch was as tasty as he'd ever eaten. The fishing had been good, and they'd caught a number of white and blue marlin, plus some wahoo and dolphin. The second night they ate there was a Friday, and Rowdy Boys had a native rake n' scrape band playing next to their tiki bar at the pool. The Friday night crowd was having a good time drinking and dancing. Seth asked the bartender who the huge white guy was, wearing a pair of XXXL bib overalls and no shirt or shoes, out on the dance floor.

"Dat's 'Big Un', he one of the Rowdy Boys … he sure can dance for a big man."

"No arguing with that," laughed Seth.

Seth backed the boat in at the fuel dock and asked John to fill the tanks while Gene made an engine room check.

After finishing a sat-phone call to Turtle Cove Marina, Seth said to Gene, "Here's my credit card, I'm going to run up the hill and pick up a cracked conch lunch for the crew while you're fueling. We'll warm it up in the microwave at lunchtime."

Seth walked up the hill to Rowdy Boys and looked south at the two beautiful white churches hovering over the bay and smiled to himself. Both of them had twin spires and were reminiscent of Moorish architecture. When he asked the marina owner about the unusual twin churches on his first visit there with Captain Toby, Mario said, "The same missionary, Father Jerome Hewes, designed both of them. He built St. Paul's when he was an Episcopalian. Later, he built St. Peter and Paul's after he became a Roman Catholic."

Lunch was waiting for him at the bar, so he hurried back down to the dock. John was finished fueling, and Gene said everything looked good in the engine room.

"Let's cast off and get going," said Seth. "We have less than 200 miles to go to Provo. If the wind stays down, we can make it into Turtle Cove before dark."

As he cleared Clarence Town Harbor, Seth pushed the throttles up until *TAR BABY* was running at 24 knots. He settled in as he headed along the top of Crooked Island, ESE. Uninhabited Samana Cay loomed northeast in the distance. Seth remembered anchoring behind a treacherous reef there with Captain Toby five years ago. They wiggled through an almost invisible break in the reef into an idyllic lagoon for the night. Most of the Cascarilla bark in the world was collected there a couple times a year by enterprising residents from Crooked and Long Island. It flavored Campari liqueur and several Vermouths. After passing Crooked, he'd basically stay on the same course; they'd leave the Plano Cays to starboard, angle south and east around Mayaguana, then run along Abraham's Bay and its south side reef. Once past the rusting hulk of a shipwrecked freighter at the end of the reef, they'd run the last 50 miles SSE across the Caicos Passage to Provo.

Seth's mind wandered back to St. Petersburg as the Hatteras effortlessly cut through the one to two foot Atlantic chop. After coming back from the successful Keys' boat salvage trip three summers ago, his semi-retirement from the family Boatworks was progressing smoothly. Charley Blevin's Huckins restoration occupied almost a full year of his time, with some time off for fishing tournaments. The *ABOUT TIME* was finished on schedule and within the insurance settlement amount. The project hadn't impacted the Boatworks regular business since Seth acted as the project manager and hired on a couple of extra craftsmen.

Seth and his girlfriend, Lori Gudentite, finally started living together, shortly after the Huckins project was complete. He moved into Lori's Beach Drive condo because he liked the restaurant and bistro scene that was developing in downtown St. Petersburg. Seth kept his townhouse out on Treasure Island, and the couple stayed there occasionally if they dined out on the beach, or felt like a change of scenery. Lori's son Greg and his wife, Delores, had their first child, and they visited grandma from Detroit a couple of times each winter, as did Lori's daughter Gladys, who was working in Lansing. Seth moved back to the townhouse on those occasions. In the summer, Lori would visit her children and grandchild when Seth went off on his fishing expeditions. The Gudentite family had a great summer house on Torch Lake in Michigan. He had also moved the *TAR*

BABY to the Yacht Club docks downtown, so it was closer for him to check and maintain.

Seth and the "Geezers" finally won an Old Salts Loop Tournament, a couple of years prior, and qualified for the World Offshore Championship in Cabo San Lucas, Mexico. Six of them flew down to Cabo in early April. They were one of 70 teams who qualified from all over the world in sanctioned Billfish tournaments. They chartered a boat for two days and practice-fished the area. When the World Championship started, the teams all drew for boats. The tournament began the next day, following an evening of pageantry, pomp, and circumstance. After three days of fishing, the Geezers, one of eight teams representing the United States, were in the top ten with a chance to win it if they had a big day. There were gala dinners and parties every night, but the Geezers played it straight. Each day they caught six to eight striped marlin, added a blue marlin on two of the days, and sprinkled in a few sailfish. On the last day, their luck ran out, and they only caught three striped marlins. They still finished in the top ten and enjoyed the experience of meeting billfish anglers from all over the world.

Seth also fished in a number of different tournaments in the Bahamas in the past couple of years, including the Custom Shootout in Marsh Harbor with Jay Hoedown on his 60-foot Rybovitch. He also did a couple of BBC legs in interesting places like Harbour Island and Cape Eleuthera on *TAR BABY*. Last year he flew down to fish with Jock, in the Caicos Classic and agreed to bring the Hatteras down this year. Jock would enter his boat in the tournament as he did every year. Seth liked Provo, and the plan was to fly Lori and John Harvey's wife, Stacy, in before the tournament and stay at Jock and Kat's house. The girls would spend the tournament days shopping and sightseeing with Kat. Then the four of them would take the boat back to Florida at a leisurely pace. The thinking was, even if the trade winds blew at 20 knots the wind would be at their backs all the way home. Freddy, Gene, and Dino would fly home after the tournament. Of course, it was all up in the air at the moment.

***

Seth also made a bold move with his son, Jeb, brought on by Seth's close call with the Tampa Mafia after the Charley Blevins – Key West episode. It concerned Seth that Jeb might have been drawn into that situation. The Mafia attempted to take Seth into custody to question him about some newly uncovered evidence linking him to the 2001 robbery of the Mafia, in Tampa, involving his brother Beau and two turncoat Mafia bookies from Miami. At that time, Seth was off on one of his adventures, which caused the Tampa Mafia to stake out the Boatworks and ponder grabbing Jeb to flush out Seth. The Mafia finally caught up with Seth in Key West and tried to snatch him while he walked along a dark back street. Unfortunately for the Mob, Dino Vino was walking along with Seth. Dino's size and martial arts skills made short work of the two Mafia enforcers, but Seth worried they might snatch Jeb in St. Petersburg to force a trade. He called Beau, who then flew in from Costa Rica. The two brothers proactively solved the problem, but Seth thought it was time for Jeb to know the truth.

During the Huckins re-fit project, Seth went to work almost every day. When the project was nearly complete, he and Jeb found themselves alone at the Boatworks one evening, working on their schedules for the next day.

Jeb walked into Seth's office and said, "You know, we've never had that promised talk about your retirement hobbies after you sent Lynne, little Cullen, and me to the Bahamas for our safety. You know, after the Russian Mafia tried to kill you down in Key West."

"I guess I've just been too busy with this Huckins project to think about it but sit down … there *is* a lot I want to tell you."

Jeb eased his six foot one frame down into a chair and looked expectantly at his dad. Seth thought he looked just like him, only Jeb was a little bigger. He was proud of Jeb and the job he did managing Stone's Boatworks. Jeb exuded a calm confidence and had patience and wisdom far beyond his years.

"Before you start, Dad. I just want you to enjoy your retirement by having fun traveling, hunting, and fishing with your buddies … instead of getting caught up in situations that should be handled by the police."

"Jeb, you're almost forty years old, and I think it's time I leveled with you … Your Uncle Beau is still alive — he didn't die in the shark tank in Key West. He cut off two of his fingers and fed them to those sharks so there'd be DNA evidence."

Jeb's jaw dropped in disbelief, and he shook his head and stammered, "b-b-but, the funeral — and you going up to Aunt Scarlett's mountain cabin to be alone … with your grief."

Seth got up and walked around his desk and sat down next to Jeb. He put his hand on Jeb's shoulder and said, "Listen, you've heard the stories about your Uncle Beau's drinking and gambling. The Vietnam War left Beau with some mental problems he couldn't handle after he got home. He was in Airborne Ranger Special Ops. operating behind enemy lines. He killed scores of enemy officers and politicians, some face to face and some from a half mile away. After a while, he realized that he started to like the killing. When it was over, he had trouble shaking the demons. He drank too much and got into debt gambling. He finally lost everything, but still owed two Miami bookies $50,000. They forced him to rob the Tampa Mafia of three million dollars. The bookies had a cousin inside the Mafia's Tampa money-drop. With a gun held to his head, Beau was told, 'agree to do it or you die right now.' He had no choice. If he and the bookie's cousin were successful Beau's debt would be forgiven, and he'd get $100,000 on top of that. Beau would wear a disguise, and the cousin would disappear somewhere in South America with a million dollars. Either way, the bookies wouldn't be suspected, as they had set up an alibi for themselves in Mexico. They pulled off the robbery and got the $3,000,000, but not without some problems. During the getaway, Beau fought with one of the money-drop guards, after the guard shot the bookies' cousin. Beau reluctantly shot the guard. In the midst of the scuffle his disguise was compromised, so they had his face on a security video. Beau stabilized the cousin's wound and hid half the money after escaping back to St. Petersburg. The next morning the wounded cousin, Beau, and the two Miami bookies took off for Mexico in the bookies' Bertram 54. Ricardo Cabeza, the cousin, died on the way to Key West and was later dumped into the shark tank, along with Beau's fingers. Once Beau delivered the bookies safely to Mexico, he would get the $100,000 and an airline ticket home. Any questions so far?"

"I'm following you, but I'm sure I'll have some questions — Go on."

"Your Uncle Beau recognized that the security video might identify him. On the way to Key West, which was a necessary fuel stop, he informed the bookies he'd hidden half the money. He outlined his shark tank plan to stage his own and Ricardo's deaths in Key West and then take the Bertram 54 to Costa Rica instead of Mexico. There he could buy a new identity and hide out. The bookies could fly back to Mexico, then to Miami, and still maintain their alibi. Beau also wanted an equal three-way split and would reveal where he had hidden the rest of the money when they reached Costa Rica. The bookies were not seasoned boaters and were basically dependent on Beau's nautical skills — so they agreed. But, it didn't work out quite like Beau had planned. The Tampa Mafia figured out the two bookies and their boat were involved. They flew two enforcers down to Costa Rica to retrieve the money and eliminate the bookies and the captain."

"But you went to the mountains!" Jeb exclaimed.

"That was a cover story. I never really believed Beau was dead. Because of his military training and experience, he is a dangerous person when his back's against the wall. I finally figured the Bertram 54 was the key. It just kept cropping up. First, it was next door at Charley's Boatyard, called *PESCADORA*, from Naples. Towed in there with two big Cuban owners aboard. I saw her again, a few days later in the Key West channel while I was down there fishing the Hemingway Tournament. It'd been renamed *CHICA*, from Ft. Lauderdale. The name and hailing port was changed, but it had to be the same boat — Schaefer outriggers and a swim platform."

"That is an odd combination for any large sportfishing boat," added Jeb.

"I realized the day after I spotted *CHICA* in Key West — was the day they supposedly found Beau and his accomplice, Ricardo Cabeza, in The Key West Aquarium shark tank. I started following the Bertram's fuel trail down through the islands to Costa Rica. I went through the motions with Beau's funeral and everything because I couldn't prove anything yet. But along the fuel trail, the captain was described by the down island dock masters as six feet tall, medium build, black hair with a black stubble beard, and two fingers were missing on his left hand. The Key West detective told me the two fingers belonging to Beau was all they recovered of him from the shark's stomachs, besides his Rolex and boat shoes. I also got reports there were two large Hispanic crew members along with the captain I described. I figured the captain could be Beau or maybe he was being held captive below. I told you I was going to the mountains, but I flew to Costa Rica and saved Beau from the Mafia enforcers."

"Did you kill them?"

"Only one ... *CHICA* was anchored out off of Los Suenos Marina, but I spotted Beau and the enforcers who were already on board. I swam out when it was dark, and had to kill one in the cockpit. Beau got loose and shot the other one with a gun he'd hidden aboard — just as the bad guy was about to shoot me."

"Did you have a gun?"

"No — just a steak knife from dinner."

"So you're in this up to your neck."

"I guess you could say that. I felt I had to save my brother from these thugs. Beau had plastic bagged and hidden half the money in the two main fuel tanks, in the middle of the night, while it was in Charley's yard. Charley fixed the bookies' props after they went aground on the trip up to St. Petersburg from Naples. They picked the Bertram up the next morning. Beau and Ricardo Cabeza joined them at the city marina fuel dock where they filled up and left for Key West."

"And you had already started down to Key West from the Boatworks with Annie three hours before."

"Right ... Now, back to *CHICA* in Costa Rica. Then Beau and I blew up the Bertram in the anchorage, dinghied ashore, and drove to San José in my rental car. We threw the deflated dinghy and engine off a bridge into a crocodile infested river on our way to San José in the wee hours of the morning. Beau took the three million and started a new life in Costa Rica. I flew home."

"How did you blow her up?"

"I soaked a hand towel in gas from the dinghy gas can and sprinkled the rest around the salon and put the towel on the automatic coffee maker's hot plate. I set auto to brew at 15 minutes. It blew the flybridge 50 feet in the air."

"So?" asked Jeb. "The Tampa Mafia thought Beau was dead and didn't really know who had piloted the Bertram to Costa Rica. They assumed the captain and their two enforcers went up in smoke along with the three million … but what happened to the two bookies?"

"Well, Beau told me he knew they would kill him as soon as he divided the 1.5 million he had hidden. Their cousin was dead, and Beau was their last link to the robbery. They had no idea the Tampa Mafia already knew they owned the Bertram. Beau eliminated both of them overboard, way offshore, in a desolate stretch of the Pacific. You could say, 'They're sleeping with the fishes.'"

"So Uncle Beau stayed in Costa Rica, you flew home, and the Tampa Mafia was none the wiser."

"Not until a year ago, when a river tour guide found the dinghy caught in a fallen tree snag, during a drought."

Jeb thought for a moment and exclaimed, "Then it was the Tampa Mafia trying to snatch you down in Key West, not the Russians like you told me. Your plane ticket, your hotel, and rental car put you at Los Suenos in Costa Rica!"

"Right, and if they'd gotten me, I wouldn't be here tonight. They probably would have tortured the information out of me, and Beau would be dead too. When I got away in Key West and sent you to the Bahamas, they tried again in the mountains at your Aunt Scarlett's, but I got away again. That's when they might have snatched you in St. Petersburg … They might have killed us all."

"So the Russian Mafia actually bailed us out when they retaliated against the Tampa Mafia after they wiped out the Russian's operatives in Key West?"

"This is the time for the truth, Jeb, no more lies. I called Beau in Costa Rica and explained the situation as I knew it then. Beau agreed we'd all be toast if we didn't get proactive."

"Holy Shit! ... You didn't ....?"

"Beau flew in, and we set the whole thing up after a couple of days of surveillance in Tampa. The hardest part was getting "No Nose" Cipriano and his capo, Luigi Scuzzi, together after dark on the veranda of his Golf View Street mansion. Beau shot them from a live oak tree on the golf course with my hog hunting rifle."

"And the other Tampa guys who knew. Did you ...?"

"No, no ... That was retaliation back and forth between the two gangs after we killed No Nose and Luigi. The Tampa Mafia thought the Russians killed their bosses. Once the retaliation started, the Russians from New York killed everyone else in Tampa who would care about the robbery."

"So we're safe."

"Yes."

Jeb sat silent for a minute looking down at the floor. He slowly raised his head, looked at his father, and said, "This has been one hell of a reality check. I had no idea our family was this tight. I mean, I knew you would always be there for me, but I didn't know to what extent — until now. I learned a lot about you when that ten-foot alligator killed one of our guard dogs a few years ago. When the state trapper said he couldn't come for three or four days, the state laws protecting alligators tied your hands. So you caught it yourself, to protect our other dog, and we delivered all 500 pounds of him to the trapper alive. You were resourceful, unafraid, and determined. I fully understand why you did what you did in Costa Rica and Tampa. I can see that technically — there have been some laws broken, but fighting back against criminals like the Mafia is a victimless crime. I'm sure they were not accustomed to normal law abiding citizens beating them at their own game. I'm all in, Dad ... but I still think you should curtail your extracurricular amateur sleuthing and just concentrate on having fun."

"Beau's phone number is in my address book in this top desk drawer. If you ever need me, and I'm out of reach, call him. I listed his cell phone under his new identity, Robert J. Cornett, a Canadian citizen from Toronto.

Beau's living in Tambor, on The Gulf of Nicoya. He's about three hours from San José. I'll call him tomorrow and tell him about our conversation. Maybe next spring the two of us can go down and go fishing with him, he has a refurbished Bertram 31."

"Thanks for leveling with me, Dad."

"I love you, Jeb … I knew you'd understand."

***

Seth checked his compass and autopilot as Crooked Island passed to starboard and the Plana Cays loomed ahead.

"Want to eat lunch up there?" called Gene from below.

"Send John and Dino up to run the boat for a while. I'll come down and eat in the salon with you."

Seth turned the wheel over to Dino and climbed down the flybridge ladder.

"Where's Fred?" asked Seth as he sat down at the salon table.

"He's eaten and is taking a nap," answered Gene.

"Man, this cracked conch is good. I'm glad I went up and got it."

"Everybody else is glad too," said Gene as he took a sip of a cold one.

"Maybe I'll take a nap too when I finish my lunch. We've been lucky with the wind — if the trades were blowing we'd be slogging thru a five-foot sea at eight knots."

"You got that right! I downloaded the *St. Pete Times* from Flying Fish's Wi-Fi while we were fueling. The only thing of interest was a report from the FBI task force stating they haven't found any new leads to Peter Petcock's whereabouts since his federal prison escape. Dr. Rhonda Fickert turned in a rental car at the Tampa airport on the day he escaped, and a week later they found an Explorer SUV, she bought used in St. Pete, in the airport long term parking lot. The authorities could not find any sign of them on the airport surveillance cameras, although they figured out how he escaped from the prison hospital. The missing prison psychiatrist also signed in a fictitious doctor when she signed herself in to do her rounds, according to a handwriting expert. A security camera shows Peter leaving in green scrubs, with a stethoscope around his neck, and a security badge pinned to his chest. They searched the psychiatrist's apartment and found a head shot of Peter wearing a scrub hat on her computer hard drive. It looks like the prison doctor helped spring him."

"Women have always been attracted to Peter. From the pictures I saw of her in the paper when it first happened, I bet he ditched her pretty quick. He probably had some cash hidden, or they would have caught him by now. My guess would be he's probably in Mexico somewhere, he definitely has some drug contacts down there. Wake me up when we get to Mayaguana, Gene, I'll take her into Provo with Freddy from there."

CHAPTER FOUR

PETER Petcock drove across Alligator Alley on his way to Miami. It was early afternoon, and the day was hot and humid. *TAR BABY* left her St. Petersburg Yacht Club slip at first light with Seth and four crew aboard. Peter checked out of the Hampton Inn and headed south on I-275 across the Skyway Bridge about the same time *TAR BABY* was running under the center span. He'd already booked a flight for the next morning on American Airlines to Providenciales with his new credit card. He also had a room booked at the Clevelander Hotel in the South Beach section of Miami Beach, a 20-minute drive from the International Airport. He was planning on a little R&R that afternoon and evening. As Peter traveled southeast on I-75, he looked out over the vast Everglades River of Grass, punctuated by its random cypress hammocks. He was happy to be out of his cell and running free. But most of all, he was looking forward to settling his score with Seth in Provo.

Sometimes it is hard to understand the motivations of men. Most men are content with the pursuit of money so they can obtain the basic necessities of life; such as food, shelter, and companionship. Others want to support a spouse and a family. Some also crave the finer things in life, such as fast machines, gourmet meals, travel, and fine wines. A very few, immerse themselves in the thrill of competition and sport, such as the pursuit of large game fish. Peter, however, more resembled the proverbial dog on the bridge gazing at his reflection and noticing the bone in the reflected dog's mouth. Driven by his flawed character, he attempts to seize the reflected bone and drops his in the water. Peter successfully escaped prison and recovered the money he had stashed along with his new identity. But, he could not transcend his narcissistic dirt-bag soul, which dictated the necessity to seek revenge on someone who was never the cause of his degeneracy.

Before long, the downtown buildings in Miami loomed ahead, and Peter arrived in Miami Beach. He checked in at the Clevelander, stowed his gear in his room, and changed into his swim trunks. Peter threw on an unbuttoned Tommy Bahama shirt he'd picked up in St. Pete, and headed for the pool. He stepped out of the elevator and into a vibrant poolside scene, tailor-made for a handsome swinger with a chiseled physique. Sitting at a poolside table, he ordered a Mojito and checked out the talent thru a pair of blue mirrored Costa Del Mars.

Within 30 minutes he corralled a pair of gorgeous bikini-clad girls who were visiting from Columbia. Blonde-haired Viviana and raven-haired Nicole were roommates at Central University in Bogota. Their English was no better than Peter's Spanish, but they were able to communicate that they were in Miami to have some unchaperoned fun. He bought them drinks and participated in some shallow end pool-time horseplay. The loud music was provocative, and the pool crowd was raucous. Even in the pool, the summer afternoon heat was almost unbearable. Peter pulled Nicole close and whispered in her ear, "Would you like to come up to my room for a *frio* shower, air conditioning, and *mas Mojitos*? I have a bottle of *Patron Tequila*."

"*Mi amiga* Viviana, *ademas*?"

"*Si*, we all have fun!"

Nicole bounced over to Viviana and whispered in her ear. Viviana looked at Peter, smiled, then said, "*Vamonos*."

***

Peter lay naked on the bed. In between shots of tequila, the girls were taking turns with him. A little cocaine would be nice, but he couldn't take any chances that might upset his mission. He'd run through as many positions as his imagination would allow and the tequila was keeping him in check. Nicole had slim hips and perky breasts. Her face was sultry, and she had a butt-floss bikini tan line. Viviana was more voluptuous than Nicole, with large brown areolas and a classic derrière. She had higher cheekbones, fuller lips, and a mischievous smile. Both were practiced and took their time. They kissed each other and then gave Peter a little lesbo show. Finally, they doubled teamed him to fruition.

The girls took another shower and left as Peter was nodding off. On the way out, they promised to meet him in the downstairs bar about 10:00 p.m., but Peter knew he'd never see them again. He smiled to himself as he drifted off to sleep.

Peter woke up with a start, soaked with sweat from the nightmare that jolted him awake. The dream started off pleasurably, with Nicole and Viviana approaching him out of a gray mist. They both wore nothing but stiletto high heels. As they slowly walked toward him, their femininity rotated in different directions within a syncopated cadence.

"You no like us no more? Viviana and I have been waiting for you in the bar all night. You break our hearts, *Papi*," said Nicole as she slowly raked her dark red nails across Peter's chest … drawing blood.

Peter started to say something, but Nicole quickly put her finger on his lips. She reached down and grabbed his rock hard member and slid on top of him. Nicole started bucking and grinding — Peter finally rolled her over and got on top. He felt Viviana's soothing hands on his shoulders and smiled. Suddenly, he felt a large object being rammed up his rectum. He looked back in horror at Seth, in his football uniform, trying to shove a football up his ass and laughing. He tried to move, but Nicole and Viviana had turned into the Crips holding him down while Seth violated him. Mercifully, he woke up — but he couldn't shake it. He became enraged and punched his fist thru the drywall, almost breaking his hand.

Peter started ranting out loud, "I'll torture the bastard until he begs me to kill him. I'm going to fuck him up no matter what it costs me!"

He took some deep breaths and started to calm down. He could only hope when he finally did kill Seth, that his mind would let it go.

It was dark outside, and the clock on the nightstand read 9:00 p.m. He noticed the music below had changed to a more Latin beat, but the driving bass was just as loud. His mind quickly returned to reality, and he realized he was running out of time in Miami. After moving a framed print from the other side of the room over the hole in the drywall, he headed for the shower. He'd have dinner at the Zen Sai around the corner at the Essex and then try for an early pickup back at the Clevelander after the Latin dance show. His Provo flight left at 10:00 a.m. so he would limit his alcohol intake. Peter knew he needed to be at the airport at 7:30 a.m. to turn in his rental car and start his international check-in at 8:00. Thankfully, the airport was only 20 minutes away. If he hustled a little, he could catch the last Clevelander show at 11:00.

Dinner was superb, easily the best meal he'd eaten since his last dinner at Louie's Backyard in Key West four years ago. When he got back, the 1020 bar at the Clevelander was packed. Luckily, he found a table for two with only one chair near the dance floor. He ordered what would be his only drink of the night — a $25, 120 oz., "Clevemosa". The waiters wouldn't push him for another drink, and if he got lucky he could just stick another straw in it.

The last show started almost as he sat down, and the music was deafening. The dancers were Brazilian and were very talented and energetic. Peter scoped the room and didn't see anything other than couples close to him. He started to watch one of the tall Brazilian dancers who had an ass like a Kardashian. He stared at her and was mesmerized by her beauty and skill. Finally, he caught her eye and smiled broadly. The next time she came near he winked at her. She didn't seem to notice. When the act was over, and the troupe was taking their bows, Peter stood up and clapped so she could get a look at him. She looked in his direction, but they didn't make eye contact. The floor show was over, and Peter sat down and looked at his watch which read 12:00 a.m. He would give the dancer 30 minutes before trolling the bar for a working girl. While he waited, he assessed the talent at the bar. There were four, maybe five, unescorted women at the bar. Two of them tried to make eye contact with Peter, tipping him off that they were probably pros. Working girls were nothing new for him. He and his Key West drug-smuggling crew had a bevy of Eastern European girls who partied with them down there. Peter supplied them with cocaine, boat rides, pool parties, drinks and food, and they supplied Peter and his crew with sex. The street value of the coke made it very affordable for a smuggler.

The best thing was there were no romantic entanglements, and they left when the party was over.

The Brazilian dancer did not materialize, so Peter walked over to the younger looking hooker and said, "Can I buy you a drink?"

She looked up at him and replied, "Why don't we go over to your table and work on your Clevemosa, you've hardly touched it."

She slid off her barstool, and Peter followed her over to the table. Peter pulled up another chair, and they sat down. He'd gotten a good look at her rear end on the walk over and liked what he saw.

She said, "My name is Evelyn," as she stuck a second straw in the Clevemosa. "Right up front, I'll tell you I'm a pro."

"I already had that figured, Evelyn," said Peter with a smile.

"I've been watching you since I sat down at the bar."

"I noticed."

"What brings you to Miami Beach ...uh?"

"Grant ... I'm just passing through. I have to fly out tomorrow morning."

"So what are you looking for tonight, Grant?"

"A little companionship, and some good sex."

"Are you staying here?"

"Yes."

"Do you want me to stay the night?"

"Probably not, I have to be at the airport at 7:30 a.m."

"Well ... it's almost 1:00 now, so we ought to get started. I'll tell you what ... I usually charge $500 for a couple of hours, $1000 for the night. But since you're staying here and you're obviously attractive ... and not drunk, I'll only charge $300 as long as you don't expect anything too kinky."

"What's kinky?" laughed Peter.

"Like a dog collar, handcuffs, rough stuff, or a golden shower."

"I'm not into any of those things."

"Well, then let's go up, Grant," said Evelyn, taking a last long pull on her Clevemosa straw.

Evelyn left the Clevelander at 2:35 a.m. leaving a thoroughly sated Peter behind. He'd given her $300, plus a $50 tip for some things she'd done to him that *he* considered kinky. He phoned the front desk for a 6:00 a.m. wake-up call, and fell into a deep sleep.

***

At 11:55 a.m., Peter looked out of the airplane's window as the American Airline's flight started its descent into Providenciales. After closing out his account at the hotel in cash, things went smoothly at the Miami Airport. When he turned in the rental car he paid cash too, just to cover his tracks. His passport cycled through the computer at the curbside check-in with no problem, and he headed for security with his new roll-around suitcase. The medium blue Columbia fishing shirt he was wearing had $9000, equally split amongst three different pockets. There was another $25,000, in $100 bills taped behind the zippered lining in the carry-on suitcase, his only piece of luggage. The rest of his money now rested in his overseas international accounts. A small black backpack, with a fishing hat, light rain jacket, Dopp kit, and other personal items, hung over one shoulder.

He gazed down at the Atlantic Ocean, it looked choppy with long white streaks, indicating winds of twenty knots or better. The pilot landed the plane smoothly and Peter deplaned onto the tarmac and followed the other passengers into the terminal door marked Customs and Immigration. In fifteen minutes he was processed through immigration, then through customs, and found himself outside the airport in a transportation area. He hailed a cab and headed for the Turtle Cove Inn, which was the least expensive hotel overlooking the marina.

Peter remembered The Turks and Caicos were a group of small islands, with their own government, protected by the British. His first reminders were steering wheels on the right side, and the death-defying roundabouts, instead of stop lights, at intersections. The cab let Peter off in front of the Turtle Cove Inn on Lower Bight Road. He checked in and found there was a car rental location a half a block away, a restaurant and bar on site, and four other restaurants within walking distance. The first floor room was comfortable, overlooked the Turtle Cove Marina, and had adequate but noisy air-conditioning. It would serve his initial purposes, but Peter wanted to have a second, more remote location before Seth and *TAR BABY* arrived in the Marina.

At 1:00 p.m., Peter walked up Lower Bight Road to Scooter Bob's Car and Scooter Rentals. Mopeds, vans, SUV's, and cars of all sizes filled the lot in front of the building. As he walked inside the one-story building, he encountered a very tan, smiling middle-aged man, with long blond curly hair, standing behind the counter. "Scooter Bob" introduced himself. There was a Canadian flag nailed on the wall behind him. In the rear of Scooter's office was a bait and tackle shop that spilled out onto the Turtle Cove docks. Peter rented an SUV for three weeks, signed for all the insurance, and paid for it with his credit card. Scooter made copies of his passport and driver's license, asked to see his room key at the Turtle Cove Inn, then handed him the keys and a road map.

Scooter took Peter out on the lot and walked over to a white Chevy Tahoe with the name *"Bonehead"* painted in small black letters on the front hood.

"What's the name all about?" asked Peter.

"This vehicle is four years old and most years it's rented for three straight months to a bone fisherman from Islamorada, Florida who holds three bonefish world records. So I named it after him, eh? I named the rest of my fleet for visiting sportfish yachts who come down here every year to fish for marlin, like that Chevy Suburban *"D.A.Sea"* over there, and the silver Nissan hatchback *"Spellbound"*, right behind you. It also lets the locals know these cars are from my rental fleet. If they mess with them, they have to deal with me *and* the police, eh? It's a small island. The thieves concentrate on Avis and Hertz. If you have any problems with the truck, call me, and I'll send another car to you immediately. The island is only 37 square miles. Oh, and remember to drive on the wrong side of the road, eh?" laughed Scooter.

CAICOS CONSPIRACY

Peter got in the Tahoe and started driving around the island. After a close call at two roundabouts and one wrong way entrance from a side road, he started to get the hang of it. He made notes on his map, which had many of the local businesses and services already indicated, and he toured the island until dark. Gasoline was $6.37 per gallon — a little culture shock for Americans.

Peter saw miles of undeveloped land, covered in scrub jungle on the east and west ends of the island. He picked up a couple of free real estate magazines at one of the very upscale IGA supermarkets along with some snacks and beverages for his room refrigerator and headed for his hotel. The large hotel parking lot also served a government office, and the Aqua restaurant and bar. After dropping off his groceries at his room, he walked around the marina and checked out the Tiki Hut restaurant, Turtle Diver's headquarters, SharkBites bar and grill, and a nice looking Italian restaurant named Baci's. Enjoying the walk after being cooped up all day, he headed back to the crowded Tiki Hut and enjoyed an excellent grilled wahoo salad and a couple of local Turk's Head beers. The large oval bar seemed to be mainly patronized by locals. He walked back towards his room in the cool evening breeze and filtered through the crowd at Aqua. They had live island music on their deck and another crowd of locals at their circular open-air bar. Peter was tired and needed some sleep. Tomorrow, he'd start looking at secluded rentals bright and early. He fell asleep reading the Turks and Caicos' Discover Magazine outlining local points of interest on the island.

***

After a restless night, Peter arose with the sun and took a swim in the pool before sitting down to a sumptuous breakfast on Aqua's deck, which overlooked the marina. He'd been jolted awake again in the middle of the night by the Nicole and Seth dream. It had to be his imagination, but his rear-end really felt like a football had been shoved up it. His arms and legs ached like the Crips had actually held him down. The memory of Seth's laughing face, framed by his football helmet, only served to increase his resolve to kill him.

Peter finally shook it off and looked out over the marina. There were seven or eight sportfish boats fifty feet or longer, all moored directly behind and to the west of the restaurant. He hoped Seth's boat would dock on this quay. Across the way, larger sailboats and mega yachts were moored along with a score of commercial parasail and dive boats. Peter had two goals for the day, to find a remote cottage and a special place to imprison Seth before killing him. He had two home rental agencies written down, both in the Grace Bay tourist area shopping district. The special place he had in mind for Seth was a dark, dank cave in some remote spot on the island. Peter remembered a trip down this way many years ago on a commercial fishing boat. They'd limped into the North Caicos Island ferry dock to fix the vessel's hydraulic steering. The crew was stuck there for three days while the engineer went over to Provo to pick up the parts to fix the problem. Peter and his shipmates rode in a cab over the stone and gravel causeway to sparsely populated Middle Caicos to explore a large group of primitive caves at Conch Bar Village near Mudjin Beach. The cab driver told them those caves were the largest non-submerged cave system in the Bahamas/Turks and Caicos island chain. The crew crawled around in the limestone caves for most of a day using flashlights. They saw hundreds of stalagmites and stalactites. Scores of bats hung from the limestone cavern ceilings, and hordes of giant land crabs patrolled the caves' floors. Many of the caverns had streams and pools supplied by the ocean tidal flow. Cave-ins blocked some of the passages, and the stench of bat guano was overpowering. The crew was glad to get back to their fishing boat, and a hot shower.

The local tourist guides alerted Peter to two cave locations on Provo. "Pirate's Cave" was near Northwest Point, perched above a deserted beach, at the end of Malcom Roads. The other was at the southern end of the island and was called, "The Hole". As he set out for Pirate's Cave in the Tahoe, downtown quickly melted away. He turned right at a sign that read "The Blue Hills — the soul of Provo" and found himself riding along the ocean through the mostly Haitian-populated Blue Hills. Some of the wooden boats that brought them to Provo were pulled up along the beach road and were slowly rotting away. He cut across the island at its widest point, at Wheeland, and 15 minutes later found himself on a rocky dirt road slowly bumping his way through the scrub jungle. The Tahoe bottomed out a couple of times but finally made it to a desolate turnaround on a cliff overlooking the Caribbean. Below was a beautiful, deserted beach covered with flotsam and jetsam. There was only one trail leading to the beach below, which Peter started down. Suddenly, two large Haitian men came out of the underbrush with machetes. He stood his ground. They sized Peter up, looked at each other, and shook their head — no, then retreated quickly back into the bush. *Probably looking for some easier prey,* thought Peter, as he hurried down the trail. He knew the Turks and Caicos had a long-standing illegal immigrant problem with nearby Haiti and the Dominican Republic, and deported any illegals they caught. The ones who hid in the hills lived off the land or resorted to petty theft or worse.

As he approached the south bluff, Peter saw the top of a ladder sticking up through a large rock crevasse. On closer inspection, it led down into a small cave whose opening faced the pastel blue ocean. He climbed down the sturdy wooden ladder and was disappointed in how small the cave really was. Multi-colored graffiti covered the walls, and an authentic carving on one rock wall by a pirate named "St. Louis" was nearly obliterated. Peter could find no passageways into any other chambers. After climbing back out, he scoured the surrounding rock formations for another opening to no avail. The ladder was probably maintained by a tour guide. He also wondered how many more Haitians either lived or lurked near the cave. It looked like it might be a fairly busy place. After finding a stout piece of driftwood on the beach, he started the trip back up the path to the Tahoe. The Haitians might still be laying in waiting for him at the top. The trip back to the Tahoe went without incident, but Peter wrote the Pirate's Cave off as a possible dungeon. He bumped the Tahoe back out the deserted road and made his way back to the Blue Hills. On one deserted stretch of road, he passed a bar called "The Boss Iguana Beach Bar". A sign over the drive-in entrance proclaimed; *Non-stop VIP.* Closer to downtown, the Blue Hills became more populated. He passed by a little seaside restaurant called "Da Conch Shack", where the lunch crowd had already filled the parking lot. Peter continued to the roundabout and took Leeward Highway east towards the Long Bay Hills to check out The Hole. After his experience with the Haitians at Pirate's Cave, Peter thought he might need some personal protection, like a pistol or knife. He would take care of that later this evening.

Peter turned off on Long Bay Road and found sparsely populated Sea Sage Hill Road. He drove slowly down Sea Sage and would have missed The Hole, except for a car pulling away near a small path worn into the scrub jungle. After walking only a few steps down the path, he passed a white limestone boulder lettered with *The Hole* in black paint. A few more steps put him precariously close to the edge of the 50-foot diameter sinkhole. Sixty feet below, the bottom 15 feet was filled with salt water. Peter could see the tide lines at the bottom levels. That meant this sinkhole connected somehow to the ocean or sea. There were no ladders or ropes leading down to the water level, but he read last night that a tour operator sometimes lowered a rope ladder down, and adventurous tourists could swim there. As Peter left, he noticed an almost impenetrable scrub jungle surrounded The Hole, as far as he could see. It wasn't what he was hoping to find, so he backtracked back to Leeward Highway by way of Long Bay Beach Drive and got a look at its stunning beach. It was about a half a mile from The Hole to the beach. Whitecaps dotted the bay, and there were eight or ten kiteboarders speeding across the luminescent blue water. After turning off Leeward at the Grace Bay roundabout, he found a little pub in the tourist shopping district called Danny Buoys. He reflected on his morning over a cheeseburger and a Turk's Head beer.

All at once it came to him, *The Hole had to link up to the sea. If he found where the water exited The Hole — and scuba dove along the passage — the chances were he might find another cave that had a small opening above it, along the route to the sea. Any sign of light would give it away.* He would need a tank, regulator, and another pair of fins, as he had thrown his fins in a dumpster in St. Pete. His suitcase contained a mask, snorkel, waterproof flashlight and his neoprene top, but he no longer had his PADI card — so he couldn't buy air. He needed to figure out a way get a tankful. Peter also needed a buoyancy compensator, weights, a compass, a depth indicator, a serrated dive knife, and a four-pound spool of #15 seine net twine. To scale the rock walls, he needed a couple of stainless steel carabiner clips and three 100 foot lengths of 5/8" polyester rope. Peter finished his lunch and paid his check. He asked the waitress where he could find the closest dive shop.

She pointed west and said, "About a block away, Dive Provo."

Peter left the Tahoe in Danny's parking lot and walked over to Dive Provo. The shop was back off the road in a little shopping area. He asked questions while he was buying the equipment. Dive Provo docked their boats in two locations, Caicos Marina on the east end of the island, and Turtle Cove Marina. As the clerk was ringing up Peter's purchases, she was also busy trying to sell him a dive trip.

"We provide the best service in Provo, sir. If you buy a two-day ticket, our dive personnel will clean and reinstall your equipment on our tanks at no charge. We also provide free pickup from your hotel. All you have to do is show up."

"Thanks for the info. I'll be back after I get my schedule organized. I want to go sportfishing for a couple of days, too."

"Here's a brochure on *PANOPLY*. Their captain, Delphine, has been really hot on marlin lately. They're down in Turtle Cove Marina, too."

"Thanks again," said Peter as he counted out some cash.

Peter stowed his purchases at the Inn, then headed back up to the Leeward Highway for the marine store just past the Blue Hills roundabout, to buy the rope, carabiners, and seine-net braided twine. All the way there, he repeated *Drive Left, Yield Right*.

Once back in his room at the Turtle Cove Inn, Peter settled in for a nap. He would wait to see where the Dive Provo boat docked. Later that night, he would relieve their boat of a couple of tanks.

When he awoke, Peter spotted the Dive Provo boat on the south side of the marina's central peninsular. It was across from the Turtle Cove Inn, 600 feet to the west. There were eight to ten dive and parasail boats in that area. As Peter ate dinner at Aqua, he watched across the water looking for some semblance of a security pattern to develop. A single security person walked around the center peninsula once during the hour he was there, and nobody walked the dock on the Aqua, Turtle Cove Inn, and Scooter Bob side. After dinner, Peter drove downtown near the airport and parked in front of the Club Zodiac. It was one of a few Dominican bars he'd frequented while he was a commercial fisherman. Provo was a good place to fuel up and reprovision for the trip back north to Florida. The Zodiac was smoke filled, had cheap drinks, and live music downstairs. Upstairs were Dominican hookers and "hot sheet" rooms. Peter sat down at the bar and ordered a rum and coke. Halfway through his drink he called the bartender over and asked him where he could buy a "piece".

"A piece of what?" asked the bartender smiling.

"A .38 or 9mm. — there's a $100 in it for you."

"You been in here before?"

"Not for a while, I used to commercial fish out of Florida."

"Hold on a minute. I'll be right back."

He ducked under the bar and went into the back room. When he came back, he pointed and said, "Go through that door and ask for Rodrigo."

Peter paid for his drink and slipped the bartender $100. As he walked towards the door, he felt for the dive knife he'd strapped to the back of his belt under his loose-fitting Tommy Bahamas shirt. He strode through the door and saw a card game going on in the corner through the dim light and smoke. He said, "I'm here to see Rodrigo."

One of the men folded his cards, turned them over on the table, and stood up. He pointed to a small table near the door and said, "Sit down there and we'll talk."

He was tall and husky for a Dominican, though not as big as Peter. His curly black hair was shoulder length, and he sported a *pistole* mustache. Rodrigo sat down and said, "My bartender tells me you are looking for a piece ... automatic or revolver?"

"I prefer a revolver."

"I have a Colt .357 magnum, or a Smith and Wesson .38 special."

"The .38, and some ammo. How much?"

"$1000 ... It includes 50 rounds."

"That seems fair. I have the money with me."

"Do you know where Tricky Ricky's is in Five Cays? It's just up the street from Pumpy's bar on Reese Street."

"Yeah, I been to Pumpy's."

"I'll make a phone call — ask for Rick at the outside bar. He'll take you to his office and give you a package — open it, check it out. If you want it, give him the $1000 cash."

Peter was in Five Cays in 15 minutes and passed Pumpy's on the right as he drove up the hill. Tricky Ricky's had an eight-foot wooden fence around it, and the courtyard was jamming with people dancing and a few topless girls splashing in a small pool. He collared the bartender who seemed to be expecting him. Peter still wasn't sure if they were scamming him, but he sensed Rodrigo was a crooked businessman, not a thief. Rick delivered the goods, and Peter was glad to put the throbbing bass and grinding hookers behind him.

After returning to his room, he opened his sliding glass door and sat out on his little patio with a cold one. He noticed there were three empty slips towards Scooter Bob's. There appeared to be tie poles missing in those slips. Below that were two 30 foot center consoles, and a 46' Hatteras charter sportfishing boat named *GWENDOLYN*. They would be his entry and exit points in and out of the water in a couple of hours.

Peter sat in a chair on the dark side of the Turtle Cove Inn pool and watched the bartender close and lock the last of the French doors around the bar, then finally walk into the parking lot. He went back to his room and got his mask, fins, B/C, and a short length of rope. He sat back out on his patio and waited for the security man to walk past on the center peninsula of the marina. All the sportfish boats behind Aqua and the Inn were dark.

Finally, the security man went by across the canal, and Peter headed for the two center consoles. He slipped off the dock into the water between them. Peter put on his fins and mask and headed for the Dive Provo boat on the other side. After climbing the ladder onto the large swim platform, he set down his fins and remained motionless for a minute. Seeing no movement anywhere, he went forward to the tank racks and lifted out one completely rigged tank and a spare tank. He tied them together, lashed his

56

inflated B/C to the ensemble, and slowly lowered the tanks over the side. After securing them to the gunnel with the piece of line, he checked the area for movement again, then slipped back into the basin.

Fifteen minutes later he was back in his room rinsing off his new gear in the shower. After sizing all of it to his proportions, he put the rest of his dive gear, rope, and other items, into his black backpack. A tourist transporting dive gear in Providenciales would hardly warrant any attention. Peter planned to be in the water at The Hole by 9:00 a.m. tomorrow morning.

CHAPTER FIVE

As El Bomba left the Silly Creek mansion he could see the drawbridge in his rear view mirror as it slowly started to open back up. He was driving one of his plain black Suburbans so he would not be too conspicuous. His alibi, if needed, rested on him being in the Dominican Republic. Almost everybody who lived in Kew Town, the Blue Hills and Five Cays sections of the island knew El Bomba drove a blacked-out Escalade with chrome spinner wheels. As a poor street urchin in Santo Domingo, he always wanted such a car. He was a grown man when he finally saved enough pesos to hook a ride on a sailboat, overcrowded with illegals, headed to the Turks and Caicos Islands. Rodrigo's street smarts had paid off handsomely in the seamy underbelly of this otherwise picture-perfect tropical paradise.

The land deal kidnapping was going well. His informant in the Provo property office related that Jock Baffert's lawyer already requisitioned the deeds, and a surveying company had picked up a property plat. Mrs. Baffert was behaving, according to his guards at the mansion. He called Jock earlier that morning, using his disguised computer voice, and instructed him where and when the closing would be this coming Tuesday.

But tonight, El Bomba wanted to check on his bread and butter island enterprises. If you weren't vigilant, someone would be sure to steal from you. He headed downtown to the Club Capri to check the receipts. This club was his biggest money maker. It was set up like a Florida titty bar. To make it even simpler, he needed no licenses, paid no fees, needed no visas for his employees, and had police immunity. His minister friend, Alistair, took care of all the details, so there was only one payoff to make each month. Club Capri had a full bar with waitresses. The girls danced to a DJ's music, and the club had VIP rooms. The dancers paid $100 a night just to dance there, and the club got $50 up front for 15 minutes in the VIP room. The girls worked the customers for $20 lap dances and tips. But, the real money maker was the escort service run out of the cocktail lounge. El Bomba rotated a group of high-priced call girls through the lounge. Well-heeled tourists could come in and pick up a girl while the snowbird residents from the U.S. and Europe could make a phone call and have them delivered by cab. Rodrigo met his manager, José "Cucaracha" Gonzalez, a childhood friend from the barrio in the Dominican Republic, in the back office to go over the books. Business was still good in the off-season but nothing like in the winter season.

Rodrigo drove a few blocks north on Old Airport Road, parked in an alley and walked across to the Club Zodiac. This was the first location that he built-up. El Bomba's business model had one business principle that most street criminal enterprises lacked. He didn't deal in drugs. No one sold drugs on any of his premises, and his core employees were required to be drug-free. Rodrigo noticed that people in the illegal drug business made huge sums of money very quickly, but they were usually caught by the authorities before long or were killed off by their competitors. You could pay off the local police or even federal authorities depending on the country. But sooner or later, the DEA would snare you. No one paid off the United States Drug Enforcement Agency. Back in 1985 two of The Turk's and Caicos' top government ministers were caught in a DEA sting in Miami, taking $35,000 each to look the other way while drug planes fueled up in complete safety on sparsely populated Middle Caicos. They did seven years in a U.S. federal penitentiary. No one ever retired from the illegal drug business, you either went to prison or went out feet first. Illegal gambling, prostitution, gun trafficking, loan sharking, and assault and battery were small potatoes. He could do that time standing on his head. Even murder on this island surrounded by miles of 4000-foot deep water and hungry sharks was hard to prove. They'd never find the body. Rodrigo was in it for the long haul. He checked the Zodiac's figures in his private office and everything there was in order.

El Bomba was just settling into a high stakes card game in the back room when his bartender came in and said there was a customer who wanted to buy a gun. Rodrigo had amassed quite a cache of weapons over the years on an island where only registered and licensed hunting shotguns were allowed. Only three hundred permitted guns existed in a country with a population of thirty thousand. The police did not carry firearms. Selling weapons smuggled in from the U.S. and Central America averaged a 200% profit. Rodrigo never touched the guns or the money during the exchange, and he used his underlings at different locations.

"Do you know this hombre?"

"He is a commercial fisherman from Florida. I remember him from some years ago. He would stop in, drink, then go upstairs and use the *chicas*. I think he is OK."

"Send him in, have him ask for me. If I like his looks, I'll deal."

The gringo looked OK, and El Bomba sent him to see Ricardo up in Five Cays. After calling "Rick", he cashed in and headed out to the Blue Hills to check his newest location. He'd stop by Tricky Ricky's bar later and pick up the $1000 in cash.

El Bomba drove out the Blue Hills Road, which ran along the ocean, to Wheeland. He passed by Da Conch Shack and "Kalooki's" and headed west along the two-lane road. The Boss Iguana Beach Bar was his latest brainstorm. It was on the way to nowhere. Rodrigo set up the beach bar on a pretty stretch of beach covering three acres of land. The parking lot and bar were at the end of a long sand drive, hidden from the road. Next to the rustic beach bar, he constructed a circular building with no windows. The air-conditioned pavilion was the bar's VIP room. He stocked the bar, seven days week, with his low end working girls from noon to 2:00 a.m. There was live local music on the weekends. The bar attracted an eclectic crowd of prosperous Dominicans and Haitians, locals of all walks, Canadian retirees, and adventurous tourists with rental cars. It was a long way from town, and so far off the road that no one could spot your car. Business was steady and building. He was happy with the crowd and planned on installing a backup generator for the VIP room after the Baffert land deal cleared.

Tricky Ricky's was his last stop. Everything in Five Cays was busy. Ricardo, "Rick", Rojas was another D.R. boy who came up with El Bomba. Rodrigo was partners with Rick in that bar. He had just put in a small in-ground swimming pool in one corner of his fenced courtyard. It was full of topless hookers at the moment. Rick was forced into making the investment by a competing bar. The Dogbite Cafe installed a small pool two months before, and it became an instant hit with the locals. El Bomba tracked down Rick in his back office,

"*Amigo*, did the Gringo buy the pistol?"

"Yeah, he was a cool customer. He didn't look like anybody to fuck with."

"A commercial fisherman probably worried about pirates."

"Here's the thousand."

El Bomba took it, counted it, and gave Rick $100.

They bumped fists, and El Bomba headed for one of his three safe houses in Five Cays a few blocks away, where his current girlfriend, Sarita, would be waiting for him. He smiled and thought about the veiled underworld that he and a few other enterprising Dominican refugees had created on Provo for its belongers, permanent residents, and visitors with prurient interests. It was out of the sight of the weekly Grace Bay tourist turnover and protected by the island politicians' insatiable greed.

***

Peter was up at dawn, loaded his dive gear in *Bonehead*, and took off east on Leeward Highway. He stopped for coffee and a breakfast sandwich at the IGA coffee shop. On the way out of the shopping center, he pilfered two orange traffic cones in front of the Digicel phone office, placed there to mark a broken curb. After continuing out Leeward, he turned on to Long Bay Drive, then Sea Sage, and stopped at The Hole. Peter carried his gear to the edge of the sinkhole and pictured what the cavern must have looked like before the roof caved in. He tied overhand knots in one of the 100-foot lengths of 5/8" rope, every 24 inches, then found a sturdy scrub tree back from the edge of the precipice, tied one end around its trunk, and lowered his dive equipment down into the water, 60 feet below. He tied another 100-foot length of 5/8" line around an adjacent tree trunk, with the bitter end trailing into The Hole. Peter fashioned himself a rappelling harness out of an eight-foot piece of line, tied a friction hitch onto the smooth line, and clipped in with a carabiner. He tested the rope with all his strength and weight. The two Provo Public Works traffic cones stood where the ropes entered The Hole. Peter rappelled down the sheer rock wall into the water. He knew he was strong enough to climb back up the knotted rope when his mission was completed and hoped the two public works cones would ensure that nobody would disturb the ropes.

Once in the water, he donned his gear and started to search for an underwater opening to Long Bay towards the southeast. The water temperature was 82 degrees, and it was dead low tide. Peter dove down and found the bottom of The Hole about 15 feet down. He was careful not to stir up the silt on the bottom and inched his way to the south with his gloved hands. As the sun moved higher, the visibility in The Hole increased. Finally, he felt a small crack in the rock just below sea level. It widened as he let some air out of his B/C and slowly sunk down. He shined his flashlight in the widening underwater gap and slowly moved forward. After removing a single weight from his belt, he tied the end of the spool of twine to it. Once the weight was securely on the bottom, he swam down the tight tunnel about 100 yards. Peter checked the depth on his gauge, and it read 12 feet. The tunnel leveled off, and he swam another 300 yards in the darkness letting out the braided twine as he went. As he continued swimming, he blew air into his B/C and rose back up in the water to sea level. His outstretched fingers touched the top of the tunnel, and he realized there was a two-foot air pocket above him. He raised his head out of the water and shined the flashlight forward. The air pocket continued as far as he could see. When he doused his flashlight, it became pitch dark again. Peter swam along with the flashlight on for another 300-400 yards, as the tunnel fluctuated from wide to wider. Then suddenly, he ran into a stone wall. After resting for a couple of minutes, he checked his tank and figured there was about an hour and a half of air left. Peter let some air out of his buoyancy compensator and started to investigate the wall. Ten minutes later, just as he was about to give up at 20 feet down, he doused the flashlight. A faint glimmer of light appeared off to his left. He swam over and felt an opening in the wall about four feet in diameter. After letting out some twine, he popped through the wall into a large chamber. A faint glow shone from above. He inflated his B/C and bobbed up to the surface. He could see one thin shaft of light coming down from a small fissure above. Shedding his mask, he shined his light up and realized he was in a large cave with a 20-30 foot ceiling. There was a scattering of stalagmite and stalactite formations. Bats were hanging from the ceiling, and the smell of their guano on the cave floor was overpowering. He swam to the edge of the cave floor, took off his tank and fins, then exited the water and explored the cave on foot. The chamber narrowed but ran another 250 feet, and the ceiling dropped closer as it sloped to the southeast. At the end of the chamber, there were remnants of a rock slide with a wide pool of shallow water in front of it. Peter crawled up the steep rubble and peered over the edge with his flashlight. The water channel continued on the other side, but the slide made it a sheer drop of better than 20 feet back to the water, as it disappeared through another rock wall. There were two large limestone pillars rising out of the rubble supporting the ceiling there. Peter guessed the last tunnel, which was wider yet, would lead to the sea. He cut the twine and knotted both ends, then tied the end of the length that stretched back to The Hole to a large piece of limestone. The four-pound spool had 5,880 feet on it to start. The played out twine would lead him back to The Hole. He would do the math subtracting the line left on the spool when he got back to the Tahoe.

Peter surveyed the cave one more time and checked his second flashlight for the return trip. He noticed a group of giant blue land crabs moving towards him, attracted by his flashlight. How could anything so ugly and nasty looking taste so good, he wondered? With his tank and other gear back on he followed his underwater twine trail back to The Hole. He was careful to check his compass reciprocals all the way back, writing them down on an attached slate with a #2 pencil. After surfacing, he saw no activity anywhere around the rim. He tied all his equipment to his rope and noticed he used only half a tank of air due to the shallow depth and the warm water temperature. The round trip had taken about 90 minutes. Peter started climbing the knotted rope, just like he'd learned in high school gym class. Slow and steady did the job, and he was up on the rim in ten minutes. After pulling up his equipment and quickly loading it into the Tahoe, he hurled the orange traffic cones back into the scrub brush. He turned around and headed northeast to Long Bay Highway, and turned right on Lignumvitae Drive, which was the straightest road down to Long Bay Beach. The odometer recorded six-tenths of a mile to the water. Next, he drove up to the Man-O-War, Curlew Drive crossroads, which was a deserted stretch of gravel road. He got out of the Tahoe, climbed up on its roof, and sighted his compass at 120° towards Long Bay then sighted the reciprocal of 300° back towards The Hole. The distinctive two-story, white roofed residence, which was a 100 yards northeast of The Hole gave him a reference point, and he calculated he was about four-tenths of a mile from The Hole. After retrieving the remaining seine twine, he put the spool on the ground and started to wind the twine between his thumb and elbow. Each loop would measure three feet. He got 1060 loops or 3180 feet. He did the math and knew the cavern was about 2700 feet from The Hole. Peter had swum within approximately 750 feet of Long Bay, underground. The fissure on top of the cave was within 300 feet of this crossroads. Back up on the Tahoe's roof, he surveyed the immediate area — an impenetrable scrub jungle in all four directions. There were two small clearings to the SSE of the crossroads with a couple hundred feet of scrub protecting them. He drove back down Leeward Highway to Building Materials Ltd. and bought two machetes, a hawksbill tree trimmer, a pickaxe, and a pair of leather work gloves. After realizing he was hungry, he grabbed a quick lunch at Club Sodax on the way back.

Peter worked through the dense scrub jungle for an hour to reach the smaller raised limestone clearing off Man-O-War West. After combing the entire area several times, he could not find the fissure. He worked west another half-hour and finally hacked through the scrub jungle to the larger clearing which had a more rugged limestone formation. After another 30

64

minutes of scouring the area, he smelled something foul. He followed his nose to a narrow fissure in the bare rock. The bats had covered that portion of the limestone rock with droppings. His nose found what his eyes couldn't. The fissure was barely wide enough for him to stick in his hand. He retrieved his pick-axe and started to work on the small limestone fissure. Within an hour, he had opened up a two-foot elliptical hole in the cavern ceiling and decided he'd done enough for one day. When he shined his flashlight thru the opening, he could see the cave floor he explored earlier that morning. The smell of bat guano was strong, but Peter was elated he'd found the cave. Tomorrow, he would buy an extension ladder and some battery powered lights. On his way out, he macheted a parking place for the Tahoe. Cut deep in the scrub, it would hide *Bonehead* from the road.

After a hot shower, Peter called a rental agent and set up an appointment for the next morning to look at cottages in the Long Bay area. He liked the remote and uncrowded aspect of that part of Provo. He ate a quiet dinner at SharkBites and turned in early after his exhausting day.

Predictably, his sleep was soon interrupted by his reoccurring nightmare.

***

Peter had breakfast at the Caicos Bakery near Grace Bay, before driving down to the Salt Mills Plaza where Island Rentals and Realty Ltd. offices were located. The friendly agent's name was Dick Gozenya. They headed for nearby Long Bay in Dick's car. After touring three cottages, Peter chose a secluded three bedroom beach cottage at the end of Long Bay Beach Road for $1400 per week. He signed a three-week rental contract with Dick, back at the office. Peter paid cash in advance and moved in that afternoon. Once settled, he went back to the building supply store and bought a 30-foot aluminum extension ladder, three tripod battery powered work lights, extra batteries, a grill lighter, a package of big black zip-ties, duct tape, and an Igloo cooler. Peter drove back out to Man-O-War and threaded his way into the hidden parking spot he'd macheted out of the scrub. It took him two trips to carry everything. He lowered the extension ladder down into the cave and set up the lights. Next, Peter secured the 5/8" rope to a scrub tree trunk 15 feet from the opening and lowered the rest of his equipment down into the cave. Backups, like the safety rope, were important.

He didn't check out of the Turtle Cove Inn because he wanted to keep that room for marina surveillance. After moving his luggage, dive gear, and an extra tank into the Tahoe, he stopped for some groceries and beer at the IGA. Then, Peter drove it all out to the beach house. Tomorrow he would take the dive gear and air tanks to the cave and follow the tidal passage out to the bay. If it were passable, he would have a shorter escape hatch if needed. He figured the remaining distance would be less than three lengths of a football field. After an early Italian dinner at Baci's in Turtle Cove, Peter checked the marina from his patio at the Inn. Seth had not arrived yet, and he didn't expect him for a few more days. He drove out to his new digs and fell quickly asleep listening to the gentle waves lap on Long Bay's beautiful shoreline.

***

Peter woke up soaking wet with sweat again, two hours before sunrise. It was the nightmare again. He realized the dream was symbolic, but when he was asleep it was terrifying. Especially the part when the Crips held him down — that was too real, and the pain and the shame took him back into the prison shower room. Peter believed his only hope of exorcising the nightmare would be the degradation and execution of Seth Stone. Finally, at first light, his thoughts turned back to the cave and his further exploration of the water passage.

***

When Peter switched on the tripod lights, they lit up the cave and cast eerie shadows in every direction. He hauled his dive gear up the rock slide and peered over the back edge with his flashlight. Peter tied the gear to the bitter end of a knotted rope and lowered it down to the rock floor next to

66

the water. He secured the other end around one of the limestone pillars poking up through the rubble. Then he tied a bowline around the second limestone pillar with the other coil of unknotted 5/8" rope, backed up, and put all his weight on the bowline knot and the pillar. They both held. Peter threw the bitter end over the sheer drop to the cavern floor, stepped into his rope harness, clipped onto the friction hitch, and rappelled down to his dive gear. Once in the water he donned his fins, cleared his mask, and tied his seine twine around a small stalagmite. The water passage grew wider as he swam east-southeast, but the ceiling dropped 12 inches in the first 50 yards. For the next 100 yards, the passage stayed much the same except there was no airspace above. Peter doused his flashlight. When his eyes adjusted, he could see a flicker of light at the end of the passage. In the next 100 yards the light became brighter, the depth increased to 15 feet, and he started to see some small fish. Finally, Peter swam out from under a three-foot limestone ledge, startling a couple of 12-pound grouper in the process. He carefully surfaced and found himself about 100 feet offshore in a 30-foot diameter depression about 15-feet deep. The surrounding water looked three to four-feet deep. A kite surfer went by between him and the shore, and Peter marked a pink beach house ashore. He submerged and made his way back to the cave. He left his dive gear and tanks on the beach side of the rockslide, and climbed the knotted rope, reset his rappelling gear, and returned to the cave. After dousing the lights, and climbing the ladder, he pulled it out of the hole, hiding it along with the safety rope at the edge of the jungle. He carefully recovered the opening with some more cut brush. Peter was ready for Seth whenever he got to the island.

The rest of the day was spent surveying the talent at the Grace Bay beaches and pool bars. Peter settled on Hemingway's Beach Bar and Restaurant at the Sands Hotel right around Happy Hour. There were tourists, locals, and an eclectic mix of age groups. Concentrating on the beach bar, he struck up a conversation with a group of bridesmaids from Connecticut, but he was far too old for them. Later, he chatted with two sunburned school teachers from Peoria, Illinois. They'd just been certified in the hotel pool and were going on their first dive with Turtle Cove Divers early the next morning. The natural beauty of Grace Bay and its world class resorts were impressive, but only a few miles away was his little cottage on an uncrowded, almost deserted stretch of beach. All of it was protected by the third longest barrier reef in the world, making it a watersports paradise. *I could get used to this*, thought Peter. But he quickly shook it off and thought of what he had planned for Seth Stone and his future in Australia.

The school teachers left and, as Peter ordered another beer, an attractive Dominican woman in business clothes slid onto the barstool next to him.

"Give me the usual Jimmy — it's been a long day," she called to the bartender.

She turned to Peter and said, "Let me guess, you're from Florida, and you just came down here to get away from it all."

Peter laughed and said, "You don't know how right you are."

She stuck her hand out for him to shake, "My name's Rikki, I'm a real estate agent."

Peter shook her hand and said, "I'm Grant ... havin' a bad day, huh?"

"Not bad, just long. I've been showing houses to a British couple, and they can't agree on anything."

Rikki's dirty martini arrived, and she clinked it with Peter's beer bottle and said, "Cheers."

They talked for a few more minutes, and Peter found out that Rikki was married to a Canadian heart specialist who worked at the Provo Hospital. They were both Turks and Caicos permanent residents based on the $500,000 plus investment they had made in their residence. Rikki met the doctor while she was an undergraduate at The University of Toronto.

"Do you have any children?"

"Not yet. I only took this real estate position because Thomas is so busy at the hospitals all the time. We have very little time together. I don't mix well with the other doctor's wives. They're all about their kids, bridge, and dinner parties. I want to make my own friends. Now, what about you?"

"First, I like women like you who are upfront ... and you pretty well pegged me. I am from Florida, I just sold my business in the Keys, and I wanted to come somewhere to relax and dive a bit."

68

"What kind of business were you in, Grant?"

"Wealth management."

"Are you married?"

"Haven't been for quite a while."

"Want me to show you the sights?"

"Well, sure ... but what about your husband?"

"He's back in Canada for a week of seminars at IntraHealth. They're planning to build bigger hospitals on Provo and Grand Turk. Where are you staying, Grant?"

"Right now ... at the Turtle Cove Inn, but I've been looking around for a nicer place. I kinda came in flyin' blind."

"I guess ... I couldn't go there, all the locals at Aqua know me. Look, this island is just like a small town. Having an affair with a local is almost impossible. Once in a while I get lucky and run into someone like you. Hey, I have an idea ... I still have the keys to all the houses I showed today. Why don't we go up to the one I showed on Sunset Bay this morning? It's the absolute best place on this island to watch the sun go down. We can stop and get a bottle of wine on the way."

"Sounds good to me, are you driving?"

Rikki stopped her BMW 7 Series Sedan at the Wine Cellar up on Leeward and bought a chilled bottle of Louis Jadot Chardonnay and some cheese and crackers. She asked Peter to stay in the car. They drove south down the ridge to the Mermaid Lagoon roundabout and headed for Chalk Sound. The house was walled and had an electric gate. Rikki's BMW disappeared inside. The house was modern, one sprawling story, with an infinity pool built on the edge of a 60 foot drop off to the beach below. Rikki opened the wine and carried it out in an ice bucket along with wine glasses from the inside bar.

""What a view!" exclaimed Peter.

"Yeah, it's five bedrooms, six baths, and a three-car garage. A bargain at a million-eight. The average upscale home or beachfront condo on Provo is about a million-five. This one's in the estate of a Swiss banker and his heirs want to fire sale it. Do you want to drink the wine in the pool or sit back here by the bar?"

"I'd like to drink it out at the infinity edge, but you don't have a suit."

Rikki laughed and finished pouring the glasses of wine. She slipped out of her jacket, wiggled out of her skirt, then slowly turned and pulled her top over her head. She picked up the wine glasses and set them on the edge of the pool. She unclasped her bra, stepped out of her black t-back, and eased into the pool.

"Cat got your tongue, Grant?"

"No ma'am, I'm right behind you."

He slipped off his swim trunks and followed her in, as she looked back over her shoulder. Her subtle tan lines made her glistening light brown skin even more provocative. A picture of the Miami Brazilian dancer popped into his mind. But Rikki's booty was even more unbelievable. They made their way to the pool's far edge, and she handed him his wine.

As they clinked their wine glasses together and kissed, Rikki looked down, smiled and said, "Welcome to Provo, Big Boy."

For the next two hours, they drank the wine, ate the cheese, and used almost every piece of horizontal furniture in the Swiss banker's house. They missed the sunset, but nothing else.

CHAPTER SIX

GENE woke Seth up as the hills of Mayaguana Island came into view, and handed him a steaming mug of coffee. Seth went up to the bridge and checked out their position. In 30 minutes he would head south along Pirates Well and Betsy Bay, then around Start Point and past the Abraham's Bay anchorage behind the reef. He thought he would call Lori on his sat-phone before he got to the Southeast Point where the water depth dropped off dramatically along the edge of the reef. If they spotted any birds working, they might be able to pick up a couple of nice yellowfin tuna. Seth knew it was going to get hectic when they got to Provo, and he would have to give one hundred percent of his time and effort to find Kat. They would only have three days to solve the puzzle before Jock's forced property closing.

"Gene, see if you can round up John. Ask him to rig a few naked ballyhoo to pull for some yellowfin tuna. Have him rig four 50-pound rods, two on the short riggers with some tuna feathers, and we'll run the other two with ballyhoo way-way back on the long riggers."

"You got it, Cappy. I can already taste the sashimi."

Seth dialed up Lori's cell phone on his sat-phone. She answered on the fifth ring.

"Hello, Lori, I've been thinking about you. How is everything at Torch Lake?"

"The weather's been nice and cool here. I checked *Passage Weather* on the web this morning, and it still looks really good down there too."

"Yeah, we've lucked out on this trip, it's been like a lake since Nassau. How are the kids?"

"Greg and Delores are here with little Hunter. He's *sooo* cute — I can hardly stand it. But, I'm looking forward to flying to the tropics to be with you."

"Me too, Lori!"

"Where are you now, and have you caught anything yet?"

"We're going to wet a line for the first time in a half hour or so. We're already down in the lower Bahamas because of the flat water."

"Well, good luck, and call me when you're settled down in Provo in a few days. Have you seen your friend Jock yet?"

"No, but I talked to him on the phone yesterday, I'll see him tonight when we get in. Say hey to Greg and Delores for me. I love you, Lori."

"I love you too, Seth ... catch the big one, and be safe."

Seth ended the call. At $2.00 a minute he never talked long, but the call was always a sure thing with *Iridium's* satellites. He actually hadn't lied to Lori. He just omitted some details. There was no sense worrying her now, and really **nobody** was supposed to know at this point. It was a small world and maybe one of her Michigan girlfriends was going diving next week or owned a house in Provo. For safety's sake, she didn't need to know yet. Seth had been up to Torch Lake a couple of times. Lori's house was right on the lake with a double door boathouse that had a party deck above it. He'd trolled for large Atlantic salmon and lake trout with a local guide and enjoyed catching both species. Torch Lake was the deepest land locked lake in Michigan at 300 feet. Though populated by many fishing boats, the fishermen shared the lake with a cadre of large houseboats, ski and wakeboard boats, and classic wood speedboats. Those types of lake boats were all about entertainment. Equipped with raucous out-sized stereos and clusters of speakers, they also displayed multi-colored LED lights above and below the water after dark. All the better to enjoy the marathon raft-up cocktail parties every weekend. It was hard to argue with people having a great time. His sister Scarlett's lake house on Lake Chatuge in the North Georgia Mountains held similar fond memories of lake boating.

Seth ran *TAR BABY* along Mayaguana's barrier reef. He spotted the old U.S. downrange tracking station support airfield above Abraham's Bay. When the space mission was over and NASA pulled out, they left all the buildings and equipment for the locals. Seth ran another 20 minutes and spotted the birds he hoped would be there, just past the Southeast Point. There the island fell away, and the barrier reef became predominant. The water around the Hatteras turned a dark inky blue while the bay inside the reef showed different shades of iridescent pastel blues. A 600 foot long, high and dry, rusting freighter sat on the very end of the reef. If the pilot had steered only 100 feet more to the east, he would have missed it. It was a stark reminder of the perils of the sea. Seth slowed down to 10 knots and lowered the outriggers. John, Dino, and Gene deployed the rods and baits. Once the ballyhoo baits were out about 250 feet, Seth trolled along the edge of the frothing bait school. They appeared to be little bonitos and skipjacks. On the second pass, both ballyhoo rigs snapped out of the long riggers starting the 50-wide Tiagra reel clickers screaming. Dino and John were on them in an instant. John worked himself into the fighting chair and hooked the reel up to the bucket harness straps. Gene quickly fitted a rod belt and shoulder harness to Dino as he braced his thighs against the gunnel in the left transom corner. Seth slowed to idle as the two fish pulled the monofilament line off both 50-wides at an alarming rate. Both anglers switched their clickers off as the fish slowed a bit. Dino's fish was into the braided backing, and John's was almost there. Since the sea was calm, Seth shifted to neutral as both fish finished their initial run. Once the fish were at a stalemate, he slowly backed the boat and helped the anglers retrieve their line. Both anglers pumped and reeled. Dino moved back and forth across the transom, lifting his line over or ducking under John's line as they fought the fish. John's fish started to circle almost straight down off the transom. Dino moved back to the left corner while John applied pressure on the fish with his body weight by winding himself off his seat and then sitting his leveraged weight back down. Before long Gene looked over the transom and exclaimed, "It's a big tuna!"

Freddy came out of the salon door rubbing the sleep out of his eyes. Gene swung the chair towards the right transom corner, then got a gaff.

Gene said, "Fred, we're going to need a tail rope."

73

Dino kept his fish tight as John worked the nice tuna up from the depths. Fred grabbed the leader and took the tuna up the right side as Gene sunk the gaff in him. After a brief struggle, Fred got the rope noose around his tail and pulled it tight. John put his rod in a chair holder, got out of the chair and opened up the transom tuna door. He helped Freddy pull the tuna thru the door tail first. The big tuna's swept-back aft dorsal and anal fins were a stunning, brilliant yellow. As soon as the tuna was aboard Gene closed the tuna door, Seth shifted back into reverse, and they started working on Dino's fish. Before long Dino's fish started circling straight down. This time, there was plenty of help and the crew made short work of landing the second yellowfin tuna.

"I make them both at about 150 pounds," called down Seth as he pulled in the outriggers. "Let's get everything else in and put away. Bleed both of the tuna back at the scuppers — let John cut the loins off them and pack them on ice in the fish box — Gene, crank the Eskimo up."

"I turned it on when we hooked up, Cappy. It's already makin' ice."

"Alright! Once we get everything squared away I want to get up and run all the way to Provo … Then I'll take a few slices of *sashimi* with Dino's famous sauce."

Soon *TAR BABY* was up and running at 24 knots, and everyone was sampling the fresh yellowfin. Two hours later they were closing on Provo's Northwest Point. There was still an hour or so of daylight left, so Seth cut back on the throttles and called Jock with his sat-phone.

"Hey, Jock, Seth here. I'm about 10 miles from Grace Bay."

"Man, am I glad to hear from you. You made great time."

"It's been like a lake all the way down, we even slowed down and caught a couple of big tuna in front of the freighter wreck on Mayaguana."

"Can I join you for dinner?"

"Of course," laughed Seth. "Will you call Crazy George and ask him to meet us at the cut and guide us through the reef?"

"I'll do better than that. I'll come on out with him and get on your boat."

"I should be at the reef in 30 minutes or so. See ya."

Seth called Turtle Cove and asked for a slip near the Turtle Cove Inn and Aqua. He ran around the reefs at Northwest Point and headed for the reef opening pin-pointed on his GPS map. As he got closer, he still couldn't find the small red and green floating balls that marked the entrance. He saw a small boat running an erratic route towards the reef and hoped it was Crazy George and Jock. He pulled back on the throttles and shifted into neutral. The skiff turned towards them and made its way through the reef. As it got closer, Seth recognized Jock and Crazy George.

"Permission to come aboard," yelled Jock as they pulled alongside. Crazy George had fenders tied horizontally all around the gunnels of his skiff so he could safely ease up to anything.

Dino and John helped Jock out of the dinghy and over the Hatteras's cockpit gunnel. Jock shook hands with the whole crew, then climbed to the flybridge. Seth shook his hand and gave Jock a big bear hug.

"I'm sorry this is happening to you, buddy. I don't know what else to say, but we're here to help."

"I'm glad you're here, Seth. I've been going fucking nuts. I took a dive trip out this morning and at least it kept my mind occupied. I got a call late this morning from the computer voice telling me that the closing will take place at 1:45 on Tuesday afternoon at Provo Title. I've got my lawyer drawing up the papers, and he's getting the property surveyed. Nobody on the island knows what's actually going on — you guys are my only allies."

"Do you know anybody in Customs? Maybe they could come down to the boat and check us through in the next hour. I'd like to get Gene to your house and have him start on the Land Rover and any other evidence."

"I'll make a call and try, Friday nights and weekends are tough. Follow Crazy George in, while I'm working on this. What's the slip number?"

"In front of the Aqua restaurant. Slip S-18."

Jock made the customs call and gave them the boat name and marina information while Seth threaded through the narrow, circuitous channel inside the reef.

"My friend, Cedric, says he'll be down here in about an hour. He and his partner are just finishing up a coastal freighter at South Dock Harbor."

CAICOS CONSPIRACY

Seth followed Crazy George through the narrow inlet leading to Turtle Cove. He left a small uninhabited spoil island, grown thick with conifers, to starboard and headed past the fuel dock and marina office. S-18 was just west of Aqua in front of The Turtle Inn, on the south side the marina's central peninsular, exactly where Seth wanted to be. From that location the crew could easily walk to The Tiki Hut, Scooter Bob's, SharkBites, Baci's and the Casino across Lower Bight Road from Aqua. They could park their rental cars in the Aqua parking lot, and if any of the crew wanted to move ashore, the Turtle Cove Inn was right there. Seth backed in, the crew tied *TAR BABY* to the dock and plugged her 50 amp cord into the dock pedestal. They all cracked open a cold one and started to wash the boat down. Seth collected all their passports, and they couldn't legally leave the vessel until they cleared customs. Seth palmed Crazy George with a Ulysses S. Grant and thanked him for his help.

George Taylor was an ex-pat American, who had worked for NASA and the Air Force during the Space Shuttle days, maintaining their downrange radar equipment. George spent time on Grand Bahama, Eleuthera, San Salvador, Mayaguana, Grand Turk, The Dominican Republic, and Puerto Rico during the program. Later the United States added St. Lucia, Antiqua, and Ascension Island. When his hitch was up, George headed for Providenciales with his oddball personality and renaissance skills. He became a permanent resident, the island's marine salvage expert, and a beloved friend to everyone.

Seth, Jock, and Gene holed up in the salon while the rest of the crew washed the boat. Jock filled Gene in on the hour by hour details of Kat's kidnapping. The former homicide detective took notes and asked some pointed questions.

"Is it possible the kidnapper has a personal vendetta against you, Jock?" asked Gene.

"I can't imagine … who would? I don't have any enemies, and the dive boats on this island can't handle all the business we enjoy. I make political donations to both political parties in equal amounts. It's something I learned from my father and American politics. I think it is just part of the political greed that has been continually increasing here over the years. They

76

can get away with almost anything, and they still get elected because of the patronage."

"So the big money revolves around land and development?"

"Mainly that, but in the last few years, there are unlicensed restaurants and bars springing up. Some establishments have illegal gambling and prostitution. There is an undesirable element forming that could undermine our upscale family-based tourist business. Roads and sidewalks are not getting fixed, the airport needs expanding, electricity and water need to be improved, and the Island's trash needs to be hauled away. Our infrastructure is starting to crumble. Parts of the island look like they could use a pressure cleaning. With fiscal responsibility and a righteous government, the Turks and Caicos could be the number one tourist and retirement destination in the Americas."

"Is the country in bad financial shape?" asked Seth.

"Not according to the present administration. But I see the signs, and I think they're cooking the books. Before every election, the elected politicians hand out an ever increasing number of government jobs. The ruling heads of the current government live like multi-millionaires. The country's debt is rising out of control. On top of it all, the government paid $600,000 in 2006 to send illegal aliens back to Haiti and the Dominican Republic. That doesn't sound like much to Americans, but for our little country of 30,000 residents, it's staggering. Tax and fee revenues are down because of the recession starting in the U.S., and the present government has proposed a new value-added sales tax. The government obviously needs this tax to prop it up. If this group of politicians loses, many of those jobs will be lost to supporters of the other party. Just so you understand — only "belongers", as voting citizens of British possessions are known, can vote here. The rest of us are either permanent or temporary residents. There are only three ways to become a belonger; first, your mother or father had to be born here; second, you can marry a belonger and vote after five years; or the Prime Minister can make you one for an outstanding social or economic contribution to the country. There are only 13,500 belongers, and they run the place. For example, they don't pay any fees to own businesses.

As a permanent resident, I pay $10,000 a year. They also don't pay many other government fees, like passports or driver's license. When they do pay, for example, it's only a quarter of what a commercial or a sportfishing license costs a permanent resident. I can't hire a divemaster or any other employee unless I can prove there's no belonger who can qualify. When I do, I pay a $1500 fee each year per employee. So the patronage continues, and the status quo survives. The level of fear and retribution that this political class employs confirms their sinister motives."

"What do you think will happen when the shit hits the fan?" asked Gene.

"I think the British Government will audit the country and find it is bankrupt. The culprits will be the politicians, right up to the highest level, who have stolen public funds, and misused government assets. Also, there are some developers who have gained advantages through bribes to those same politicians. On a lower level, the Brits will find officials taking bribes to look the other way concerning licenses, code violations, and illegal activities. The only answer will be to suspend the present government, and appoint a temporary governor. Then bring in a team of outside prosecutors and judges to ferret out, indict, and prosecute the violators. Lately, jury trials of politicians caught with their hand in the till almost always result in acquittal. The Governor will shut down the illegal activity, and suspend trial by jury. The juries can only be belongers, and they're all related in one way or another. The British will have to bring in impartial judges to decide guilt and innocence. The Governor will put the whole country on an austere budget until it works out of bankruptcy. The cushy patronage jobs will disappear, and the incarceration of the guilty politicians will hopefully serve as a deterrent to future Turks and Caicos elected politicians from behaving similarly. The sooner that happens the faster our country will recover."

John opened the door and said, "The Customs guys are here."

Jock thanked Cedric for coming over so quickly and went outside in the cockpit. Cedric welcomed Seth to the island and got right to work. Seth filled out the Customs and Immigration forms for himself and the crew. Cedric stamped all the passports while his partner Percy checked out the boat.

"Good luck in the tournament, Captain Stone. Remember to get fishing licenses at the marina office before you go fishing. Enjoy your stay in The Turks and Caicos."

"Thank you for coming so promptly, Cedric. Would you and Percy like a few pounds of fresh yellowfin tuna? We caught some big ones on our way past Mayaguana this morning."

"Well, you can thank Jock for our promptness. He is a good man, and I count him among my friends. But, we will accept the tuna from our new friends from America as a gesture of good will."

They shook hands and Seth gave them two big bags of iced tuna, as they left.

Jock came back in and said, "Why don't you all come up to the house for dinner? We can grill the tuna and have a salad and whatever else I can scare up. I can take you all up in my Suburban."

"We need a few minutes to take a shower and clean up. But it will give us a chance to start our investigation. You retrieved the Land Rover, right?" asked Seth.

"It's in the garage. I used latex gloves to bring it home."

Seth called the crew together, and they headed for the showers. An hour later Jock pulled into his driveway on Blue Mountain with the whole crew. After a quick house tour, Dino, John, and Fred got busy with dinner. Jock, Gene, and Seth went into the closed garage.

"I haven't disturbed anything, I opened the hood and plugged the coil wire back in. Then I opened the driver's door, got in, took the keys from behind the sun visor, and started it. I drove home, hit the garage door button, pulled in, and put the transmission in park. The keys are in the ignition, and I spotted her purse stuffed under the back seat."

"Do you have any more latex gloves, Jock?" asked Gene.

"'There's a whole box over on the workbench."

"Can you find me some baby or talcum powder and some clear scotch tape? Oh … and maybe Kat has one of those fluffy brushes women use to put on cheek blush? I'll need all that stuff to lift some fingerprints."

"I'll look."

79

CAICOS CONSPIRACY

Gene put on a pair of latex gloves and opened the driver's side back door. He lifted the seat up like he was going to lay the backrest down and picked Kat's purse straight up. He took it over to the workbench, spread out a couple of paper towels and set the purse on top of them. Seth helped him clear more tools and things off the workbench. Gene put down more paper towels, then carefully unloaded Kat's purse, item by item.

"Get a pad of paper and a pen from the office off the kitchen and catalog each item, Seth. If you can find some sticky notes, you can number them. Don't touch any surface that could hold a fingerprint."

"Here's what you asked for, Gene. I had no idea of how much stuff she'd rat-holed in her vanity and under her sink in our bathroom."

Dino interrupted with a "Dinner is served" announcement. They all retired to the dining room for lightly seared yellowfin tuna steaks topped with Dino's brown sugar bourbon sauce, a Balsamic tossed mixed green salad with walnuts, craisins and hashed brown cheddar cheese potatoes. They washed it down with an ice cold Turk's Head Ale. They could all tell Jock was glad the Geezers were in the house.

After dinner, Jock and the crew cleaned up the kitchen and dining room, while Gene and Seth dusted the car, Kat's business cell phone, and purse for fingerprints. The majority of them were most probably Kat's, but Gene found several similar prints on the driver's door and handle that were not. The cell phone held the same odd prints, as did the gold MK logo on the purse. The driver's sunshade and the car keys did not yield any of the odd prints. When Seth was finished numbering and cataloging the contents of Kat's purse, he went inside to make a phone call.

"How's the fingerprinting going?" asked Seth when he walked back into the garage 15 minutes later.

"It would be faster with a real kit, but this baby powder works pretty well," said Gene as he finished lightly brushing some powder on the driver's side door. He pursed his lips and blew some air to clear off the excess powder and lo and behold three fingerprints appeared. Next, he carefully covered each of them with a piece of scotch tape, pressed down lightly and peeled them off. Gene pressed each piece of tape on a blue sticky note and

80

made a recognizable print. Finally, each print was numbered and recorded on a sketch of the Rover.

"I never realized how painstaking police work was, Gene."

"Yeah, it's all about the details. I'm always surprised if we get a perp's print, you'd think they'd wear gloves. I see they wiped some parts of the door. Maybe whoever put the keys and the purse back in the SUV got careless? They were in a hurry since they snatched her in a public place. Did you call Bobby Thompson in DC?"

"Yes, I just called him on my sat-phone. He said he could run these prints through the FBI and Interpol, but stressed fingerprints take a little time. He wants you to send photos of them taken on a phone. Jock has one of those new Apple iPhones that has an HD camera. It's better than anything we have. He'll be out with it in a minute."

"I'm about done here. I want to lift a couple of prints from Jock, and also, lift a couple of Kat's ... like on her hairdryer and hairbrush. That way I can eliminate the majority of these and only send Bobby a few."

"Smart ... I'll get Jock."

Gene found like prints on Kat's hairdryer and brush and lifted a few fresh prints from Jock. He had Jock take pictures of the odd prints and email them to Bobby.

"They went through ... how can Bobby access all the top federal agencies?"

"Bobby was a CIA agent for years. Now his security company has contracts with the United States and most of its allies, including NATO. He provides guards, security systems, and cyber-intel. It might be the largest private company of its kind in the world."

"It would be nice if they could identify one of the perpetrators ... It would at least give us a clue. This iPhone actually takes as good a photo as my Nikon. I wish I could use it underwater. I bought four of them in Miami right after they came out after Christmas. Now our whole family keeps in touch, by text, email, and phone. We send pictures, and can access the internet, from all over the world."

'So, I don't remember seeing an iPhone on your wife's purse inventory," said Gene. "Does she carry it with her?"

"I can't believe I forgot that," said Jock hitting his forehead with the palm of his hand. "She carries it every waking moment, in case one of the kids call."

"Let's scour the Land Rover for it."

They searched the SUV thoroughly and didn't come up with it.

"You know, she usually carries it in her back pocket when she wears shorts or jeans because she leaves her purse on her desk at the rental company."

"Look," said Gene. "What I'm getting at is, by law, all the new cell phones have to have a GPS chip in them. We used to subpoena phone records so we could put a perp in a certain area at a certain time from the cell phone tower locations. Now the government wants exact locations for 911 emergency calls. It takes a special app."

"Well, we can't call the police here."

"Bobby Thompson!" said Seth.

Seth went outside again and called Bobby. He was back inside in ten minutes.

"Bobby needs Kat's iPhone username and password. He also needs the phone's area code and number, and her provider's name. According to him, there are a couple of ways to gain the phone's location if it's still turned on. He said a fully charged 2G battery will last 250 hours on standby, and has eight hours of talk time. So we have a good chance of it lasting for a week or so. His tech will basically hack her phone, install a couple of apps, and see which one works the best."

Jock found the info in his password storage app and emailed Bobby, straight away.

"Well Seth, it's getting late, and the kidnapper told me he'd have someone watching me every minute. I told him I was expecting y'all for the tournament, and he told me just to act normal. I guess I ought to take you back to the marina. We can start to follow any other leads tomorrow. Like, maybe you and Gene can check out Las Brisas where they took her?"

82

"OK, in the morning we'll get a couple of cars from Scooter Bob so we can move around the island. I want to get myself and the crew prepaid cell phones so we can all communicate. Is Digicel still the place?"

"Yeah, up by the IGA on Leeward."

"We also need to reprovision the boat and get settled. We'll go over and get fishing licenses, in case someone is watching us too. But, I doubt it. If Bobby calls me back tonight with any information, I'll call you right away. I'll plug my sat-phone into an external antenna when I'm inside the boat."

"Okay, let's get everybody loaded up, and I'll check with you in the morning. I'm glad you're here Seth. I'm starting to feel positive."

"We're gonna need some luck, buddy."

CHAPTER SEVEN

PETER drove toward Turtle Cove and checked his rear view mirror. Rikki had dropped him off at his SUV, saying she was heading home, but he wanted to make sure she wasn't following him. He didn't want her or anybody else to know about the Long Bay beach cottage. Depending on how things worked out with Seth, he didn't want her showing up there unannounced. He pulled into the Aqua/Turtle Cove Inn parking lot, locked up *Bonehead* and walked past the busy bar to his room. Rikki was quite an experience. She was the closest thing to a walking porno flick he'd ever encountered. There seemed to be nothing she wouldn't try. When Peter asked her if her husband had similar sexual tastes, she called the doctor her "Missionary Man". Rikki wrote her cell phone number on the back of her business card and asked him to call her when he changed hotels. She suggested he rent a small house or get a suite at one of the upscale resorts. Peter understood why, from both points of view. Making love to her in a small hotel room would be dangerous. Rikki handed him her card and said with a smile, "Don't lose the number."

He took a shower at the Inn, toweled off and put on a pair of fresh shorts and a Polo shirt. There were still a couple of shirts and pairs of shorts, along with some personal items in the bathroom to make the maid think he was still living there. He rinsed and wrung out his black swim trunks. Next, he pulled down the bed and rumpled it, throwing the spread over a chair. Then he walked over to the sliding glass door and pulled open the drapes and peered out at the marina. Peter was startled by what he saw and quickly pulled the drapes together. He peeked out again just to be sure. There it was, one slip to the east of his room, the transom of the *TAR BABY*. Seth had gotten here five days ahead of his float plan. After turning out the lights in the room, he opened the drapes a crack, pulled up a chair, and started his surveillance. There was no movement in the dimly lit salon. Peter figured *they were probably out to dinner*. His dive watch read 10:00 p.m.,

84

they'll be back soon — I'm sure they're tired after traveling all day. Peter fought to stay awake, but the wine and recent physical activity caught up with him. He nodded in and out of sleep, waking up with a start every five or ten minutes. Finally at 11:30 he was jolted awake from a deeper sleep by his nightmare. Quickly, he shrugged it off and looked out at *TAR BABY*. The lights were on, and it looked like the whole crew was aboard. Ten minutes later the lights on *TAR BABY* went off, and the boat was still. Peter would stay put at Turtle Cove tonight, so he called the desk for a 6:00 a.m. wake-up call. Once he sighted Seth, he wanted to check out the cave to make sure no one had stumbled upon it. He would then watch Seth's movements when he wasn't fishing. Seth was entered in the Caicos Classic Billfish Tournament so he would be here for the next two weeks. Peter knew a pattern would emerge after a few days. Where they ate breakfast, lunch, and dinner, and what bars would they frequent. Who would go to the IGA, the tackle store, and hardware store? Peter would find a way to catch Seth alone and unaware. He only needed a moment; then he would take him.

***

El Bomba drove up Chalk Sound Drive in the hot Saturday afternoon sun and called ahead to Diego, who was in charge of keeping Mrs. Baffert comfortably captive.

"Close the bridge, Diego, I'm about ten minutes away, is everything cool there?"

"Been very quiet, *Jefe*, our guest is being a good girl. Conchita is taking good care of her, she gave her a shower and cleaned her clothes. We borrowed a robe from the master suite. Conchita took the shackles off one at a time to get her clothes off. I waited at the door in case there was a problem. Conchita didn't wash her hair, she put a shower cap on her head and left the blindfold on, of course."

"How do you know?"

"I admit it, *Jefe*, I peeked. She is a beautiful woman."

"Treat her with respect, Diego; those were my orders."

"She doesn't know I peeked. Conchita wants to keep her in the robe until it's time to leave, easier for her bathroom trips ... *Ah, Bueno*, the green light just went on, the bridge is closed and ready for you, *Jefe*."

El Bomba drove his black Suburban over the drawbridge, its tires making a clacking sound on the tightly fitted boards. As soon as the SUV cleared the bridge, it started to revolve back open, exposing the sheer rock walls that lined the channel below. He checked in with Diego, then went outside and talked to Paco and Ramon, who took turns walking the small Cay, 24/7. There had been no suspicious boats or car traffic, just the occasional tourists taking pictures of the estate from across the moat. He went back inside the palatial main house and told Diego, "I'm going to move Mrs. Baffert to one of our houses in Five Cays before the closing on Tuesday. But, I want you to stay here with Paco. I'll need you to standby to open and close the bridge for me the day of the closing. Paco will provide you with security."

"No problem, *Jefe.*"

"I'll put *Cucaracha* in charge of the Five Cays house."

"A good choice, *Jefe*. José is a smart *hombre*."

El Bomba went into the minister's office and closed the door. He pulled a stolen prepaid cell phone out of his pocket and dialed the minister's clandestine cell phone in the Dominican.

"Alistair ... Rodrigo. Everything is going smoothly. The closing is on for Tuesday at 1:45."

"*Bueno* ... I will send the helicopter for you at exactly 12:00 noon, just to be safe."

"*Sí*, I will have your *dinero*. My men will wipe your *hacienda* of all fingerprints, and they'll drive my Suburban back to Five Cays where I'm moving the *Señora* Monday. They'll be no trace that anything went on at your *casa*."

"Call me when you take off in the helicopter Tuesday afternoon, Rodrigo."

Rodrigo ended the call, found Diego in the kitchen and said, "Close the bridge, I'm leaving. I'll be back sometime *mañana*... call me if there's any problem. And remember Diego — the utmost respect."

El Bomba headed for the Blue Hills and Boss Iguanas. He wanted to check out the hidden camera system that had just been installed in the VIP building, kitchen, and bar. As he passed Da Conch Shack and Kalooki's, he noticed the packed parking lot. It was a balmy Saturday night in Provo, and business should be good all over the island. He phoned a special contractor that he used for security and enforcement. Jacque Mehoff was an ex-pat Frenchman, who had lived on the island for 15 years. He'd been an elite member of France's DGSE, France's version of Britain's M-16 and the United States CIA, for ten years, but ran afoul of his socialist superiors because of his heavy-handed tactics. Disgraced and jobless in France, he dropped out of sight and surfaced in Providenciales. After getting the lay of the land in Provo, Jacque approached Rodrigo and offered to do his heavy lifting. But he added a unique twist. He would pose as a private investigator, working for lawyers and suspicious spouses, but would also be on Rodrigo's payroll. With that kind of cover, he was able to encourage El Bomba's welching customers to pay, eliminate enemies, discourage business competitors, and uncover disloyal employees. Jacque was a master of disguise and never left fingerprints or clues. He operated from the shadows when a hit was necessary, and El Bomba's hands never got dirty. Jacque moved as easily among the island's social and political elite as he did through the sordid Provo underworld. At the moment, El Bomba had him working on two projects. He was watching Jock Baffert's movements, and also supervising the security camera installation at Boss Iguanas.

"Jacque, *qué pasa?*"

"I've been tailing Baffert, and he seems to be just entertaining his fishing guests. They've been up to his house a couple of times, and he's gone down to their boat in Turtle Cove Marina. They're all here at Da Conch Shack for dinner right now. None of my police sources have called so I would say he's playing by the rules so far. But, I will keep my eyes on him."

El Bomba laughed and said, "I just passed there, and it's busy. What about the cameras?"

"The security cams are all installed in the kitchen, bar and VIP building. I had the two guys from Miami install the VIP cameras between 3:00 a.m. and 6:00 a.m. the last two nights. Nobody on the island knows they're there except you and me. The installers from Miami flew back this afternoon. I'll get the invoices to you when you have time. I paid them in cash."

"You can show me how it all works after this land deal closes — after I return from the D.R."

"It's a cool system; the cameras are all hidden, and the VIP cameras automatically switch to a night vision mode when the light is too low. Everything is motion activated. They all go to a hard drive that you can watch in your office at the Zodiac or at home. You can monitor your employees and have the goods on your VIP customers if you need them."

"So, they are working right now?"

"They are. When you get there, go behind the bar, and walk back in the kitchen. Note the time. Then walk into a couple of the VIP rooms. When we get together in your office, I'll show you how to go right to the dates and times."

"I think they'll pay for themselves before long. *Gracias,* Jacque you're a good *amigo.*"

"I got you covered, *Mon Copain.*"

El Bomba drove out to Boss Iguanas. It was already busy. As he walked through, he chatted with the employees and noted the times he thought he was on camera. On the drive back into town he called Sarita, who was cooking dinner for him at one of his houses in Five Cays.

"I'll be there in 15 minutes, Baby. Make me a mojito."

"I make you *Sanchoco* for dinner, Rodrigo. I been cooking all day."

"My favorite, Baby … what do you have on?"

"*Yust mi* cooking apron, high heel *choes,* and Chanel No. 5."

"I got somethin' *especial* for you too," chuckled Rodrigo.

He was looking forward to a quiet night of dinner and romance.

***

At 6:15 a.m. Saturday, Peter was back in his chair looking out the small slit he opened in the drapes. The trade winds had begun to blow again from the southeast. He was drinking a cup of coffee he brewed in his room. It was possibly the worst cup of coffee he'd ever tasted, but it was better than nothing. Later, he'd get a good cup at the Caicos Bakery on his way out to Long Bay. Finally, at 7:10, the salon door opened, and one of the crew stepped out into the cockpit. He was about six feet tall, muscular, had curly black hair, and a close-cropped beard and mustache like Pablo Escobar the famous Colombian drug lord. "Pablo" appeared somewhat younger than the rest of the crew and moved with a confident grace. He climbed out of the cockpit and took off jogging down the beach road towards Baci's. A few minutes later, Seth and three crewmen appeared. Every one of them was six feet tall or better, except the last man on the dock who was about five-foot-five and stocky. All of them appeared to be in good shape as they hopped up on the dock and walked up the ramp to Aqua. Peter waited for a couple of minutes then put on his sunglasses and donned a black Scubapro ball cap he'd picked up at the Dive Provo shop in Grace Bay. He left his room, walked to the other side of the pool, and sat down at an umbrella table near a palm tree and some lush tropical foliage. He watched a hostess seat Seth and his crew for breakfast out on the deck overlooking the marina. The tops of the palm trees shading the deck swayed in the 20-knot breeze. Peter decided to run up to the IGA coffee shop and fetch a breakfast sandwich and a large coffee. He would be back before they finished their breakfast. Peter headed for the parking lot and pointed the Tahoe east toward Pratt Road thinking, *Drive Left, Yield Right*. He passed "Pablo Escobar" jogging back to Turtle Cove halfway to Pratt.

When Peter returned 20 minutes later, Seth and the crew were still eating breakfast. He sat by the pool and ate the second sausage, egg, and cheese croissant he'd bought. He'd downed the first one on the way back because he was famished after his tryst with Rikki the night before. He felt a tingling in his loins just thinking about her. He'd try to find a way to schedule an encore before her husband returned, without revealing his Long Bay location. Seth and crew finished breakfast at Aqua and headed

89

back down to the boat. Peter hustled back to his room in time to see Seth and the gray-haired guy, who helped provision the boat in St. Petersburg, walk by towards Scooter Bob's or the marina office. The other three crew members busied themselves in the cockpit rigging lures and changing wind-on leaders on eight rods. Peter figured they would also need to rent a couple of vehicles, reprovision, and buy fishing licenses. That should be enough to keep them all busy until early afternoon.

He decided to check out the Man-O-War cave, stopping first to replenish his bottled water, ice, and snack supplies. He also wanted to transfer some clothes back to the marina room since he realized he might be there more than he originally planned. Just seeing Seth with his fishing buddies and fancy Hatteras got him riled up again. Everything kept working out for Seth in his life while nothing worked out in Peter's life because of Seth. He needed to cool down, think calmly, and pick the right moment to snatch him. One well-placed whack behind Seth's ear with the butt of his .38 special would put him in "La-La" land. When Seth woke up, he would be in a living hell.

He pulled *Bonehead* into the hidden parking spot off Man-O-War and carried the cooler, ice and provisions down the scrub jungle path. Peter pulled the brush he'd cut off the entrance hole and shoved the ladder down inside. He threw the safety rope down, climbed down the ladder into the dark cave, and switched on a light below. The cave lit up in surreal shadows and iridescent dripping stalactites. The bats stirred on the cave's ceiling, as he stowed the cooler and supplies. He cut and burned the ends of some ropes to hold Seth. He planned to tie his wrists and feet tight and hoist him up between two large stalagmites that rose from the cave's floor like giant incisors. After tying bowlines in the ends of two 20 foot pieces of the rope, he cut and looped them over the top of the 12-foot stalagmites. As he worked his emotions started to calm and he began thinking clearer. After hiding the ladder and safety line and covering the cave entrance with the brush, he headed the Tahoe towards the nearby beach cottage for some lunch. Before heading back to Turtle Cove to watch *Tar Baby*, Peter packed a few things in his backpack at the beach cottage and ate a sandwich. When he returned, he parked in the small parking lot at the hotel's entrance rather

90

than the bigger lot to the east that also serviced Aqua and the south dock. He didn't want to chance Seth seeing him walk, fearing he might recognize his limping gait. His brown hair and mustache disguise probably wouldn't fool Seth either.

Back in his room, he checked *TAR BABY* from the sliding glass door. Two of the crew members were loading groceries on the boat from a marina push cart. The shortest member of the crew was rigging rubber ballyhoo on an umbrella dredge in the cockpit. He watched for an hour, but Seth never appeared. "Pablo" and the tall crewman, who looked a lot like John Wayne, started pulling and adjusting drags on the eight rods in the cockpit. Finally, Seth and the gray-haired guy returned and got on the boat. Seth reached into a bag given to him by "Pablo" and handed a cell phone and charger to each crew member. They fiddled with the phones for a while, calling each other, then stuck them in their short's pockets. A few minutes later they were joined by a large man who arrived via the Aqua Restaurant ramp. He was easily six-foot-five, weighed a trim 250 pounds, and had a ruddy complexion framed by sun-bleached curly brown hair. They all greeted him, but no one shook hands with him when he got aboard, which told Peter they'd already met him last night. They all went inside the Hatteras.

An hour later the whole crew filed off the boat and headed up the Aqua ramp. Seth and "Pablo" each carried a large duffel. Peter hurried out to his vehicle in the parking lot in time to see two vehicles drive past. They turned up the hill towards Suzie Turn and the Leeward Highway. He jumped in his Tahoe and started after them. It was a green Chevy Suburban, followed by a white four-door sedan of some type. Peter caught the caravan at the top of the hill as they coasted down to the stop sign at Suzie Turn. The Suburban drove across the left lane and turned right on Leeward Highway. The smaller white car, which was a Subaru, followed. Oncoming traffic held Peter up, then he followed their lead. They traveled a little less than a mile, and the Suburban got in the right turn lane that read Cherokee Road. The Subaru lined up behind it. Peter kept going for a half of a mile and entered the Blue Hills roundabout. He went all the way around and came out going back the other way. When he got to Cherokee, he turned left and eased up the road. The road ran along a high ridge, and the homes were all upscale. He was almost to the end of the road when he spotted both cars parked in the driveway of the last house on the road. The residence was a sprawling ranch with a spectacular view of Turtle Cove and Grace Bay. Peter backed up, turned around, and headed for a side road which ran off of Cherokee. He turned around and sat facing Cherokee near the stop sign on Point of View Drive. He'd sit there until Seth moved.

An hour and a half later, the green Suburban and the white Subaru drove by Peter. He waited about 15 seconds before following them. They drove towards downtown, shooting out of the first roundabout on Millennium Highway towards the Blue Hills. Both cars took Blue Hills Road, along the beach, for about a mile then pulled into Da Conch Shack parking lot on the ocean side. Peter motored by, turned around further down the road and came back. He parked in the same lot, but closer to Kalooki's Bar at the other end. Peter walked over to Da Conch Shack, ambled through the outside entrance, and stood behind a cluster of palm trees near the restrooms. Seth and his friends sat down at a large round table in the center pavilion facing the beach. Seth unfolded what appeared to be a map and traced some lines on it with his fingers. Da Conch Shack was too small of an establishment for him to walk into without being conspicuous to everyone present. It was nothing more than three open-air pavilions built in a semi-circle around a grove of palm trees. The stretch of sugar-sand beach in front of the tables gently tumbled into the reef protected, crystal clear, blue lagoon. There was a little bar, with a small restroom outbuilding near the entrance, and a cook-shack between two of the pavilions. Everything was painted white, with pastel blue trim that matched the water. The focal point was a conch corral located about 50 feet offshore in about four feet of water. From his vantage point, Peter could make out two natives cleaning conch on a makeshift table next to the corral. He was hungry too, and the aromas wafting from the cook-shack made his mouth water. He walked back over to Kalooki's. As he passed in front of the green Suburban, he noticed it had "Frigate" painted on its front hood. Another Scooter Bob rental. He found a table overlooking the parking lot on Kalooki's deck, ordered a cracked conch platter and a Turk's Head Ale, and prepaid his check so he could leave without hesitation. The conch was ocean fresh, battered lightly, and tasted even better than he'd remembered.

Forty minutes later he watched Seth get into the green Suburban along with the big curly-haired guy, "John Wayne", "Pablo", and his gray-haired buddy. The short, stocky crewman took the white Subaru, called "*Sushi*". The cars headed back towards Leeward Highway. The green Suburban turned left towards Turtle Cove while the Subaru went around the roundabout and turned south towards Five Cays. Peter followed the Suburban, as he was only interested in Seth. The green Suburban took a left at Cherokee and Peter followed, ducking into Point of View Drive. Seth drove back by almost immediately. They must have dropped the big guy off at his house. He followed them back to the marina, where he parked and hurried to his room. Seth and his three crewmen went aboard the Hatteras, and soon the salon lights went out. Peter was sick of the little hotel room and decided to drive out and stay at the beach cottage for the night. He would be back in his Turtle Cove room by 7:00 a.m. Sunday morning to continue his surveillance. Peter knew he had to be ready and stay close to catch Seth in that rare moment his crew did not accompany him.

CHAPTER EIGHT

SETH'S phone rang at 6:30 a.m. on Saturday. It was Bobby calling from D.C.

"Sorry this took so long, I've had two techs working on it all night. A GPS in a phone is brand new technology, but they finally got the apps working. We have a good stationary signal this morning."

"Shitfire ... Bobby. Jock and I appreciate any help you can give us, buddy."

"The Google maps available for Provo are pretty primitive, but the iPhone appears to be at the end of Silly Creek Road. Does anybody else there have an iPhone or a Blackberry?"

"We're all getting those little-prepaid Samsung's later this morning, and I have my Motorola sat-phone. But, Jock has an iPhone ... he took the fingerprint pictures with his and emailed them to you."

"They were good! Have him text me his username and password at this number and I'll set him up to read the map on his phone, then you can see her iPhone's location in real time. I'm still waiting on the fingerprints from Interpol. They didn't match anything in the FBI's databank."

"I'll call Jock now, and thanks, Bobby."

"Hey, I'll jet down there with some operatives if you need me, but it sounds like you need to stay undercover at this point. Remember how I sprung you when the Sandinistas had you, back in the 70's, in Nicaragua?"

"How could I forget? The family boat business looked awfully good to me after that Nicaraguan gig."

"I'll come down there right now, Seth ... he's my buddy too."

"I'll keep you posted, Bobby."

Seth dialed Jock and filled him in.

"The end of Silly Creek Road, huh? They're just a few big houses out there on the end."

"Text your info to him now. We'll have a quick breakfast at Aqua while we're waiting for him to gear up your phone. Make sure it's fully charged."

"Okay, Seth."

"After breakfast, we'll get two vehicles from Scooter Bob's. Then Gene and I will come up to your house. Call me if Bobby's techs get your phone set up before we get there. The other guys will get the prepaid cell phones at Digicel, some groceries, beer, and water. Then they'll stay busy in the cockpit pulling drags and rigging lures, just in case someone's watching."

When Seth arrived at Jock's, he was sitting at the breakfast bar staring at his phone.

"It looks like Kat's iPhone is out on the very end of the road. The only house out there is a large estate on Emerald Cay. It's a five-acre island connected to Provo by a rotating swing bridge. The last I heard, our Minister of the Interior was leasing it. It doesn't make sense."

"Let Gene and me do a drive by in our rental car and check it out. Maybe we'll spot something."

"It is a spectacular sight, and a lot of tourists drive out there to see it. I guess it can't hurt. Let me mark the map Scooter Bob gave you. There's a large cul-de-sac at the end of Silly Creek Road. That's where the drawbridge is. It's about 20 minutes from here."

"Call my sat-phone if Kat's phone starts to move while we're gone."

Seth drove *Frigate* around the east end of the airport's runway, past the concrete mermaids, then traced Chalk Sound until he turned onto Silly Creek. The homes were upscale and got larger as they drove out the narrow peninsular. The lots increased in size, and the houses became fewer as they neared the end. The last quarter of a mile had just a few houses close to the road, then just scrub jungle and a couple of long driveways to hilltop estates. A cul-de-sac, with a central island planted with large palm trees, appeared. Seth drove around the central island, and there, across a narrow chasm filled with sea water, stood the magnificent Emerald Cay Estate.

"Holy shit," exclaimed Gene, "I've never seen anything like this. Look at the rotating swing bridge, this place must be worth mega-millions."

"Jock said it has ten guest bedrooms, 14 bathrooms, a tennis court, pool, two private beaches, boathouses, servant's quarters, and a heliport. The house must cover an acre itself. I wonder what the other side looks like."

"I think you could only see it by boat."

They stopped and got out. Seth surveyed the whole scene while Gene took lots of pictures. They got back in the car and left.

On the way out Seth noticed a pink villa, with its white hurricane shutters fastened down tight, about 500 yards from the cul-de-sac. The house had a vacation rental sign outside its three car garage courtyard. Gene took a picture of it.

"Unbelievable estate, huh Gene?"

"I saw a guard patrolling along the edge of the tennis court, and he carried a small caliber rifle slung over his shoulder. I took his picture."

"I didn't notice him. I wonder how the bridge works."

"I took a picture of a set of gears on the cul–de-sac side, they sit on a concrete foundation attached to the rock wall … it's the front part of the bridge that rotates open."

"You never cease to amaze me, 'Dick Tracy'," laughed Seth.

"Nothing but the facts, ma'am, and only the facts," quipped Gene, doing his best 'Sargent Friday' impression.

They drove back to Jock's house and found Jock sitting in the same spot staring at his iPhone.

"What did you think of the estate, Seth?"

"World class … Gene spotted a guard patrolling the grounds. We didn't see any other movement or people visible, but there was a white van, and a black Suburban parked up near the main house."

"The guard was probably there to shoo the tour boats away," said Jock. "I can't imagine that the Minister has Kat and her phone. We would have to be sure before we make a move, it would be disastrous if we were wrong."

"I hope it becomes clear sooner than later. The little island would be a tough place to storm, and we'd have to do it by boat."

"I think we should put a man out there to watch for any traffic in and out of the estate," said Gene. "That empty pink rental house would offer a pretty good vantage point, and there are no neighbors nearby. The little white car will be inconspicuous out there, and we can rotate the crew using the green Suburban."

"Should we rent the house Jock? There was an Island Escape Rentals sign on it, and Gene jotted down the number."

"Rent it. I'll pay you for it, but you'll have to rent it."

"Gene will take care of it. Let's ride down to the boat and get our local cell phones and pick up some of the guns I have hidden on the boat. Do you have any guns, Jock?"

"I have permits for two hunting shotguns. Both of them are side by side double barreled, one 12 gauge, the other 20 gauge."

"Somehow, we have to find out if they're holding her in the estate house; we can't just bull our way in there with an assault team. If she's not there, we run the risk of the kidnappers killing her, and maybe some of us."

"I'd rather take the eight million for the property and be sure of getting Kat back. We're going to need really good odds to get proactive."

"I agree," said Seth. "But let's get ready in case the odds do turn in our favor."

They arrived at *TAR BABY* ten minutes later with Jock a couple of minutes behind them in his Suburban. The crew was working in the cockpit rigging lures and pulling drags as planned.

"Were you able to get the phones, Dino?"

Dino handed Seth a bag from Digicel and said, "I had them load 250 minutes of local text or voice, and 60 minutes international for each phone."

"That should work. Listen up guys," said Seth as he handed out the phones and chargers. "Put all four numbers plus Jock's and my sat-phone in your speed dial, then call them to make sure they're all correct. When we're all connected, come inside the cabin for a quick meeting."

Seth went into the salon as both his phones started to ring.

When everyone arrived, Seth started the meeting.

"Bobby Thompson came through, and we know Kat's iPhone location. Surprisingly, the location is where a high ranking politician supposedly lives. It's a large estate about 20 minutes from here on a small island connected to the mainland by a drawbridge. We can't be sure Kat's actually there, and the little island is easily defensible. We've decided to set up one man on a 24/7 surveillance at a vacant rental house nearby. We'll rotate all four of you in and out every six hours using the green Suburban. Jock will be driving the Land Rover Sport now. Gene will familiarize everyone with the situation, he's got photos, and he'll also participate in the surveillance. Jock will either be on the Hatteras or up at his house, and I will be on the Hatteras. Hopefully, we'll get some clue she's there and figure a way to go in and get her out. But we're looking for good odds. There were two vehicles parked on the island, a white van, and a black Suburban, and we know there is at least one armed guard. Gene will brief you and give you the marked up map. Then we'll all go up to Jock's house for a while, and have an early dinner at Da Conch Shack. The Subaru will deploy from the Conch Shack after dark — Put Freddy in there first, Gene. He was our best stakeout man in Key West."

Seth and Jock went into the owner's cabin, and Seth opened his starboard hanging locker. He lifted out the jackets, shirts, and slacks on hangers and stacked them on his bunk, revealing the back wall of the teak wood locker. He took out two foul weather jackets hanging on bronze hooks fastened to the rear panel. Next, he grasped the two hooks and pulled the Velcro-fastened false back wall out of the locker revealing a cache of racked guns.

"Man, is that slick!" exclaimed Jock. "Quite an arsenal."

"Yeah, I developed the false-backed weapons locker during the late seventies for our around the world and down island cruising customers. All the foreign countries' gun laws were different. But the reality was the drug-runners were hi-jacking the larger cruising boats. They'd kill the crew, dump them overboard, haul a load of grass back from Jamaica, and abandon the boat. The bad guys always had guns."

98

"Wouldn't the customs officers find the guns with those metal detecting wands?"

"I always put a self-contained air conditioning unit in the bottom 15 inches of the locker with front louvers and a removable shelf over it ... they'd figure the a/c unit metal was setting off the wand."

"Some of that pirating is still going on. The human smugglers steal boats to run the illegals over from Haiti and the D.R.," said Jock

"As my old dad, Robert E. used to say, 'Better safe than sorry'. I think we'll take the Mossberg Tactical 12 gauge shotgun with the pistol grip, the Remington 700 rifle with the scope and laser sights, and two of the Glock 9mm pistols up to your house. I'll keep my Ruger LCP .380, both .38's, the other two Glocks, and my .357 magnum pistol here, along with the Remington 870 tactical 12 gauge. Both shotguns have sawed-off, $18^{1/2}$" barrels. Get two of those long duffels from under the bunk storage and we'll load up the guns and some ammo."

"What are those black and yellow plastic guns?"

"They're Tasers. The Monroe County Sheriff gave those to me after we helped him find the boat thieves that stole a boat from one of my customers. It turned out they were running drugs with his boat. The sheriff got a big drug bust out of it."

"Have you used them?"

"Not yet. He figured if we were going to recover stolen boats they might come in handy. Shooting somebody with a gun, even in self-defense, gets messy. These Tasers incapacitate the perp for 15 minutes. You can shoot them from 10 to 15 feet away. He also gave me some lightweight Kevlar body armor — they're the rolled up mesh you see at the bottom of the locker. The sheriff also gave me another tip. He told me to use cans of 20-foot wasp spray you can get at the grocery store. He thinks it's twice as effective as pepper spray. If you get them in the eyes or face it will incapacitate a perp for 20 minutes."

They drove up to Jock's house leaving his white Suburban down at Turtle Cove. Once at Jock's, Gene helped him clean up the fingerprint dust off Kat's Land Rover, now that Jock would be driving it. Finally, the whole crew sat out on the veranda and watched the sun drop lower in the west. They each pondered in silence how this adventure might turn out. It was hard for them to comprehend the length and breadth of all the intrigue and turmoil that boiled behind the scenes in this pristine tropical paradise, as they sipped a cold one and looked out over the windblown Atlantic.

The sound of Seth's sat-phone broke the spell of silence and introspection, and he quickly retrieved it from the kitchen.

"Yeah, Bobby give me a minute to get a pen and some paper." He quickly scribbled some information down, then filled Bobby in on the Emerald Cay estate situation.

"See if you can figure out who owns it, without tipping our hand ...... OK, call me back anytime; I should be back at the boat by 9:00 p.m."

Seth turned to his crew and said, "The only prints Interpol were able to identify was a José Guzman-González's, aka 'El Cucaracha', born in Santo Domingo, Dominican Republic; 17 arrests ranging from petty theft to forgery, mail fraud, and assault with a deadly weapon. Expatriated to Turks and Caicos in 2002, four arrests here for operating a bawdy house, pandering, human trafficking, and assault and battery. No convictions, imagine that! He's reported to be the manager of the Club Capri in Providenciales. Residence address unknown, and his mug shot is blurry. Bobby also got some information for us on a possible consort of Gonzalez. Rodrigo Moreno, aka 'El Bomba', is listed as the owner of the Old Airport Road property that the Club Capri occupies. He also owns three houses in the Five Cays Settlement area, an oceanfront parcel in Wheeland, and another commercial building downtown. His reported residence is 2505 Reece Cl. Interpol suspects he is the Dominican 'Boss' on the island. He was granted full 'belonger' citizenship in 2005 and has no arrest record, so there's no mug shot."

"Gonzalez must be part of the Five Cays Dominican gang," said Jock. "I wouldn't think they would be involved in anything this sophisticated. They do gambling, titty bars, and hookers."

"Well, maybe they're moving uptown," said Gene. "Do they control the drug trade?"

"I really don't know much about it, but I heard that some white Bahamians from Spanish Wells control it, and their dealers are all Haitians. We're still considered Bahamian territory by a lot of folks in the Bahamas."

"Where is the Club Capri, Jock?"

"It's behind the airport on Old Airport Road just down the street from the small airplane FBO."

"Sounds like a field trip for me and Dino tomorrow night. Are they open Sunday?" asked Seth.

"Every day's the same to them."

"Let's head for Da Conch Shack, before it gets dark. We need Freddy to get in place right after sundown."

"I think it would be smart for us to go fishing for a half-day early tomorrow morning," said John. "If someone is watching us it might convince them we know nothing about the kidnapping and are just here to fish."

"OK, we'll change out our man at Silly Creek before daylight. Jock can drive down to the boat at 7:00. We'll leave at 7:30 and be back around noon. Then we'll change the lookout — he can always call us if something goes down. We'll only be four or five miles off the island."

Twenty minutes later they were sharing a couple of cracked conch appetizers and enjoying a Turk's Head Ale. First timers Freddy and Dino were mesmerized by the waves breaking on the distant reef, and the lilting sounds of the island's reggae music. They sat wiggling their toes in the pure white sugar sand while listening to the palm fronds rustle above them in the trade winds.

"This island will get to you, Fred. We're definitely in the mango latitudes," said Gene.

"No wonder it's so good, they're pulling the live conch out of the pen out there in the lagoon and cleaning it right in the water," gushed Dino. "This will be my first stop when I bring my dive trip in here. It sets your clock to island time."

The crew was mellow when they pulled out of the parking lot for the trip back to Turtle Cove after dinner. Freddy peeled off at the roundabout and headed for Silly Creek, and Seth dropped Jock off at Blue Mountain.

"What time does the fuel dock open, Jock?"

"7:00 a.m."

"OK, meet us at the fuel dock at 7:30 ... We'll probably take on about 600 gallons so it will take a while. When we're topped off, we'll throw the lines off and be gone. We'll all be up early to change out the lookout and move the boat over. If the lookouts report anything important tonight, I'll call you. We have coffee and sweet rolls on the boat, and we'll cut up a couple of fresh pineapples while we're fishing. Think about a good place for the whole crew to go to lunch after we get in."

"You got it, Seth! See you guys bright and early."

***

Seth steered *TAR BABY* out the narrow Turtle Cove channel into Grace Bay and turned north. He was glad to have Jock with him as he idled along the shallow, circuitous channel that turned easterly through the bay. Finally, the channel markers turned abruptly north and took him through the small cut in the barrier reef. The Hatteras motored smoothly between the breaking waves on both sides, and into the Atlantic. A short 15-minute run put them at the 1000 foot drop-off where they let down the outriggers. Seth trolled east towards Parrot Cay and the rusty freighter wreck. The wind was blowing a steady 20 knots, but the seas had only a light to moderate chop out to four miles in the lee of Provo Island. Seth knew he could fish east another 10 or 15 miles until he almost reached North Caicos Island. Then he would turn around to the west and enjoy a long downwind ride towards Provo's Northwest Point.

They put out four 50-pound class bent-butt boat rods with large marlin lures trailing #11 J-hooks in their skirts. The Caicos Classic was a release tournament, so the idea was to catch the billfish as fast as possible and release them unharmed. Size didn't matter, whichever boat caught the most targeted fish won the tournament. The 50-wide Tiagra reels were spooled with 80-pound Hi-Viz green mono and rigged with 400-pound bright orange mono and Dacron wind-on leaders. The bright color helped Seth know where the lines and leaders were during the heat of battle. The rigs were heavy enough to put some serious pressure on a big marlin if he decided to head for the depths. Seth asked Gene to put out a bowling pin teaser, while Freddy and Jock deployed an umbrella dredge rigged with soft plastic split tail mullet. Dino was sleeping below since he'd caught the graveyard shift on the Silly Creek surveillance early this morning. John Harvey replaced him an hour before dawn. There was no ingress or egress from Emerald Cay last night; just different interior lights turned off or on throughout the dark hours.

Seth zig-zagged *TAR BABY* back and forth for a couple of hours and worked up parallel with the rusty freighter. The swells and chop built as they started to motor out of the lee of North Caicos. He turned his attention from the lures and eased the Hatteras into a trough and slowly worked her bow downwind. The seas began to flatten out, and Seth cut the engine RPMs to keep his speed at eight knots. Freddy cut up the pineapples and handed the slices out to the crew. Seth turned his helm seat aft again and began to watch the spread. Fifteen minutes later, out of the corner of his left eye, he saw a large shape make a move on the left long rigger. Seth saw a splash but couldn't identify what species had missed the bite. The fish didn't get hooked but managed to knock the line out of the outrigger clip.

"Something tried to eat the left long," Seth called down to the crew.

Gene must have seen it too because he grabbed the line above the reel and pulled the line three times in rapid succession. That made a ruckus back at the lure and the fish piled back on the lure and was hooked in the process. Gene took the rod out of the holder as the big fish made a long, blazing run. The fish fought hard but never jumped. Gene was fitted with a harness and a rod belt and fought the fish standing up in the left corner of the cockpit. He pumped and reeled against the fish's steady pressure. Twenty minutes later he saw the double line finally clear the water. Seth backed down on the fish and lo and behold it was a huge wahoo. Jock made a nice gaff shot on the wahoo's head and Freddy sunk another in his tail. They brought the huge Caicos wahoo aboard through the tuna door.

Dino came out of the salon door, rubbing his eyes, to see what all the commotion was about and said, "Holy Shit! It's a giant."

Gene was recovering from the battle and remarked, "Except for the initial run, he never acted like a wahoo, he never stopped and shook his head like they do. I thought it might be a small foul-hooked marlin."

"Let's weigh him ... just for grins," called down Seth.

Freddy got the scale out of the tackle center and handed it to Jock saying, "The fish is easily six feet long, you're the only one aboard who can lift the scale high enough."

Gene put on a pair of gloves and hooked the scale under the wahoo's gills, then he helped Jock get positioned. Jock took a deep breath and raised his hands and the scale over his head, making it look easy.

"94 pounds," exclaimed Gene. "Not a record ... but a damn big wahoo."

"Nice fish guys, let's get the lines back out and we'll finish this downwind run. Maybe we can pick up a marlin near the Northwest Point before we go in. We still have an hour before noon. It looks like we'll be eating grilled wahoo tonight."

They trolled downwind for another hour and a small blue marlin bit the right long rigger. It took a couple of jumps and threw the hook as the crew started clearing the other rods. Seth had the crew continue to wind everything in, and they called it a day. They'd start their next fishing day near Northwest Point, where they got the marlin bite.

As they ran toward the break in the reef, Jock climbed into the flybridge.

"Nice wahoo, Seth. Maybe we can use it to our advantage. We'll get some dock buzz out of it for sure, but I can call some people I know at the newspaper and the local TV station. We'd definitely get some press buzz."

"It couldn't hurt. If the kidnapper *is* watching us, it will certainly disarm him."

"I'll make a couple of calls."

Thirty minutes later, Seth pulled in next to the tournament scales across from *TAR BABY'S* slip in the marina. There was a small throng of people already standing there waiting, and Jock got off the boat and shook hands with a couple of them. He swung the boom, holding a digital scale, out over the cockpit. Gene and Dino hooked the magnificent wahoo up to it. Jock pushed the up button on the electric hoist control and suspended the wahoo over the cockpit. The digital scale lit up and read 95.2 lbs. The *SUN* newspaper photographer took a picture of the wahoo surrounded by *TAR BABY'S* crew from the dock, also capturing the boat's name and hailing port on the transom. The TV crew took some video and interviewed Seth, Gene, and Jock. The *TCI SUN* reporter got the captain and crew names, and also interviewed Gene and Jock.

Once back in their regular slip, the wahoo continued to draw a crowd from the lunch patrons at Aqua. Gene cleaned the fish, and it was packed in ice, provided by Seth's Eskimo icemaker. Freddy slipped away and drove out to relieve John at Silly Creek in *Frigate*.

The crew had just finished washing down the Hatteras when John came back aboard.

"Freddy told me about the wahoo, Seth, quite a fish!"

"Really big for this time of the year. How did your surveillance go?"

"I went up on the pink house's second story porch. There's a spiral staircase and some big cactus plants to hide behind. Using your Steiner binoculars, I spotted two guards patrolling the grounds once it got light. Around 11:00 this morning they rotated the bridge closed and another black Suburban, with limo tint windows, drove in. I couldn't get a good look at the driver … but he was tall, had long black hair, and wore black clothes. He went in the house and was still in there when I left. I briefed Freddy, left him the Glock, and showed him the porch. I did get the license plate number, TCI plate, 20065. Red letters on white. It really stood out on that blacked out SUV."

"Good eye, John. We're starting to put some info and a pattern together. Jock's going to take us down to Bugaloo's on the water in Five Cays for lunch. We were waiting for you to get back. He says it's *what's goin' on*, on Sundays. A Dominican owns it, but it's straight up. Just good food and good entertainment. Tonight, Dino and I are going to check out the

Club Capri to try and get a line on this "Cucaracha" character whose prints were on Kat's car."

***

Peter parted the drapes carefully and looked out of his sliding glass door as he had every half hour since 7:00 this Sunday morning. Seth's Hatteras was already gone when he arrived at Turtle Cove. He could only guess they were out fishing. This time, he spotted *TAR BABY* backing in at the marina's fish weigh station across from the Inn. He looked at his dive watch; it was 12:31 p.m. There was a small crowd gathering, and soon he saw a very large wahoo swing over their cockpit. A TV van and another photographer were taking pictures, and two reporters were interviewing Seth and his large curly headed friend. His hate for Seth boiled over again, and he cursed out loud, "That fuckin' asshole, he's in town two fuckin' days, and he's already on television and in the newspaper!" *In all my days' of commercial fishing,* thought Peter, *I never caught one that big … his life gets better and better, and mine keeps getting shittier. The prick has fuckin' friends everywhere. I'll put him in the newspaper, wait until they find him dead on their island with a broomstick two feet up his ass.* Peter knew he had to get control of himself or he was going to start trashing the room, and that would compromise his whole plan. He sat on the bed and took deep breaths and thought about Rikki.

CHAPTER NINE

EL BOMBA left Emerald Cay about 1:30 Sunday afternoon after he phoned a takeout lunch order, for three, into Bugaloo's Conch Crawl Restaurant. A waitress would bring it out to the black Suburban when he pulled up behind the bandstand. He'd driven out to Silly Creek earlier to check on Mrs. Baffert and to go over the plan to move her Monday afternoon with Diego, Ramon, and Paco. They would travel to the Silly Creek mansion in two of his black Suburbans. He would drive the one he'd been using and bring Frederico along with an AK-47 rifle. José would bring Antonio and Chico in a second black Suburban, and both would have Uzi 9mm machine pistols in addition to the Glock 9mm's they all carried. Ramon and Chico would drive Conchita and Mrs. Baffert out in the third black Suburban that was already at the mansion. Diego and Paco would stay behind and maintain security on Emerald Cay. If something went wrong during the move to Five Cays, they could head out in three different directions, and any pursuer would not know which Suburban carried Mrs. Baffert.

Mrs. Baffert was given a daily shower and was being fed three meals a day by Conchita. She'd reportedly been sleeping well and been escorted around the mansion's hallways for exercise twice a day. Rodrigo's land buyer confirmed his arrival by private jet on Tuesday morning from Jamaica. Jock's lawyer had completed his end of the deal, and according to Jacque Mehoff, Mr. Baffert was playing by Rodrigo's rules. The helicopter was scheduled for touchdown on Tuesday at noon on Emerald Cay. Everything pointed to a successful conclusion at 1:45 on Tuesday afternoon.

El Bomba was anxious to get back to his private Five Cays house on the hill above the safe house. Sarita planned a take-out lunch from Bugaloo's, some skinny-dipping in the pool, topped off by a *ménage a trois* including her best girlfriend Fabiana, who had just flown in from the Dominican Republic. Rodrigo hadn't seen Fabiana naked yet, but he was already salivating just thinking about her. *Life was good and getting better — wait until I get the 1.5 million in my hands,* thought El Bomba.

***

Kat got back to her bed from her afternoon walk around the halls of the house where she was being held captive. She knew she was in a large house, with long wide hallways and high ceilings. As the sounds of their walking resonated, the house felt spacious to her. Some of the floors were marble or textured stone travertine; others were smooth wood that creaked in places. In certain parts of the house, she could hear waves breaking on rocks or a reef. Some stretches were not air conditioned, and she could smell the salt air and feel the same trade winds breeze on her face that she felt in her house on Blue Mountain. Back in her room, the matron put her ankle cuffs back on and told her to sit down on the bed. Normally the matron immediately flipped on the room's TV to a Spanish speaking station and sat down in front of it. But this time, she heard her walk into the bathroom and sit down on the toilet. She didn't hear an immediate *tinkle* sound so decided the matron might be in there for a few minutes. Her hearing had definitely become more acute over the past three days and nights while being continually blindfolded. She also hoped there would be some response from Jock concerning her iPhone. She was worried the battery might be wearing down. She thought she might try something more positive with it, to jog his imagination. Kat laid down on her side and rolled over on her back and positioned her manacled hands over the phone. After slipping her hand under the mattress cover, she grasped the phone. She arched her back and rolled up a little more to get more comfortable. Now she pushed the bottom indent, then slid her thumb across the bottom of the phone's smooth glass face to open it. Quickly moving her thumb to the approximate position of the message icon, second in from the top, she clicked. Her last message the day of the kidnapping was sent to Jock. He left for work early while she was still in the shower running a bit late. He texted her on his way to the dive shop to say he was sorry for not kissing her goodbye. She thought that was sweet and answered; *I love you.* She moved down to the keyboard's left bottom corner, using the bottom control button indent as a reference, then touched the bottom left corner and heard a click. She clicked the same spot again, moved higher and clicked a letter. Kat tried for the letter x, but any letter would do, if she could just hit send. She measured with her thumb to the middle of the screen, while holding the phone with her other hand. She moved her thumb across to the right side and pressed. A reassuring little *whuump* sound rewarded her efforts. Kat slid the phone back under the mattress pad as she heard the toilet flush in the bathroom. She heard the matron walk over to the bed, then stand over her breathing softly.

"The walk around the house got you all sweaty, *Señora.* Would you like to take a shower now and maybe a fresh robe?"

Kat nodded enthusiastically.

***

Seth followed Jock down to Bugaloo's in Five Cays in the green Suburban. Dino rode with Jock. The parking lot was overflowing, so they parked out near the road that led to the fisheries on the south point.

The crew walked to the front entrance and Jock said, "Look at this concrete tidal pond the owner built, it's full of small tarpon slurping up little crabs."

They walked through a small open-air renovated beach cottage which housed ten or twelve booths and a long bar. Delicious cooking odors wafted from the kitchen in the back. The restaurant opened onto a series of decks, shaded by a large, mature palm tree grove. The grove overlooked a beach and the pastel blue waters of Five Cays Bay on the Caribbean side of the island. The hostess sat the crew down at a wooden table built around a double-trunk palm tree. An energetic Dominican waitress soon arrived with the crew's order of ice cold Turk's Head Lager. She recommended the cracked conch and their American cheeseburgers, and everyone ordered. An island band was playing a spirited rendition of Bob Marley's *No Woman, No Cry* on a makeshift bandstand under a sailcloth canopy. The sun was shining, and the trade winds were cooling the island with its constant breeze. There were chickens strutting among the tables doing the work usually reserved for potcake dogs or iguanas.

Seth's cell phone rang, and he picked up.

"Yeah, Freddy ... No, no, you were right to call — big Hispanic, long black hair and a mustache, black shirt and jeans, and you got a picture of him — Great! Is everything else quiet? — alright — Gene will relieve you in a few hours." He looked at John and the crew, then said, "The black Suburban that John ID'd this morning just left Emerald Cay ... same license number. I wish we could follow it."

Their lunches came, and the crew ordered another round of beers. Except for Seth and John, who'd been perusing a surprisingly good wine list. They ordered two glasses of Belle Gloss, California Pinot Noir. They noticed the restaurant's patrons were both tourists and local citizens of Dominican descent. A child's birthday party was in progress a few tables away. Jock explained that the restaurant's owner, Mike, had named his restaurant after Berlie "Bugaloo" Williams, who started the whole island conch mania at his original conch shack out in Wheeland on the beach in the Blue Hills. As they finished their lunch, John nudged Seth, who was sitting next him.

"Look behind the bandstand. A black Suburban just pulled up."

"Don't look at it again, John, but slide out and walk through the restaurant like you're going to the men's room. Go out the front door, check the license plate, and come right back."

Just as John came back, a waitress walked past their table with three large Styrofoam boxes in a plastic bag. She continued past the bandstand and handed them through the now open driver's window of the black Suburban.

"Same one, Seth. What's the odds?"

"Pretty lucky, but it's a small island. Let's follow him, John — **Jock**, don't look anywhere but at me — we just made the black Suburban that just left Silly Creek. John and I are going to follow him — Pay the check, take Gene and Dino back to the boat, and wait for us there. We'll call if we need you."

Seth and John got up and ambled through the restaurant and walked to the green Suburban. The black Suburban rolled by them, and they never looked up. Seth started the engine and pulled out a good 20 car lengths behind the black Suburban and slowly followed. The black car bore right when it reached Five Cays Road and drove a half-mile past a police sub-station, turned left and climbed the steep hill through a rough looking neighborhood of walled and fenced houses. The neighborhood's vacant lots were strewn with garbage and rubble. He reached a small plateau and turned left on a road with better paving and continued to climb to the top of the ridge, where he made a right on Matilda Way. Seth hung back and waited for a couple of minutes. When he turned the corner, the black Suburban was just pulling into a concrete-walled compound. Seth went by and saw a tall Latino with long black curly hair, dressed in black, entering the front door of the house. The heavy iron gate was almost closed in front of the entrance, but John got a glimpse of what looked like a black Escalade parked inside the block wall. He and John rode down to the road on the plateau below, turned right on Reese Cl. and passed some houses, a small grocery bodega, a seafood restaurant and bar named Pumpy's, the Dogbite Café, and a walled club called Tricky Ricky's. He followed the road back out to Five Cays Road, which led him down to South Dock Road. They drove back past the Mermaids' Lagoon to Leeward and on to Turtle Cove.

"Looks like the Dominican side of town," said John.

"Well, I'll mark our map with the location and the street names. If we can connect José Gonzalez into this caper tonight, it looks like we're dealing with the Dominican gang for sure. I wonder where the big, black-haired guy we followed fits in. Maybe Jock can shed some light."

They parked and walked down to the boat. When they walked into the salon Dino, Gene and Jock were sitting there looking strange.

"What's up?" asked Seth.

"On the drive back, I got a text message from Kat. She's in the Silly Creek mansion," said Jock.

"What! Let me see it," said Seth excitedly.

Jock handed him the phone. Seth read the letter z.

"We figure she was trying to send an x — like x marks the spot — but hit the z next to it."

"Wow! This certainly changes things."

"Yeah, how did your tail go?" asked Gene.

"We followed him up into a Dominican neighborhood in Five Cays. He pulled into a walled compound at the top of the hill, and we only got a glimpse of him. He was a big Hispanic, with long black hair, dressed in black. It looks like we're dealing with the Dominicans."

"Do we do a re-think on an assault of Emerald Cay, Seth?"

"That has to be Jock's decision," said Seth looking in Jock's direction. "Right now I'd say there are four or five people guarding her at the mansion."

"I have no real reason to trust this kidnapper. I think I'll get the money for the land and Kat back. But we'd be looking over our shoulders for the rest of our lives. The only way we could be safe would be to sell our house and businesses and move somewhere else. We already know it's one of the Dominican bosses. If this crook thought I was close to figuring out who he was, he'd kill us in a heartbeat. It's hard for Americans to understand how it works here. Our government has almost no financial information on its citizens. The only tax they collect is on imports, and they charge fees for government services. There's no income tax, so there's no record of business profits, salaries, or rents. There's no sales tax, so there's no record of businesses sales volume. There's no property tax, except a 9% one-time tax when you buy the property. So, the one-time tax is why Interpol knows Moreno owns some property here. Businesses are licensed and inspected for codes, but a bribe can result in no enforcement. There are codes and fees for zoning changes and building permits, but a bribe only costs pennies on the dollar. Rodrigo Moreno hides in the shadows. If I ask anybody on this island about Rodrigo, José Gonzalez, or the minister ... they might be an informant. That's how deep the climate of fear permeates this island. Somebody has to make a stand here, and it might as well be Kat and me. In fact, I've just made up my fucking mind! … I'm not going to let these bastards run us off of *our* island."

The Geezers all looked at Seth and nodded.

"We're with you Jock, let's figure out a plan," said Seth.

Jock regained his composure and said, "We'd have to do it at night … silently … by boat. We could anchor my sportfish, *SEACOLT,* up behind Silly Cay, the little, uninhabited island across the creek from Emerald Cay. We'd go in by kayak or on paddleboards. I've got a whole rental fleet of those."

"We would have to take out both of the guards who walk the property all night, silently … Jock and I can do that," added Dino. "It might be better if the two of us scuba in, and you guys paddled in once we've got the guards Tasered, zip-tied, and gagged.

"Then we have to get in the house, and neutralize two or three people before they can call for reinforcements."

"We can disable the rotating bridge," said Gene.

"How … cut the wires?" asked Dino.

"No, just kayak in and stick a tire iron in the gear set," said John.

"How about a glass cutter to open the doors, cut a circle, reach in and open the door," offered Jock.

"What about the alarm system, I'm sure they have a good one," said Seth.

"They would only arm the windows and the doors at night. There wouldn't be any motion alarms inside or outside so they could move around," said Dino

"What about going in from above," said John. "When I was scoping out the house from the pink house's porch with your Steiners, I noticed a couple of those plastic bubble skylights on two of the lower roofs. They're probably over the bathrooms — at least a roof toilet vent was near each one. We can take one off with a battery operated drill. Eight fasteners and it's off. Then we drop in down a rope."

"How do we get on the roof?" asked Gene.

"Kat's got every size extension ladder there is," said Jock enthusiastically. "We'll float one in with a couple of lifejackets attached to it, pulled behind a kayak."

Seth said, "Looks like we have a plan, when do we do it?"

"Tomorrow night at midnight," said Jock.

"Well our timing is good," said John.

"You mean with the property closing scheduled for Tuesday?"

"That too, but we're just coming off the new moon, it will be very dark."

"Let's have dinner at Aqua tonight, they'll do a nice job with the wahoo, and we can just relax," said Jock.

"Sounds good," said Seth. "We'll get a good night's sleep. We've got all day to get organized for the assault tomorrow night."

"Gene, how about driving out to relieve Freddy. John will come out later to relieve you, and we'll keep some dinner for you in the fridge. Check out the skylights and the roof vents with the binoculars while you're out there."

The dinner at Aqua was good. The wahoo was grilled medium rare, and they served it with coconut rice and fresh French-cut green beans. Jock treated the table to two bottles of Meomi Chardonnay. After dinner, Jock drove back up to his house. John took a nap on *TAR BABY* and set his alarm to relieve Gene at midnight. Freddy watched a baseball game on cable TV in the salon, and Seth and Dino headed for Club Capri.

"I'm going to try and chat this José Gonzalez up about organizing a bachelor's party for my nephew," said Seth as he and Dino drove up Old Airport Road looking for the sign. "If he's the manager he would be the go-to guy. With what we know now, I just want to know what he looks like in case we run into him later. The mug shot Bobby sent was hard to make out on the phone."

"There's the sign, Seth. This place looks a little fancy for this neighborhood."

Seth parked the green Suburban and they walked under the large CLUB CAPRI neon sign. As they passed through the front door, they were greeted by a large Hispanic in a suit coat with slicked back hair.

"Welcome to the Capri, *Señors*, my name is Antonio. The cover is ten dollars U.S."

Seth handed him a twenty and Antonio showed them to a table.

"I'll send your waitress over for your drink order. The girls dance on the center stage and then circulate. We have VIP rooms upstairs, or you may negotiate to take them back to your hotel room. Let me know how I can help you."

The main room was smoke-filled and dimly lit. There were ten tables, and plush booths lined the left and back walls. A long service bar dominated the right side of the room, along with a staircase with a brass handrail leading upstairs. The DJ spun records behind the stage, which sported a floor to ceiling brass pole. At the moment a slim hipped, brown skinned girl with large silicone breasts was slowly sliding down the pole head first, totally naked. The throbbing music was a sub-woofer dominated rap version of the Temptations, *My Girl*.

Camila, the waitress, arrived and they ordered two Turk's Head Lagers.

Eboni finished her number, and the DJ struck up a round of applause as she gathered up her thong and bra and got ready to circulate. She was replaced on stage, with much fanfare, by *Mei-ling*, an exotic Asian and Dominican mixture, with a gorgeous pair of "slopers". She soon revealed all of her assets, including excellent flexibility and obvious athletic ability.

Seth caught Antonio's attention and motioned him over to the table.

"I want to talk to José, your manager, to possibly arrange a bachelor party for my nephew who's getting married down here in a couple of months. Your club comes highly recommended by my friends in Miami."

"*Si Señor*, I will see if he is available."

A few minutes later Antonio walked past and nodded. Behind him walked a stocky Dominican in a black suit and matching t-shirt with the customary slicked back hair. His pleasant face was marred only by his scarred eyebrows and a nose that had been broken a time or two. He smiled, showing two gold teeth among the otherwise perfect whites, and said, "I am José, you asked to see me?"

"José, I'm Michael, this is my friend Don … this club was recommended by a friend as a place I could throw a spectacular bachelor's party for my nephew. So far I like what I see."

He smiled at Seth and gave Dino a long look, while sizing him up, before saying, "We host quite a few of those each year for the destination weddings. The groom and his groomsmen can party with selected girls down here and take the girls upstairs if they wish. We also have a large private suite upstairs, complete with a bar, hot tub, and two bedrooms. Most choose the private suite."

"What's the approximate cost for a groom and six groomsmen for … two hours?"

"All inclusive … the suite, bartender, girls, DJ, drinks and appetizers, cabs back to the hotel, plus tips … four thousand."

"Sounds good."

"When do you want to book, Michael?"

"The wedding's been scheduled for the end of August. Let me run it by my nephew and I'll call you. Do you have a card?"

José reached inside his suit jacket and handed Seth a card.

Seth said, "Thanks, José," as he and Dino got up to leave.

"Get back to me, Michael," said José smiling.

Seth acknowledged Antonio as they walked out the door to the strains of Sam the Sham's *Wooly Bully*.

As they pulled out of the parking lot, Dino said, "They looked like a couple of bad actors."

"It's always better when you know what you're getting into."

"Yeah, the harder we fall," laughed Dino.

"Let's get some rest. Tomorrow's gonna be a long day … and night."

***

Peter Petcock didn't know what to think. First, he'd tailed Seth and his crew down to Bugaloo's this afternoon. He watched him eating lunch with his buddies through a pair of binoculars from the fishery parking lot a quarter of a mile away. Then Seth and "John Wayne" took off by themselves and went sightseeing in the worst section of Five Cays. What was he doing in that neighborhood — looking for trouble? Next, he suffered through their dinner at Aqua, sitting back in the shadows near the Inn's pool. The whole time Peter wished Seth would maybe, just maybe, take a walk after dinner around the marina by himself so he could snatch him. Sooo, what does he do? He and "Pablo" leave the rest of the crew and drive to the most notorious titty-bar brothel in Provo. I mean — just when you think you know somebody. Seth was a straight arrow, but maybe he had a dark side. A fucking hypocrite is what he was. Peter thought he needed a day away from Seth. He thought he might call Rikki and rent a big time suite in a fancy hotel for a day. It might help his sanity.

CHAPTER TEN

THE *TAR BABY'S* crew was up with the sun the next morning. Dino relieved John at the pink house just before dawn. Seth, Gene, and Freddy were already working on that night's assault plan. Jock arrived, poured himself a cup of coffee, and joined in on the planning. They created a timeline, penciled in who was responsible for what, and listed all the logistical equipment and weapons each man would carry.

They would arrive at Pirates Cove at the western end of Provo just before dark in Jock's sportfish, loaded with paddleboards, kayaks, and a ladder. They'd anchor and wait until 10:30 p.m., then idle into Silly Creek with no lights. Jock would use his Flir Scout hand-held night vision scope to navigate in and out. Once they were on the northwest side of Silly Cay, they'd anchor up again. At 11:20, Jock and Dino would scuba in and handle the two sentries. The rest of the flotilla, on paddleboards and in kayaks, would gather at the south end of Silly Cay. Once Jock and Dino had neutralized the sentries, they would meet at the west end of the tennis court. They'd signal the crew with three short blips of their dive flashlights. The flotilla would paddle silently across the mouth of Silly Creek to the tennis court. Freddy would continue under both spans of the mansion's entrance road and jam a tire iron into the swing bridge gears. When he returned, the task force would assault the mansion. John and Dino would carry the extension ladder that John floated in on an extra paddleboard. Dino would sling 50 feet of 5/8" diameter rope over his shoulder. John would have an 18-volt Ryobi drill in a holster and a socket and bit kit in his pocket. The whole assault team would be supplied with gloves and watch caps with eye-holes. The target was a flat first story roof 35 feet left of the main entrance portico. Seth, Freddy, Gene, and Jock would set up a perimeter across from the front of the house, in case the drop-in thru the skylight tactic didn't work out. They planned to arm the crew with Tasers, cans of 20-foot wasp spray, pistols, and shotguns. Seth would have his hog rifle slung over his shoulder for any eventuality. They all would have flashlights and several jumbo black zip-ties to hog-tie the kidnappers. Once John had the skylight off, Dino would slide down the rope, check the corridor outside the bathroom, then secure it. At that point, John would signal the rest of the crew with two quick flashlight blips. The crew would move silently up the ladder and into the house. They'd form into two man crews and systematically check each of the house's ten bedrooms. It would be over fast. They would neutralize the kidnappers with the Tasers and wasp spray, then zip-tie them. The Geezers would not kill or wound any of them unless it became absolutely necessary. If a kidnapper did meet his end, he would be deep-sixed far offshore on the way out. The assault crew would leave en mass, with Kat and her iPhone. They would photograph any captive kidnappers. One would be forced to turn off the door alarms before he was securely trussed up. They weren't worried about the captives calling the police. Once the kidnappers worked loose of their bonds, they would probably all disappear.

When the plan was complete, Jock said, "If we can pull this off, I will go to the local newspapers and the British Consulate with my story. Once it is all out in the open, I doubt anyone will retaliate. The police will be forced to investigate and make some arrests. My lawyers will have the buyer's information, and the Provo Title Company has the transaction information. The buyer may be able to identify the parties who set up the deal. It will put one more nail in this government's coffin, and this island will be one step closer to getting cleaned up and back on track. None of the remaining conspirators will admit anything, but we've got José Gonzalez's fingerprints on the Land Rover, and a time/dated picture of the black Suburban's driver at the mansion. Somebody on this island can identify him, and then he'll have to explain what he was doing there that day. The Minister of the Interior can explain why they held Kat against her will in his house. Hopefully, this will spur the British to take a closer look at the reality of what's going on here."

"You've got a pair of *grande cojones*, Jock, let's take it to them," said Freddy.

"Let's get some breakfast at Aqua on the way out, and then we'll start putting the rest of the logistics together," said Gene.

During breakfast, the planning continued.

"We can load the guns and other equipment in my sportfish just after dark and take off — it's docked behind the dive shop right here in Turtle Cove. The paddle boards and kayaks are in outside racks, so we'll load them in the fishing cockpit and on the foredeck. We'll put a couple of tanks and the scuba gear aboard for Dino and me," said Jock.

"How are we going to get the extension ladder aboard?"

"I'll get the ladder this afternoon from our rental warehouse, along with the drill and bits. I'll tell Cecil I need it for some rain gutter work at the shop. I'll tie the ladder on the Suburban's roof rack and bring it around the back of the dive shop tonight. We'll lash it to the bow pulpit, inside the toe rail. Nobody will notice it after dark."

"While you're doing that, Gene and I will run up to NAPA and get a half dozen Maglite waterproof flashlights. We'll stop at the IGA and get some drinks, snacks, and deli sandwiches for dinner tonight on Jock's boat. As ol' Robert E. used to say, 'An army marches on its stomach.' Freddy, why don't you grab a nap, and we'll let John sleep until this afternoon."

Gene was just pulling out of the IGA when Seth's cell phone began to ring.

"Yeah, Dino? … They just pulled in — two black Suburbans, one with the 20065 TCI plate. Five guys got out and went inside the mansion — José and Antonio from the Capri — really? — And the big guy in black with the mustache and long hair we saw in the picture Freddy took earlier. Call me as soon as they come back out, and get some pictures."

"Sounds like a major pork shift," said Gene.

"We'll see, maybe they're just relieving the troops?"

Gene drove them back to Turtle Cove, and they carried the groceries and flashlights back to the boat.

As Seth put the sandwiches in the refrigerator, his phone rang.

"Yeah, Dino … Shitfire! — They're leaving in all three black Suburbans — you took pictures of a tall blond woman with a blindfold coming out of the mansion — and a short Hispanic woman — one of the mansion guards and a new guy got in that SUV — the other four guys got back in the cars they came in — you got pictures of all of them, OK! Get the other plate numbers on their way out if you can, then follow them. Wherever they end up, call me — and don't get too close."

Seth dialed up Jock, "They're moving her — they just left the mansion in a three-car caravan. Dino is following them. Drive down here and I'll fill you in when you get here. I want to keep the phone line clear."

"I was just on my way out to get the ladder and drill. I'll be there in five minutes."

Ten minutes later Seth's phone rang.

"I'm on South Dock Road going towards the airport. They just turned right at the gas station on Five Cays Road — I have a two car buffer — I'm slowing down for the turn — Shit! Neither of the cars in front of me turned, so I pulled into the station — Now I'm starting up the hill — the first car is bearing right at the top of the hill. I'm going to put the phone down on the seat."

"I'm standing by, Dino."

"Passing by a place called Pumpy's bar — goin' by Tricky Ricky's — they're pulling in further up the block —— I just went by it — a green ranch house with a wood stockade fence around it — they were closing the gate, no house number — I just picked up the phone, could you hear me?"

"Loud and clear, a green ranch house, stockade fence."

"The first two Suburbans pulled inside the fence — the last Suburban parked outside across the closed gate."

"Go straight down the hill and turn left on Five Cays Road, it will bring you back to the gas station on South Dock Road. Come on back to the boat, we've got a lot of planning to do, and I want to see the pictures you took."

Dino strode into the *TAR BABY'S* salon 15 minutes later and handed Seth his phone.

"Look at these pictures on Dino's phone, Jock. See if you recognize anybody."

"I can't say I recognize any of them, only Kat. There's the big, long-haired Dominican, Seth. But I don't know his name."

"Well, Antonio and José are identifiable to Dino and me."

"This swarthy looking guy, with the shaved head, is one of the house guards, Seth," said Dino.

"We need to download and print all these pictures for Jock," said Seth. "Look, let's get reorganized. We need to come up with a new plan. First, we need to watch the green ranch house in Five Cays, but we'd stick out there like a sore thumb. Second, I think we need to continue to watch Emerald Cay. Does Kat have any trucks that she rents to contractors?"

"She has three flatbed trucks with portable diesel generators on them, four dump trucks, and two semi-tractor trailer rigs," answered Jock.

"Are the trucks marked?"

"They all have TCI Rentals in black on both doors."

"If we cover the "Rentals" with white duct tape, we can park on the street, hook dummy wires to the nearest overhead transformer to the green house, and run the generator all night. It will look like we're preventing a brown-out, by by-passing a weak transformer — also, nobody would question an employee staying with the truck in that neighborhood. Do you have any traffic cones?"

"Yeah, and we can put a couple of ladders on the truck. I can make it look even more official. The truck lettering is a vinyl graphic. I can peel it off and replace it with FTCI. We can get the stick–on letters from the building supply store. The electric company is a private business. A diesel generator plant up on Leeward generates all our electric. Fortis Energy Inc. of Canada owns the plant. They letter all their trucks FTCI. If anybody in Five Cays asks, we can say the repair crew is scheduled for Tuesday sometime. I can rig a jumper wire that won't conduct any electricity, at the dive shop after hours."

"When can you have the truck ready?"

"I'll get it after five when Cecil closes, along with the ladders and traffic cones. Why don't you go to the building supply and get the stick on letters,

100 feet of 1-0 welding cable, and four big alligator clips? I'll meet you at the Turtle Cove dive shop at 5:30."

"OK, I think Dino is the best choice to take the truck to Five Cays. He looks Hispanic and actually speaks pretty good Spanish. We've got 5-Hour energy drinks aboard so he can pull an all-nighter. He can just hook the dummy wires up above two of the transformer's ceramic insulators. Gene, why don't you drive Jock out to the rental lot to get the truck at 5:00 and then set up surveillance at Silly Creek? Take something to eat and drink; we'll send Freddy out after midnight to relieve you."

"OK," said Gene as he headed for the galley.

"Hold on a minute, Gene … We have a couple of hours to kill right now, why don't we ask Jock the next **Big** question while we're all together?"

"Ask away," said Jock.

"Now that they've moved Kat to Five Cays do you want to try and pull her out of there?"

"I think it's more important now than it was before they moved her! Why did they move her onto their turf? I would have never imagined she was on Emerald Cay. But … I also think it's more dangerous now because of the close quarters there. I'm reluctant to ask you guys to go in there after her."

Seth looked around the salon and one by one the Geezers gave him a thumbs up.

"How many rooms do you think are in the house, Dino?"

"It looks like a typical cement block ranch. Probably a living room-dining room 'L', a small kitchen, three small bedrooms and two bathrooms. The wooden stockade fence surrounds the whole lot. They could park four or five cars inside the front and side yard. The backyard opens to a dirt alley through a small gate."

"I think we've lost the element of complete surprise, and whatever armed personnel they have will be close at hand. I'm still reluctant to ask you guys to risk your lives."

"Maybe we can make the compactness of the house work in our favor," said John. "It certainly will take less time to locate Kat and get her to a vehicle in a three bedroom 2000 square foot house than in a ten bedroom 30,000 square foot mansion. What we need is a diversion. Let's scout it out before it gets dark."

"Jock, you stay here ... Dino, John, and I will scope it out, and pick up the wire, truck letters, and alligator clips on our way out. We'll see you at your dive shop around 5:30."

**

Seth eased the green Suburban past Pumpy's and Tricky Ricky's. Neither was busy on this Monday afternoon. Dino gave directions from the back seat. They passed the green ranch house, which still had a black Suburban pulled across the outside of the front gate, then turned up the hill towards Matilda Way, the same street Seth had followed the TCI 20065 plated black Suburban up on Sunday. They turned at the dirt alley halfway up the hill, drove slowly behind, then clear of the green ranch house. The alley was higher than the parallel front street and afforded them a better view of the compound inside the fence. An armed guard was sitting on the hood of the second black Suburban 20 feet inside the gate, smoking a cigarette. The kidnappers backed the third black Suburban into the side yard. There was about ten feet of yard between the back of the house and the stockade fence. A pipe and rope clothesline set-up dominated the small backyard. The back gate lined up with a door that opened out of the kitchen. It was obvious the bedrooms were on the left side of the house when facing from the front. Seth continued down the bumpy alley, past the music blaring out of Pumpy's, and turned up the hill he'd come down yesterday. He bore left at the top and went past the walled house where the big Dominican turned into yesterday. There was a black Escalade parked inside. Seth followed the road back down to the highway and drove back to Turtle Cove and Jock's dive shop.

"Did you spot a transformer close to the house, Dino?"

"The closest one is between the green ranch house and Pumpy's in the alley. It should attract little attention there, and I can see inside the fence."

"The bedrooms are on the right side going in the back door," said John. "The back gate has a padlock on it. The backyard of the big, longhaired Dominican is across the alley from it. The wall is block and too tall to see what's in there. But the house has a pool deck that looks down on the green ranch house."

Seth pulled into Turtle Cove and drove through the Tiki Hut Restaurant's parking lot to Jock's docks behind it. The generator truck was already sitting there with a couple of ladders lashed to it. Jock was peeling the rental graphic off the driver's door.

"Here are the letters for the doors, where do you want the wire?"

"Take it into the shop, and we'll cut and crimp it in there."

Jock showed Dino how to start the generator and where to dummy up the welding cable. The whole group was gathered in the shop when Jock said, "What did you see in Five Cays?"

"The house is compact, and the property is completely surrounded by a six-foot stockade fence. There is an alley in the back. We saw an armed guard inside the fence, along with two of the Suburbans. They pulled the first Suburban across the outside of the front gate. I think John has got a plan brewing in his head."

"After seeing the compound,' said John. "I think we need a diversion. Tonight, Dino might be able to figure exactly how many people are guarding Kat. We know they have the woman tending to Kat, and maybe two men inside and one outside. The big Dominican who Seth and I tracked yesterday lives up behind them in a big house on the next street. Their backyards meet at the alley."

"What kind of diversion are you thinking about?" asked Jock.

"Well, these guys are not trained mercenaries, they're street criminals," said John. "The Suburban outside the gate was put there so nobody could crash through the gate and gain entrance. There was nobody in it or standing out there with it. I can slither down there through the vacant lot on the south side of the compound and stuff a gas soaked rag in the gas filler pipe and light it. I'll be long gone when the whole car bursts into flames. They'll lack discipline and all run out to save it. It will eventually blow-up and wreak havoc. Gene will take over the generator truck, Dino will pair up with Jock. When they run out front, Gene will un-hook the dummy wire from the generator, turn it off, and get back in the truck. Dino and Jock will pull up from behind the generator truck in the white Suburban. We'll all wear one of the sheriff's Kevlar vests. Seth will get the wool watch caps out of the storm locker and cut eye holes in them like we were going to do for Emerald Cay. We have five pistols and a couple of tactical shotguns. We'll cut the lock off the gate with a bolt cutter — take the one hanging on that pegboard behind Seth over there. Dino and Jock will take a sledgehammer, and break the backdoor in and find Kat. If anybody but the woman is still in the house, we'll Taser and zip-tie them. If they shoot at us, we'll shoot back. I'll cover their backs with a shotgun and a can of wasp spray. Seth will cover the backyard and alley with his hog rifle. Seth and I will follow y'all in the green Suburban. We'll all drive back to Jock's house."

"Sounds like a good plan ... What about the two copper welding cables left hanging from the transformer?"

"I'll bet they won't last five minutes after we leave," laughed John.

"I think you're right ... Jock, why don't you drive home and come back early tomorrow morning. We want to start the Five Cays assault at 11:00 a.m. Freddy will relieve Gene around midnight tonight at Emerald Cay. Everybody make sure you charge your phones."

Dino drove out in the generator truck wearing Kevlar under his black long-sleeved t-shirt, and a green hardhat supplied by TCI Rentals. He had the bolt cutters and a sledgehammer in the cab along with a 9mm Glock pistol. He moved the truck into position in the alley and set out his traffic cones. He put up the ladder and clamped the dummy wires in place atop the transformer. When he started up the generator, some curious Dominicans filtered into the alley from both directions. One large scruffy neighbor dressed in a sweat stained wife-beater approached the truck.

"Qué pasa, Señor?"

Dino answered without hesitation, *"El transformador es malo, el generador va a mantener las luces encendidas, una tripulacion reparara, mañana, eh?"*

"Bueno, gracias compadre."

He turned to the advancing neighbors and repeated Dino's explanation; the transformer was bad, but the generator would keep the lights on, and it would be fixed tomorrow. They all muttered *Bueno* and headed back to their houses. Dino breathed a sigh of relief and settled into the truck's driver's seat. He could see some lights in the green ranch house, and spotted one guard in the yard. There were two under-eave spotlights illuminating the front yard and side yards. A single light fixture next to the backdoor lit the back yard. The Suburbans had not moved. The blinds were down in all the windows he could see from the truck. Dino munched on a sandwich and drank a bottle of water. He screwed the top off a bottle of 5-Hour energy drink and drank it down. It was going to be a long night in the generator truck.

***

Peter Petcock watched the Hatteras intently from behind the drapes of his hotel sliding glass door Monday morning. The crew had been coming and going for a couple of hours. One or two of them was always with Seth. Finally, he went over to the phone and called The Alexandra Resort and checked the availability of a suite that day. He was in luck — they had three available for $595. He called Rikki's cell phone. She answered almost immediately.

"Rikki, this is Grant, can you get away later today? I'll get an oceanfront suite at the Alexandra and buy you lunch and dinner."

"I wondered when you were going to call me, Big Boy. I thought you might have lost the number. How about dinner and breakfast? But it will have to be room service. The doctor is in Cockburn Town until Tuesday afternoon helping the new Canadian Hospital set up their cardiac wing. I have a client for lunch today and then a couple of house tours. I can meet you there about 4:00 this afternoon."

"I'll call you after lunch with the suite number."

Peter hung up with a smile on his face. His luck was starting to change. He could also feel his flaccid penis start to swell. He fumbled with the

127

phone and booked the suite. He'd go back to the beach cottage and take a swim, then shower. Once he checked into the suite he'd call Rikki.

***

El Bomba got out of bed early Monday morning. He was naked and still groggy from the night before. The lunch and swimming went well Sunday afternoon. He could still visualize Sarita and Fabiana taking turns jumping up and down on the diving board naked and diving in the pool. Later that afternoon, the three of them started drinking shots of José Cuervo Silver Especial Tequila, and the ménage a trois started in the pool, then traveled to the living room, and finally the master bedroom. Rodrigo did not remember dinner — if there was one. The threesome rekindled sporadically throughout the night depending on who was awake. The two girls were still passed out in different positions on the king-sized bed. Two empty bottles of tequila sat on the nightstand. Rodrigo's hangover dispelled the myth that 100% pure blue agave silver tequila would not give you a hangover. He took a long second look at Sarita and Fabiana before heading for the shower.

An hour later he was on his way to Silly Creek with Frederico to move Mrs. Baffert. José and his crew followed in an identical black Suburban. On the way, he called Jacque Mehoff.

"Anything new, Jacque?"

"Not really, Jock went fishing with his friends, and they caught a huge wahoo. It'll be in the newspapers, they hung it up and weighed it at Turtle Cove. Otherwise, he's either home, at his dive shop or with his fishing friends. They're all eating breakfast at Aqua right now. It looks like he lent his white Suburban to his fishing friends. He's using his wife's Land Rover. I don't think he's going to cause us any trouble."

"We're moving Mrs. Baffert over to Five Cays. I don't want her to hear the helicopter come in tomorrow, and I don't want any traffic leaving Emerald Cay when we let her loose out past Wheeland in the Northwest Point Park."

"Sounds smart."

"I was thinkin' of just droppin' her overboard out in the Atlantic and lettin' her husband take the heat. The cops would have a fuckin' field day with him. He'd go to the police with the story, and they'd look at the eight million dollar land sale, and figure he wanted it all for himself. He has no proof there was a phone call. They'd ask him why he didn't call the police. There's no proof anybody kidnapped her. Her car's in their fuckin' garage."

"Yeah, he'd be on the hot seat. They couldn't charge him, though, without a dead body. But it might get some of the straight police to start looking around. Holding up your end of the deal is cleaner, and you know some rumor might get started. If you ever wanted to use this scam again, it wouldn't work."

"Yeah, I figured the same thing. Hey, why don't you come over for dinner tonight? Sarita has this friend visitin' from the DR. She's a knockout and very friendly ... if you get my drift."

"OK, I'm going to check out the surveillance system at Iguana's this afternoon, and I'll check the Baffert's house on the way back, just about dark. Then I'll come over for dinner. Should I bring my swimsuit in case we want to swim after dinner?"

"You won't need it."

"That friendly? *Bon Ben, amigo!*"

129

CHAPTER ELEVEN

DINO watched Tuesday morning's sun come up and wash the shroud of darkness from Five Cay's dusty hills. The daylight revealed the overgrown weeds, rubble-strewn vacant lots, and the shabby dust covered houses. This was the low-income section of Provo. The street above the unpaved alley had larger homes than those that spilled down towards the industrial structures to the west, and the water's edge to the east. The high ground in Provo enjoyed the constant, cooling ocean breeze while living below the ridge could be stifling. From first light, a steady stream of women in housekeeper uniforms, and men in all manner of dress made their way down the streets on their way to their jobs at the resorts. Dino thought; *every tourist destination has its own Kew Town and Five Cays that the tourists were not meant to see. Nassau, Jamaica, Miami, Rio, and actually all of them in the world. But, Provo looked to him like it had a job for anybody who wanted to work.* Three potcake dogs fighting over the contents of an overturned garbage can near the truck ended his muse, so he called in at 7:35 a.m. Seth was already drinking coffee and picked up immediately.

"Hey Dino, everything OK?"

"I've been wide awake all night thanks to 5-Hour Energy. The outside guard was relieved every two hours. The same two guys traded off. One was the guard from Silly Creek, the other I couldn't make. José from the Capri came out of the house once and talked to the Silly Creek guard about 1:00 a.m. and put an AK-47 in the SUV parked right inside the gate. I'd guess there are two or three men inside, along with the woman attendant."

"Any trouble with the neighbors?"

"A crowd started to form when I started the generator up, but I explained it was temporary, and we would replace the transformer tomorrow."

"Good, we'll be there just before 11:00 this morning. We're going to stage from behind your truck. You and Jock will make the backdoor assault to get Kat, with John and me covering you. Gene will drive the generator truck out. John and I will bring up the rear in *Frigate* ... any questions?"

"No, but I wanted to tell you that the lights and loud music were on late at the big Dominican's house up on the hill last night. They finally packed it in about 2:00 a.m."

"Keep your eyes open, and have another 5-Hour Energy drink. We'll see you soon."

Jock showed up about 8:00 at the boat and said, "I brought down the guns you stowed in my house, and my double-barreled shotguns."

"I hope we don't have to use them, but we'll get everybody armed before we leave. Everybody put on the Kevlar body armor under a long sleeve t-shirt. Pull the watch cap down over your face so they can't identify you, and don't wear flip-flops. The terrain is rocky and littered with broken glass and sand spurs."

The crew drank coffee and picked at a coffee cake, as Seth went over the assault plan one more time. John cut an old cockpit towel into long strips and retrieved a two-gallon red plastic dinghy gas can from the cockpit and put it in a black garbage bag. Seth issued each Geezer a pistol and put his hog rifle and three shotguns and some ammo in a long duffel, along with three Tasers. Each man took extra ammo for his pistol. Jock would also carry his own shotgun which was fitted with a leather sling, like Seth's tactical shotguns. The Geezers fidgeted with their weapons and made nervous small talk. They were like a football team waiting for the game to begin. Seth and John did some stretching exercises.

"Is everybody's cell phone charged up?" asked Seth.

Everybody nodded. Seth called Freddy out at the pink house.

"Is everything OK? ...... only the guard ... the bridge is open. Yeah, we're going in there just after 11:00 a.m. ... I know you'd rather be with us,

131

but you have to watch the mansion, especially if something goes wrong … there may be a tie-in, maybe by boat … I'll call you when the smoke clears."

Even as the minutes went by like hours, the Geezers continued to kid each other good-naturedly. Finally, it was 10:30 and time to go.

"OK guys put on your game face and let's go — nice and easy — like we're going out for a late breakfast."

The two Suburbans loaded up and headed up the hill with Jock in the lead in his white one. They started towards downtown, turned onto South Dock Road at the first roundabout, and continued to Five Cays Road where they turned left. Jock turned right on Reese Cl., which led to the green ranch house, but turned up the hill on Matilda Way and then left at the dirt alley. Both cars eased past the back of Pumpy's and stopped behind the generator truck. Gene got in the truck, and Dino came back and slid in the back seat of *Frigate*. Seth handed Dino a black watch cap.

"Don't forget to wear this. I cut the eyeholes really big."

"Thanks … FYI, the big Dominican with the droopy mustache walked down from his house and entered through the back door about a half hour ago. So, I figure there's four of them plus the woman in there now. The yard guard has been sitting on the front fender of the SUV inside the gate most of the time."

"OK … get the bolt cutters and the sledgehammer and get into Jock's SUV. Put this Taser and holster on your belt, Jock and John already have theirs. We're going to try and not kill anybody if it's possible. In five minutes, John is going to sneak through the vacant lot next to the fence and set the Suburban outside the gate on fire. By the time he gets back, it ought to be about ready to blow. Have Jock watch in his side mirror for my signal to go. I'll be talking to Gene on my cell. He can see the whole thing from his higher vantage point. Leave the engine running when you shift it into park."

John took his black garbage bag and slipped into the overgrown vacant lot. He worked his way over to the outside of the green house's fence and came out on the road below. After ducking around the corner, he squeezed between the gate and the black Suburban. Using a screwdriver, John pried open the gas port lid and removed the cap. Crouching behind the vehicle, he opened the garbage bag and pulled out a strip of towel, soaked it with gasoline, and stuffed it down the filler pipe with the screwdriver. John splashed gasoline from the open can on the front tire, the gate, and the fence. Next, he stuck another gas soaked wick into the filler neck of the now partially full gas can and set it next to the gate. After lighting both wicks with Seth's grill lighter, he quickly traced his steps back through the vacant lot. By the time John reached the green Suburban, up in the alley, he could see white smoke starting to billow up over the fence.

"What do you see Gene?" asked Seth on his cell phone.

"The guard is yelling toward the house and running towards the gate. He's trying to unlatch the gate, but he's coughing from the smoke."

KA- BOOOM!!!!!

"You heard it. The explosion blew the gate in on top of the guard — three men just ran out of the front door into the yard."

Seth gave Jock the signal and the two SUV's moved up the alley. Jock and Dino stopped at the back gate and flung their doors open and converged on the gate. Dino cut the gate lock off, and they moved towards the back door. Jock hefted the sledge hammer, swung, and the splintered door sprung open. They disappeared inside with John right behind them. Seth took up his position at the back gate.

"Talk to me Gene!"

"They're trying to get the front gate off the guard, but the whole front fence is burning. It's hard to see because of the smoke. One of them is trying to spray the gate with a garden hose. Another is running back towards the front door. The big one, with the long hair and mustache, is running around my side of the house — you'll see him in a second."

Seth shoved his phone in his pocket and readied his Remington. The big Dominican came around the corner and Seth aimed and shot over his head, and the bullet ricocheted off the concrete block house. The Dominican dropped down and scrambled back around the corner.

Seth got back on his phone, "Where is he, Gene?"

"He's headed back to the front door."

At the same moment, Seth heard two loud shotgun blasts, as Jock emerged from the house with Kat over his shoulder. Dino came out through the billowing smoke, 15 seconds behind him. They hustled through the open gate, and Jock put Kat in the back seat. He and Dino jumped in, slammed the doors shut, and accelerated away in a cloud of dust and gravel. John emerged from the smoky house and launched another shotgun blast down the hall before starting up the hill. He was almost to the gate when two shots slammed into the fence right next to the gate.

"Get down John," yelled Seth as he hit the dirt.

"Gene, where did those shots come from?"

"There's somebody up on the deck behind the big Dominican's house with an AK-47."

Seth stayed low and angled around the green SUV. He heard another shot, and it splintered part of the fence. John rolled behind the fence as Seth steadied his rifle on the *Frigate's* rear bumper step-up. As he sighted through his scope, he clicked his laser sights on. A tall white man with black hair wearing only "swing-easys" sighted through his rifle sights looking for a shot from the pool deck above. Seth put his laser dot right on the man's hairy chest and squeezed the trigger. The shot blew the shooter backward out of Seth's line of sight.

"Let's go, John, it's all clear, get in the truck!" yelled Seth. "We're pulling out, Gene," said Seth after picking up his phone.

"The big Dominican just jumped in one of the Suburbans, Seth. The whole front and side of the fence is in flames, and the Suburban outside the gate is still burning with black smoke. I don't think he can get out."

Seth heard some distant sirens as he ran down the alley to try and shoot out the Dominican's tires. As Seth got in position, the black Suburban backed up and then was floored forward, with tires squealing and gravel flying, towards the burning fence. The black Suburban crashed through the burning fence landing on the road, and the fiery remains of the fence flew everywhere. The Dominican wrenched the bouncing SUV left and floored it again, and it took off in a cloud of smoke and flames for parts unknown. Seth's first shot blew out the back hatch window. The second hit the body somewhere but missed the tires.

"I'm going to follow him, Gene, take the truck back to Jock's," gasped Seth as he ran to the *Frigate*. He jumped in, did a skidding turn around, and sped back past Gene, who was shutting down the generator.

"I guess we'll just follow the burning debris until we get on his tail, eh, John?"

"Why do you want to follow him, we've got Kat?"

Seth answered, "I think he's the key to finding out who is actually behind this conspiracy, and I think he's the Dominican boss … but not the mastermind." He skidded to a stop at South Dock Road. Seth turned left to follow the smoldering wood strewn all over the left lane and started passing cars and trucks.

"We're hitting 85. We should see him soon, John."

"You just concentrate on your driving. I'll look ahead for him."

"How did it go inside?"

"They found Kat in the front bedroom, the woman who was tending her just put up her hands. There was a guard looking out the front bedroom window at the flaming front gate. Jock rushed him, picked him up over his head, and slammed him to the floor so hard it knocked him out. He zip-tied his hands and feet, and Dino duct taped his mouth. Jock is no one to fuck with. The living room was clear. I watched the open front door from the hall. The rest of the Dominicans were outside. Dino finished cuffing the matron's hands and duct taped her mouth. Jock came out of the bedroom with Kat over his shoulder. I started up the hall in front of them to check the kitchen, dining room, and the backyard. Dino was covering our rear in the smoke filled the hallway. On his way out of the bedroom — *(horn blaring)* **Fuck!** — That was close! — Anyway, Dino almost ran smack into a stocky Dominican entering the smoky hall. Dino grabbed his gun hand, broke his wrist, and flipped him on the floor. I could hear the gun hit the floor. The bad guy scrambled for the gun with his other hand, and Dino tasered him in the chest as he brought it up to shoot. He shivered and shook from the electric shock, and his eyes rolled back in his head. Dino recognized him as José, the manager from the Capri. By the time he hit the floor, he was out cold. Dino pulled the Taser darts out of the perp's chest while I covered the hall and kitchen until everyone was by me and up the hill. I think the roof was starting to burn because the whole house was filling up with smoke."

"The wind is blowing its normal 20 knots, and some of the flaming debris from the SUV explosion could have landed on the roof."

"As I was backing out, two more of them started into the smoky hall, from the living room, and I gave them two blasts with the Mossberg. If I hit them, they're only hurt 'cause it was only #8 shot. I fired one more shot, before I left, just to buy us some time."

"Who do you think was shooting at us from the top of the hill?"

"We may never know."

"Hey! There's the black Suburban up ahead."

"I see him, and it looks like he's headed for Emerald Cay."

Seth pulled out his cell phone and speed-dialed Freddy.

"Freddy, we got Kat … John and I are chasing the big Dominican. Is the bridge still open?"

"Yes."

"Get the tire iron out of the *Shusi's* trunk and wedge it in the gears under the bridge, they're on the cul-de-sac side under the concrete apron. You've got about ten minutes — take your gun with you."

"No problem."

"Freddy, when he turns at Chalk Sound, we're going to put some serious heat on him."

***

El Bomba drank the strong *Barahona* coffee Conchita made earlier and looked at his watch — it was 11:15 a.m. He'd come down the hill earlier to make sure everybody was doing their job. Last night there'd been a little too much pre-celebration, and the steaming coffee was helping to wipe the cobwebs from his brain. Rodrigo guessed Jacque Mehoff hadn't experienced a night that sensuous, since coming to Provo. Watching Jacque and Fabiana progress from strangers to lovers had been fun for him and Sarita to watch.

El Bomba impatiently checked his watch again. It was just a little over two hours to the closing and 35 minutes until the helicopter landed at Emerald Cay. After he collected the deal money and was ready to take off in the helicopter, he would call Jock Baffert and tell him where and when to pick up his wife. José and Ramon would drop her off in the Northwest Point Nature Preserve on the far end of the island. By the time Jock found her, El Bomba would already be in the Dominican Republic and be a million and a half dollars richer.

Suddenly he heard someone in the front yard yelling, ***Fuego, Fuego!*** El Bomba pushed back the living room drapes and saw flames shooting above the front gate. As he ran out the front door, an explosion almost knocked him down. Ramon disappeared under the flaming wood gate, and El Bomba was showered with burning debris. His first reaction was to pull Ramon out from under the burning gate. But, the exploded Suburban was burning so intensely and putting out so much acrid black smoke that it was impossible to get near him. Chico ran out and turned a garden hose on the flaming gate, and José helped El Bomba pull Ramon to safety. El Bomba checked Ramon's vitals — the explosion had killed him.

José yelled, "I'll check the hostage, you check out back, *Jefe*."

As El Bomba ran around back, he noticed the roof was beginning to burn. When he turned the corner near the clothes line, a shot ricocheted off the back of the house above his head. He dropped down, pulled out his pistol, and crawled back around front. Smoke was starting to billow out of the front door. Chico ran to the closest Suburban and got the AK-47 out of the backseat.

"C'mon Chico, let's get everybody out of the house, it's going to burn."

They entered the smoky house and saw José laying on the hall floor outside the master bedroom in a heap. Conchita stood terrified in the open bedroom door with her hands cuffed behind her back and a piece of duct tape over her mouth. As El Bomba and Chico stepped into the hall to pull José back into the living room, they were greeted by two blasts from a shotgun. El Bomba dropped his pistol and stumbled back into the living room. Chico dove headfirst over José into the bedroom as Conchita ran for cover. El Bomba's right arm stung and bled from the shotgun pellets, and he knew then his plan had somehow unraveled. He ran through the open front door and looked at his watch, 11:40, the helicopter should be landing in 20 minutes. As the sound of distant sirens filled the air, he headed for the Suburban in the side yard. El Bomba jumped in, started the engine, and surveyed the flaming wreckage in front of him. The hulk of the outside Suburban was still a burning inferno. The front and side fences were engulfed in flames. There was only one way out. He got low in the seat and backed up quickly. A bullet shattered the rear window. El Bomba shifted into drive and stomped the accelerator. The big SUV fishtailed toward the flaming fence, punched through it, and carried a flaming section out onto the paved road. Another bullet thumped the car somewhere. He kept the pedal down and wrenched the steering wheel left as the rear end drifted towards a parked car. The smoking tires caught and the big Chevy rumbled down the street shedding its flaming cargo as it picked up speed. He turned at the bottom of the hill and headed for Silly Creek. He looked at his right arm and decided it looked worse than it was. Luckily, the shotgun was loaded with target loads. His goal now was self-preservation. He and Jacque had underestimated Jock Baffert, but he doubted Jock knew his identity. The police would probably chalk up the Five Cays assault to a gang war, and it would be forgotten. Nobody really cared when criminals killed each other. As he turned onto Chalk Sound Drive, he noticed a green Suburban coming up quickly behind him. El Bomba increased his speed, but the SUV stayed right with him. He could see two gringos in the front seat. His right arm and hand hurt with his every movement. Somehow he got his cell phone out of his right pocket and speed-dialed Diego at the mansion.

"Diego, close the bridge, **pronto!** Then open it back up — as soon as I'm across. I'm just about to turn up Silly Creek Road ... tell Paco to set up on the bridge with his AK-47. I've got two gringos on my tail in a green Suburban. Tell him to shoot to kill — did the helicopter get there yet?"

"I can hear it landing right now — I've flipped the bridge switch, *Jefe.*"

El Bomba laid his cell phone on the seat, increased his speed to 70 mph, and flew up the narrow winding road. He wanted to put some distance between himself and the green Suburban so they would run into a hail of bullets when they reached the cul-de-sac. As he neared the cul-de-sac, he glanced in the rear view mirror. They were further behind him — he could hear some chattering from his cell phone on the seat, but couldn't make it out. He looked ahead and drifted the careening Suburban around the palm trees and bougainvillea plantings in the center of the cul-de-sac, then gunned the Suburban towards the bridge. El Bomba realized too late that the bridge was not closed. He wrenched the steering wheel to the left and stood on the brakes. All he managed to do was to roll the SUV over. It slid on its side in a shower of sparks, went airborne, crashed into the open bridge structure on the other side, and exploded in a ball of flames. The flames were finally extinguished as the black Suburban slowly sank to the bottom of the rock-sided canal below.

***

A guard with a rifle on the other side of the open bridge took off running for the mansion house as Seth skidded to a stop behind the palm trees, just in time to see a Bell Jet 412 helicopter take off near the tennis court and fly southeast at a high rate of speed.

Freddy appeared out of the scrub jungle perimeter of the cul-de-sac carrying a tire iron. He walked slowly over to the *Frigate*. Seth rolled down his window and said, "Are you OK?"

Freddy just smiled and said, "Fuckin' A."

***

Antonio Arroyo hoped he'd made the right decisions. There wasn't any time to think. Chico called him and told him everything was turning to shit in Five Cays. El Bomba had just blasted through the burning fence in the second Suburban and was gone. Ramon was dead out in the compound, killed when the Suburban exploded. Now the house was starting to burn. José was unconscious and was bleeding from one of the shotgun blasts. Chico had taken some pellets in his butt and legs but was otherwise okay.

139

He'd cut Frederico's zip-ties off and pulled the duct tape from his mouth, but he acted like he might have a concussion. Chico left Conchita's hands tied behind her and the tape over her mouth so he wouldn't have to listen to the whiny bitch. The third Suburban was inside the fence and was not burning.

"Get everybody out of the house, and into the good Suburban, *pronto*. Leave Ramon — he's an illegal so it won't matter. Drive through the hole in the fence and go up the hill to El Bomba's house and hide out there. I'll be there in ten minutes. *Vamoose* before the fire trucks show up! I'll call Sarita to open the gate."

Flames were shooting from the roof of the green ranch house down near Pumpy's as Antonio drove up the hill to El Bomba's house. One fire truck's hose was trained on the roof, and another was racing back to a hydrant two miles away to refill with water. Antonio knew there were only two firetrucks and four firemen stationed near Five Cays. The island's fire department depended on volunteers, so the response was slow. The lack of a viable hydrant system made it hard to save a house. Dr. Fonseco was on his way to El Bomba's house, to check out José and the others. He checked the working girls for STD's every week and ran a small clinic for the Dominican community in Kew Town. Antonio had attempted to call El Bomba, but his phone went to voicemail. He honked his horn, the gate to Rodrigo's house slid open, and he pulled in between the Suburban and El Bomba's Escalade. Sarita met him at the front door as the doctor honked from outside the gate.

"Get him through the gate and parked, then bring him inside," said Antonio as he brushed by her and walked into the living room. José lay on top of a bloody sheet on the couch, with another covering him. Frederico sat in a chair across the room holding a bag of ice on the back of his head.

"Where's Chico?"

Frederico motioned towards the kitchen.

Chico stood on a towel in the middle of the kitchen dressed only in a t-shirt as Conchita plucked birdshot out of the back of his bleeding legs and butt with a pair of tweezers. He held a cell phone in each hand.

140

"Ah, I'm glad you're here, *amigo*. The fuckin' gringos kicked our asses. Diego just called on José's cell phone. El Bomba crashed and burned at Silly Creek with the gringos chasing him. He is dead at the bottom of the creek, and the helicopter took off and flew back to the D.R. He and Paco are getting ready to leave Emerald Cay in a skiff. They're waitin' for your orders."

"Call Diego and have him and Paco stand-in at the Capri for José and me. *Jesus Christo,* what the fuck else can go wrong?"

"Well, El Bomba's friend Jacque Mehoff was shot dead out on the pool deck. Sarita brought the rifle he was shootin' back in the house and covered him up with some beach towels. There's much blood on the deck."

The doctor pronounced that Frederico had a mild concussion and some cracked ribs and should take it easy for a few days. Conchita was instructed to put iodine on all of Chico's shotgun pellet wounds. After examining José, he concluded he'd broken his right wrist and died of heart failure due to an electric shock from a Taser. Something called ventricular fibrillation, which meant nothing to Antonio.

"How do you know he got Tasered?"

"Look here, Antonio, see the two puncture marks on his shirt and skin, that's where the darts hit him, look at the burn marks around the wounds. Also, he was hit with quite a bit of bird shot, but not enough to kill him."

Antonio thanked the doctor and he left.

As Sarita walked back into the living room, Antonio asked, "What are your plans now that El Bomba is dead?"

"I guess I go back to de working girl's life. I still have *mi* two *ninos* and *mi madre* in Santo Domingo to support."

"What about your friend who was staying here?"

"I drop her off at de *aeroport* early this morning, she back in Santo Domingo now."

"What was Jacque Mehoff doin' up here this morning?"

"He and Fabiana party with Rodrigo and me last night. I make Rodrigo and heem breakfast when I got back from de *aeroport*. Rodrigo walked down to the green *casa*, and Jacque was in the *baños* when I hear de explosion."

141

"How did Jacque get shot?"

"He run out of de bedroom in his underwear, he see what happens. He run in and grab Rodrigo's rifle and start to shoot in de alley. A shot from down dere heet heem and almost knock heem in de pool. He dead, dere was nut'ting I could do."

"How about you stay here and help me run the girls on and off the island? I'm going to need a lot of help with Rodrigo and José gone. Conchita will work for you. I will make it worth it for you. Our Santo Domingo partner's commercial fishing boat *EL CALAMAR GOTEO* came in late last night with some new girls. They'll be moving into our apartments in Kew Town, and the girls who are scheduled to leave will start back late tonight. If you want to leave, you can go on the boat."

"If it works out, can I bring *mi ninos* and *mi madre aqui?*"

"This is a big house, and we could be one big happy *familia.*"

"I will stay, *Jefe,*" said Sarita … giving Antonio a seductive look.

Antonio smiled and said, "*Bueno*, you and Conchita can start today. You and I will go down to the wharf later this afternoon so you can meet *Capitan* Martinez. After dark, Diego and Paco will deliver the girls that are leaving and pick up the new girls in a couple of vans. Chico will call Rafael at Iguanas to help him take José's and Jacque's bodies down to the boat. The *EL CALAMAR GOTEO* will sail for Santo Domingo just after midnight. José and Jacque will be dumped at sea, 50 miles out in the Atlantic. But first, I'll put Chico and Conchita out on the pool deck to clean up all the blood and wrap the bodies in tarps with duct tape."

Antonio stifled any feelings of anger or revenge. This was a time to make rational business decisions and keep order in their organization. Paybacks could wait to later and would have to be approved by their political partners. With their belonger gone, their very existence on this small island rested with their political connections. He helped Chico carry the bodies out to the garage while Conchita cut a large blue plastic tarp in half. Chico and Conchita wrapped and taped the bodies in the tarps. While they cleaned and scrubbed the blood from the pool deck, Antonio called the managers at Iguanas and the Zodiac from the kitchen. From the back window, he could see the fire was dying out below, and the remains were just smoldering now. Both men had already heard of El Bomba's death. It was a small island. He told them the bad news about José and assured both of them that everything was under control, and it would be business as usual. El Bomba's death would be chalked up to an auto accident, and if asked, they were to say José went back to the D.R. for family reasons. Jacque Mehoff's disappearance would never be solved. Everybody would move up a couple of notches, and all the gang members would get a bigger share of the profits. He figured that there would be no repercussions from the authorities. It had been a whirlwind couple of hours since Chico's phone call, but Antonio was already getting used to being *El Jefe*.

Antonio called their partner in Santo Domingo on José's cell phone and explained the situation. The partner commended him on this quick thinking and follow through. He said he looked forward to meeting him soon and wanted his business relationship with the Provo gang to remain the same. Antonio felt even better later when he rode over to South Dock with Sarita sitting next to him in the black Escalade. He wondered when Alistair Hixon would call him.

CHAPTER TWELVE

SETH, John, and Freddy arrived at Jock and Kat's house 30 minutes after El Bomba's spectacular crash to a surprisingly somber crew. They were all sitting around Jock's pool yawning away the effects of the huge adrenaline rush they'd just experienced. Jock came out of the kitchen with a cooler full of beer and handed them out to the crew. Dino went inside and helped Jock make sandwiches for everyone. As they ate their sandwiches and drank their beers, the Geezers slowly began to perk up. They stood in a tight group in the shallow end of the pool holding a post-mortem and sipping their cold ones. With each recollection, their conversation became louder and more animated.

Jock and Seth sat at the pool bar, "How is Kat holding up?"

"She cried all the way back from Five Cays. She was scared to death when the assault started. But, by the time we got home they had turned into tears of relief. She took a hot shower and is taking a nap. I think she'll be all right when she wakes up … she's a tough girl."

"Did you cancel your closing yet?"

"Yes, just before you rolled in. My lawyer is coming over later this afternoon for an explanation. We need to talk about whether we should present the whole thing to the British Ambassador and maybe then to the local authorities — or not. My lawyer is an old friend and is keen on the island's political situation. He can help us assemble the actual evidence we have and advise us if we have any possible exposure to criminal charges. He's also a friend who I trust."

"Gene will be helpful too. I think I'll go back to the boat now, shower, and change clothes. I want to put the Tasers, guns, and body armor back in the boat's gun locker. What time do you want Gene and me back here?"

"Rex said he would be over at 3:30. Make sure you bring the pictures that Dino took on his phone."

"I can print them. I have a computer and printer on *TAR BABY*."

"Why don't you leave a couple of your pistols here, in case there's any backwash from today?"

"OK, I'm going to carry my little Ruger .380 in my pocket. Hey, give me your keys. I'll bring Kat's Land Rover back up when Gene and I return. Do you need any help with the generator truck?"

"Nah, Kat and I will handle that."

Seth and the rest of the Geezers went back to the boat in the *Frigate* and *Sushi* and hit the showers. Dino, Freddy, and John settled in for a well-deserved nap.

***

Jock, Seth, and the Geezers sat out on Jock's veranda nursing cold ones as they waited for Jock's lawyer to show. Kat walked out in white slacks and a flowing navy blue tunic, looking fresh as a daisy.

"Seth, Gene, and John it's so good to see you!"

Seth stood and said, "You look great, Kat. Meet two more of my friends, Dino and Fred."

She hugged each of them and gave them a peck on the cheek, and said, "Only thanks to you and your merry band of Geezers, as you call them."

"Maybe, but if you hadn't played it smart with your iPhone I'm not sure we could have found you," said Seth.

Kat smiled demurely and said, "I think I'll pour myself a stiff one," and headed for the bar.

"You've earned it," said Seth. "How did they treat you?"

"Actually, very well. A Hispanic girl took care of me the whole time, and the only thing that was demeaning was when they frisked me — and thank God he was an amateur."

The front doorbell chimed, and Jock went to answer it. A minute later the lawyer strode onto the veranda dressed in a pair of beige slacks, a light blue Tommy Bahama shirt, a Brighton belt, and a pair of dark brown Sperry Gold-Cup driving loafers with no socks. He carried a thin, legal-size leather briefcase under his left arm.

145

"Sorry I'm late ladies and gentlemen, but I thought I'd shed the three-piece suit I wore for the canceled closing today."

Jock introduced Rex Hodson all around emphasizing that he was an old family friend. He had an athletic build, was of medium height, with a thick shock of brown hair crowning his ruddy good looks.

"Where should we start, Rex?" asked Jock.

"At the beginning ... with you Jock. I'll take notes," said Rex, as he pulled a legal pad and a pen from his briefcase. "I want you to know you are all protected by the attorney/client privilege, so there's no need for you not to be forthcoming."

Jock recounted the surprise call from the kidnapper and his decision to call Seth on the high seas since he could not call the authorities. He told Rex he didn't call him because he was afraid a mole might work in his office, or the kidnappers might be tapping Rex's phone. He recalled how unsettling it was to hear the kidnapper's computerized voice barking orders at him. Next, Jock launched into Gene's fingerprint lifting skills and his realization that Kat or the kidnapper might have her Apple iPhone. Jock asked Seth to explain their relationship with Bobby Thompson and his far-reaching intelligence capabilities. He explained once Bobby's techs put the apps on his and Kat's iPhone, it revealed the phone's location at the end of Silly Creek Road on a Google map. Seth jumped in and detailed how they maintained a 24/7 surveillance of the mansion on Emerald Key. He also showed Rex the surveillance log and the printed and time-dated pictures; including blow-ups of pictures taken by Dino and Freddy from the pink house. Gene explained the Interpol results of the fingerprints samples they sent to Bobby which identified José Gonzalez, as well as revealing his arrest record, present activities, and consorts on Provo. He also enumerated how Seth and Dino had scouted José Gonzalez at the Club Capri.

"Tell me about how you got Kat back," asked Rex.

"I should tell you first, I started to get a bad feeling about maybe not getting Kat back when we found out the iPhone's location. The kidnapper could've deep-sixed her offshore, and I would've had a hell of a time, standing there with eight million new dollars in my hand, explaining why I didn't know where she was. I had no real proof of her kidnapping, and I told people she was in Miami. Then I would have changed my story and what would they believe after that? The kidnapper doesn't know about the fingerprint ID, the iPhone location, the photos, and the license plate number. We still really don't know for sure who made the phone calls or who the mastermind is. It could be Gonzalez, Moreno, or Hixon. We are not sure who the big Dominican with the long black hair and the droopy mustache is."

"After seeing the pictures, I recognize him as Rodrigo Moreno — known in Five Cays as 'El Bomba'. He was at a political reception I was invited to at the Emerald Cay mansion a couple of years ago. I asked Alistair Hixon, the Minister of the Interior, who is leasing the residence, who he was. He told me he was a Dominican businessman," said the attorney.

"How can he afford that mansion?" asked Jock.

"Good question, old chap. All of our ministers live like multi-millionaires. But someday there will be a day of reckoning. In this particular case, the mansion was built by an American millionaire from Colorado. After completing the project, the builder was bribed to value it at half-price to lower the one-time 9% property tax. Someone in the government accepted that ridiculous figure, but the previous government filed a 1.8 million dollar lien on the property to collect the just value tax. After the last election, it was leased to the newly elected Hixon for an undisclosed sum, and the whole matter has been in limbo ever since."

"How did you get invited to the reception?" asked Seth with a wry smile.

"I took a cue from your big U.S. law firms. I donate equally to both political parties."

"You got me," laughed Seth.

Jock started explaining the plan to assault the Emerald Cay mansion. He mentioned using Tasers instead of using guns. He stressed that they didn't want to kill anyone unless they had to; they just wanted to free Kat.

"Then the Dominicans moved her to Five Cays, up the street from Pumpy's and Tricky Ricky's — there were guards, and a Suburban pulled across the front gate. But on a positive note, when they left Silly Creek we got the pictures that showed us who we were up against. We rigged a generator truck to look like an FTCI maintenance vehicle and put it in an alley close to Kat's new location for surveillance. We came up with a plan to create a diversion out front, so we could break in the back of the house and get Kat out using the element of surprise."

"What kind of diversion?" asked Rex.

"John snuck down and started the Suburban on fire, shortly after 11:00 this morning, using the old 'gasoline soaked wick in the fill pipe' trick. When she blew, it drew most of them out front — that's when we went in the back door and got Kat."

"Did anybody get hurt?"

"The guard stationed right inside of the front gate probably got hurt bad or worse — it was quite an explosion. As we were exiting the house, Dino was suddenly confronted by one of the kidnappers in the smoky hallway. Dino took his pistol away from him in those close quarters and broke his wrist. Then he threw him down and Tasered him. He recognized the perp as José, the Club Capri manager. He was unconscious when we left, but he should be alive. I sacked a guy in the bedroom when we first went in. He was knocked out, but breathing all right when I cuffed him. The roof on the house started burning just before we left. John shot at two guards who entered the hallway as he covered our retreat with Kat. But, he was only using #8 shot, so I doubt that killed anybody. Seth shot a white guy, who was shooting down at us from Moreno's pool deck as we were leaving, with his hog rifle. We don't know his condition, except he quit shooting at us. Seth and John followed Moreno out to Emerald Creek where he crashed into the canal at the drawbridge at high speed. He didn't notice it was open until too late. There was a Bell Jet helicopter there waiting for him. It took off when his SUV exploded. El Bomba, as you call him, is dead for sure."

Rex finished taking notes and asked, "Kat, can you add anything you saw or heard while you were captive?"

"Well, I didn't see anything … they kept me blindfolded the entire time. The first house felt and sounded large, and I could hear the ocean. The second house was small and smelled of mildew. I guess the biggest thing is they were all Hispanic. All the kidnappers spoke Spanish to each other and Spanglish to me. The woman watched Spanish TV 24/7. I wish I could tell you more."

"Thanks, Kat. Now, after hearing all this, I don't think any of you should jump to any conclusions, post-haste. These people are criminals and their reaction to this situation may surprise you. They might not want the authorities to get wind of any of this. They'll probably hide their dead and wounded. The police may think it's all part of a gang war in that part of town. Let me make some inquiries to the police and fire department and see what I can find out."

"Do you practice criminal defense law, too?" asked Gene. "I thought you were a property lawyer."

"Yes, I do criminal defense, divorce law, estate planning, personal injury, property, and civil law. Let me put this in perspective for you. The Turks and Caicos have just over 30,000 people living here, 23,000 of them live on Providenciales. St. Petersburg is a small city in Florida and has 240,000 people living there. Tarpon Springs is 30 miles from St. Pete and has 23,000 people living there. Imagine that Tarpon Springs is a country and its GDP is created wholly by those 23,000 people. How many attorneys can a country that small support?"

"We get it, Rex, please don't take it personally," said Seth. "We were just asking."

"No offense taken. I'll check my sources and give you an opinion tomorrow morning. I couldn't figure out why Jock wanted to sell his beach property after owning it all this time, especially with all the new hotels coming down his way. At least now, I know why. Jock, I will call you before our meeting tomorrow. Oh, one more thing, Jock. Can you locate Kat's iPhone on your app for me?"

"Sure. Come over here and I'll show you."

Jock pulled out his iPhone and unlocked it. He found the "findaphone" App and touched it. He entered Kat's Apple ID and password and tapped go. A Goggle Map of Providenciales appeared and shrunk down to the end of Silly Creek Road. It showed a pinging target at the end of Silly Creek Road over Emerald Key.

"Unbelievable," said Rex, as he took a picture of it with his cell phone. "I wanted to get a picture of this before Kat's iPhone battery went dead."

"It is amazing."

"Gentleman, I'll see you all on the morrow," said Rex as he picked up his briefcase and left the room.

Everyone left in Jock's house was exhausted. They had four pizzas delivered and drank Turk's Head Ale and a Ridge Geyersville Zinfandel from Jock's wine cellar. When the pizza was gone, the Geezers left for the marina, except for Dino, who stayed behind in case any retribution from the Dominicans surfaced. Jock closed up the house, switched on the air, and set the perimeter alarms. They all fell into their respective beds and bunks for their first good night's sleep in almost a week

***

Wednesday dawned to another sunny, warm, and breezy day in paradise. The crew slept in, then enjoyed a leisurely brunch at Aqua under the swaying palms. The call came from Jock about 1:00 p.m. The meeting was on with Rex at 2:30 at Jock's house. They drove up to Jock's in their swim trunks and t-shirts at 2:00. Jock and Dino were already out on the veranda.

"Where's Kat?" asked Seth.

"We got a call late last night from Jordan. He sailed into Miami yesterday from Rio. They won the Rio to Miami leg. But they leave in a couple of days to race to Lisbon. Kat caught a plane out about two hours ago for Miami. She wants to see him. She'll be back Friday at noon. It will fit her original cover story if we decide not to go public."

"The Volvo around the world race is grueling."

"That's an understatement, but he wanted to do it. We're going to have a little dinner celebrating Kat's "homecoming" Friday night at Opus. Just a little something to show you Geezers our appreciation."

"You don't owe us anything, ol' Buddy, but we'll go!"

150

There was a lot of conjecture flying back and forth concerning what Rex might have discovered. Rex finally arrived, and they all assembled in the living room for privacy.

"I'll get right to it, Gentlemen. My suspicions were confirmed. The Fire Chief on Provo confided to me the fire was started either by a car bomb or perhaps a leaking fuel system or tank dripping on a hot exhaust. There was one death caused by the explosion and the resulting residence fire. A Ramon Pena, a Dominican illegally in the country, died at the site from fourth-degree burns and smoke inhalation. The house and its contents, owned by a Rodrigo Moreno, a belonger, was a total loss. I called several of my police contacts and found they'd spent very little time investigating the fire. First, the investigators interviewed numerous neighbors, who heard nothing but the explosion and could not get near the blaze because of the burning fence. Nobody saw or heard anything suspicious or saw anybody coming or going from the residence. Apparently, nobody in that neighbor *ever* sees or hears anything suspicious. The police figured the fire department cut the chain lock on the back gate and broke in the back door. The prosecutor I queried thought it might be gang related but stated there was no evidence, and if there was it had burned up in the fire. Nobody has filed any missing person reports, and none of the emergency clinics or the hospital have any gunshot or trauma victims on their books. Any questions so far?"

"What about El Bomba?"

"Rodrigo's death has been listed as an automobile accident. The desk sergeant at the Five Cay's Police station said it took two wreckers and a couple of divers all afternoon to haul the wreckage of the SUV out of the Silly Creek canal. They recovered Rodrigo Moreno's badly burned body, but it was unrecognizable. He will have to be officially identified by his dental records. I asked what they thought he was doing out there at Emerald Cay. The sergeant said, 'It is common knowledge that he and Minister Hixon are friends.' I called the Minister's office and they informed me he has been attending a political conference for the last ten days in Santo Domingo. They said they would inform him."

"Any questions now?"

"What do you think I should do? Now I think that Hixon is behind the whole thing, and we have the evidence to bring a good case against him," said Jock.

"Not really ... I thought it all through, and it's all circumstantial. With him out of the country during the whole thing, it would have to be a conspiracy. All your major players are missing, except for maybe José. Proving that Alistair had anything to do with it would be tough."

"But what about the iPhone in his house, the fingerprints, and the photos?"

"They only prove that Rodrigo and José are suspects in the kidnapping. If Alistair admitted he gave Rodrigo permission to use his house, we still can't prove he was involved in the kidnapping. The same thing goes with the land deal. First, we didn't have a closing, so it's a non-entity. Second, our leverage would have been a bribe or excessive commission if we could have tracked it. Third, we would wait for the inevitable instant zoning change. We could have threatened the buyer with some jail time. They usually give up everybody else to avoid doing the time. But, the truth probably is that Rodrigo was his only contact. So Alistair would walk. These politicos have experience at this game, and they know if there is a jury trial they'll win it every time because our jury of their peers all owe the politicians. If I were you, I would lay back right now. I think this government will self-destruct in the next year or two. They've stolen so much money and crown land that the complaints are piling up in Britain from the owners of the high-dollar hotels and restaurants. The country's infrastructure is not keeping pace with the foreign investment. I can see London investigating the country's finances, then shutting the government down and installing a governor until it's all straightened out. I think a lot of the recent developers and politicians will be indicted and convicted. It will warn future politicians here not to take bribes or put their hand in the till. It will be a tough couple of years, but when it's over ... The Turks and Caicos will return to its rightful place as the jewel of the Caribbean. In the meantime, I will document everything we have. I would suggest we send a copy of the pictures of the Dominican gang leading Kat out of the mansion, including the picture I took of her iPhone's Google map location on Emerald Cay, to Alistair. I'll send them in a manila envelope with my law firm's return address, and an unsigned note reading: 'Cease and desist. If any harm comes to my client, his family or friends, we will send these photos and other pertinent evidence to the British Embassy and Scotland Yard in London.' I'd like to be there to see Hixon sweat when his chambermaid hands him Kat's iPhone."

"I know we've talked all about our country's future before, Rex, and I had hoped the turnaround would happen sooner rather than later. But now, it really hits home — the audacity and arrogance of this group of politicians have gotten to the point where they think they are untouchable."

"My point is, why should you become the poster boy of their downfall when they're going to self-destruct within a year or so anyhow. It will be much easier for you to live here after the reformation if you're patient."

"I think that's good advice, and it will keep my friends here from suffering any possible repercussions."

"Right, but there is one loose end I think we need to tie up … José Gonzalez. He would be the obvious choice to be the new Dominican boss. Depending on his frame of mind, and what Alistair tells him to do after receiving our photos, he may decide to concentrate on their core business rather than revenge. Let's see if he's back at work at the Club Capri. It will give us an idea of how badly he was hurt yesterday."

"I'll go back up there tonight with Dino if you want," volunteered Seth. "I'll book my fictitious nephew's bachelor party. But tomorrow, Rex, why don't you go fishing with Jock and the rest of us?"

"What a bloody good idea. I'd welcome the chance to get to know you hardy bunch of blokes better."

***

After an early dinner back on *TAR BABY* with the crew, Dino and Seth got all shined up, dressed in long pants, and put on their Tommy Bahama shirts. They looked like two up-scale gringo tourists from Miami, looking

153

for some fun. They drove to Kewtown, walked under the Capri portico, and were greeted by a different bouncer than their first visit.

"Welcome to Club Capri, ten dollar cover, *Señors*."

"We're just here to see José and book a party," said Seth.

"Step inside and wait at the bar, I call the manager."

The bouncer said something unintelligible in Spanish into a lapel microphone while adjusting his earpiece. A few minutes later a tall, middle-aged, dark-haired Hispanic arrived in a black suit at the bar.

"You wanted to see the manager. I am Diego."

"Oh … I was in here the other night and talked to José about a bachelor party for my nephew, in August. José suggested the private suite and gave me a price, is he here?"

"No, José went back to the D.R. We don't know when he'll be back. I'm the manager now."

"Ok … José said for two hours in the suite, open bar, hors d'oeuvres, DJ, girls, and tips, $4000 … We'll have seven young men at 9:00 p.m. in the evening, on August 23rd. I'll be with them … but down here at the bar with a friend."

Diego called to the bartender over the loud music, "Hector, bring me the booking calendar and the receipt book. What is your name, *Señor*?"

"Michael Martin."

"Well, Michael Martin … that date is available. I need a $500 cash, non-refundable deposit, and I will give you a receipt."

Seth counted out five "Big Bens". Diego wrote his information on the calendar and wrote Seth a receipt. They shook hands as Seth and Dino exited.

As they drove back to Turtle Cove Dino asked, "So what do you think happened with José?"

"I'd guess he either suffered complications or thoroughly displeased someone in upper management," replied Seth sarcastically. "He was in no shape to travel anywhere. Either way, I don't think we have to worry about José anymore."

CHAPTER THIRTEEN

PETER'S tryst with Rikki ended late Tuesday morning after a room service breakfast and a playful shower. He headed back to his Turtle Cove Inn room and observed that no one was aboard the Hatteras, and all their vehicles were gone. Seth's friend's Blue Mountain house was the first place he checked, but none of their vehicles were there. Peter drove out to his Long Bay rental house, changed into a t-shirt and cargo shorts, then checked out the cave. Nobody had been near the cave, but he cut some fresh brush and piled it over the entrance anyhow. He wasn't hungry, but was tired from the activities of last night, so he settled back into his Turtle Cove room to take a nap. Rikki had been insatiable before and after dinner in the suite. She sorely tested his staying power, and he popped his second Viagra an hour after dinner at 9:00 o'clock last night. Every time he fell asleep, she would wake him up in a different erotic way. The price of the suite, dinner, and three bottles of champagne had been worth every penny. He drifted off into a deep sleep with a smile on his face and when he awoke it was dark. When he peeked out of the drapes, the lights were on in the Hatteras. The lights went out early, and Peter walked down to SharkBites for a late dinner.

The next morning he was on station at 7:00 a.m. The Hatteras's crew slept unusually late, left the marina just before 2:00 in the afternoon, and drove up to the Blue Mountain House. Peter followed them, and they appeared to have an early dinner out on the veranda, before returning to the marina. Peter resumed his watch in his room and saw Seth and "Pablo" leave the boat about 10:00 p.m. He followed them in *Bonehead* to the Club Capri where they stayed for about 30 minutes, then drove back to the boat.

The *TAR BABY'S* lights went off 15 minutes later. Peter figured they must be closet perverts or something.

Early Thursday morning Peter watched the *TAR BABY* pull out of the slip with the whole crew aboard, along with Seth's big curly-haired island buddy, and a new passenger who arrived with a large cooler. They put all the rods out, so he figured they'd be fishing most of the day. Peter headed towards Long Bay for a leisurely breakfast and a day of R&R on the beach. He planned to be back on station mid-afternoon, to see if the one opportunity he needed to get Seth all alone might present itself tonight.

***

"C'mon aboard, Rex. Dino will help you with the cooler," said Seth. "What's in it anyhow?"

"A case of cold Turk's Head Lager, seven Cuban sandwiches from IGA's Deli, and a couple of fresh pineapples. I appreciate you taking me fishing ... it's the least I can do."

Seth started the engines and the generator. "Disconnect the shore power and let's cast off, guys. The fish won't wait for us. I want to troll around the Northwest Point to see if there's a marlin bite out there."

Jock climbed to the flybridge as Seth threaded his way out of Turtle Cove and Grace Bay. Rex stayed down in the cockpit in the middle of the bait preparation and some lively conversation.

"Rex's courier delivered the photos to Minister Hixon's office first thing this morning. The next few days will tell the tale," said Jock.

"Yeah, like my ol' dad Robert E used to say, 'Forewarned is forearmed'. Personally, I don't think we have much to worry about."

"Rex's idea is gutsy, but it notifies Hixon that we know he was involved. I think he'll cool it and concentrate his greed on a less proactive project."

"I see some birds working up there off the point," said Seth quietly as he slowed to idle. "Let's ease the outriggers down so the boys can get the spread out."

Seth worked *TAR BABY* around the Northwest Point and trolled through the whirling, swooping, and diving seagulls who were feeding on the fast moving schools of bait from above, while a school of large yellowfin tuna attacked them from below. The crew caught a few of the 50 to 60-pound tuna on a cedar plug that was run 250 feet back thru the shotgun rigger mounted on the flybridge top. Once around the point, he headed in towards the rocky cliffs where the reef ran right up to the shore, and the Atlantic dropped to 1000-feet deep, 150 feet off the rocky beach. As the Hatteras moved closer to the cliffs, the seas smoothed out. Seth zig-zagged a couple of hundred yards from the dive boats that were drifting the sheer wall outside the reef. Suddenly there was a loud "pop" and the line came out of the right long rigger clip. An instant later the left rigger was knocked down too.

Seth shouted down, "Marlin behind the left rigger!"

He turned the boat seaward towards the left rigger and accelerated slightly out of the turn. The Moldcraft wide range lure slowed and sank a little in the middle of the turn, then sped up like a frightened baitfish as Seth came out of the turn. The marlin aggressively piled on the lure, making a big splash, before racing away with the lure in his mouth.

"What a bite!" yelled Jock, as the 50-wide Tiagra reel started screaming.

"Let Rex take her," shouted Seth, "get him in the chair and harnessed up … it's a big fish."

During its initial run, the marlin surged first and then started jumping. While the crew cleared the other four rods, two teasers, and the dredge, they whooped and hollered at every jump. After telling Rex to back off on the drag a bit, Seth turned the boat and ran the bow towards the fish. Rex reeled hard and retrieved most of his line. Seth slowed down as they got close to the fish and spun the boat until the fish was off the transom again and swimming up-sea.

"Get ready to reel again, Rex. I'm going to back down on this fish hard, and we'll try and get the leader for a quick release. We don't want her to sound in this deep water, or you'll be pumping her up for at least another half an hour."

Seth started backing aggressively while John and Dino put on their leather gloves and headed for the transom. Water splashed over the transom half filling the cockpit as the exhaust pipes belched black smoke. Rex was covered in sweat and soaked with salt water, but he obviously welcomed the cool relief. The hi-vis green mono line inched aft off the transom, and the fish finally rose and jumped fifty feet behind the boat. Rex dug in, reeling relentlessly, and was rewarded with the appearance of the double line. A few more revolutions of the reel brought the leader to the rod tip. Dino took a hand wrap on the 400-pound test leader and put all his weight back on his haunches as the fish jumped close to the boat. Seth put one engine in gear at idle speed and moved the boat forward. Two more wraps brought the big fish to the transom, and Dino guided her up the starboard side of the cockpit. John leaned over and controlled her bill with two hands as Gene tagged the magnificent fish, grabbed the lure, and de-hooked her. They towed the fish for a couple of minutes forcing water through her gills and released her back to the sea. The awesome fish was still lit up in shades of neon as she slowly swam away, then with one parting flick of her enormous crescent tail — she was gone.

"What a fish!" Seth yelled down at an exhausted but elated Rex in the chair. "Easily six-hundred pounds."

Rex was speechless, but the rest of the crew continued to shout and high-five while pounding Rex on the back. Jock climbed down the ladder and shook Rex's hand after handing him a well-deserved cold one.

Once Rex regained his composure, he raised his beer and said, "Thank you, gentlemen … That marlin was at least twice the size of any I've caught here over the years. What a great captain and crew. I would have never thought I could catch a fish that big at my advanced age of 60."

"Hey Rex, we have an 80-year-old member of our St. Pete fishing club who caught two marlin over 450 pounds on our Costa Rica trip last year," said Freddy. "Tell Rex what Harvey's advice to us old Geezers is, John."

Already laughing, John said, "Number one, 'Never trust a fart'. Number two, 'If you're not thinking about sex 24 hours a day, your mind's wandering'. Number three, 'If your wife asks you which of her friends you would pick for a ménage a trois, don't give her two names'."

Rex and Jock cracked up, and the rest of the crew laughed — even though they'd heard it many times before. But the truth was ... Harvey Daniels was a truly amazing 80-year-old.

"Thanks again lads, this is a day I'll always remember!"

"Our pleasure, Rex ... let's get the spread back out and see if there's any more action along the wall, guys," said Seth with a smile.

Five minutes later Freddy and John put the dredge back in the water, and the spread was complete. Seth continued to zig-zag the Hatteras along the western rock wall as close to the dive boats as politeness and discretion dictated. Dino cut up the fresh pineapples and passed a plate up to Jock and Seth on the flybridge, before sharing the rest with the crew. Spirits remained high.

Down in the cockpit, Rex said to Gene, "You know I've been thinking about the tall, dark haired white guy you saw shooting down from El Bomba's pool deck. I've seen Moreno, now and then, with a private investigator that fits your description. He's a mysterious French character who lives on this island."

"Ah, the French," said Gene. "There's no end to those pricks!"

Everybody in the cockpit laughed, and Freddy said, "You know, I caught French pneumonia once."

"What in the bloody hell is that?" asked Rex.

"I could only catch my breath in snatches," laughed Freddy.

"I've been had again," said Rex smiling, as the cockpit crew cracked up.

After only twenty minutes of trolling, the left long rigger was knocked down again. The right rigger remained in the outrigger clip, so John moved to the left long rod located in the fighting chair's rocket launcher. He grabbed the monofilament line right above the reel and gave it three quick pulls, causing the lure to lurch ahead, then he let the lure drift slowly back. A small blue marlin suddenly appeared behind the lure and pounced on it like a hungry tiger.

"Blue marlin on the left long!" yelled Seth as the marlin surged away.

John climbed in the chair and loosened the drag a few pounds as the young fish sped away.

"Fell for the old escaping baitfish trick," laughed John as Freddy turned the fighting chair towards the jumping fish. Dino, Gene, and Rex cleared the lines and teasers. John kept the pressure on the game fish and dialed up the drag a bit as he brought him closer. Seth started backing on the acrobatic marlin, and Dino had the leader in his hand in under ten minutes. He and Gene made a clean release.

"Let's head in boys — we've fished enough for one day. It looks like a thunderstorm is headed our way from Mayaguana. If we leave now, we should beat it in. It looks like we found a good spot here, we'll try it in the tournament during the same tide phase if the wind speed and direction is similar. Next time we're out we'll try our luck around Fort George and Parrot Cay."

TAR BABY made it back to the dock in 25 minutes, flying two blue marlin release flags, just moments before the sky let loose with a 30-minute downpour. The crew was enjoying the fresh sashimi and some cold ones in the salon as the driving rain washed the salt off the boat for them. Freddy set the Cuban sandwiches out on the galley counter on paper plates, and the hungry crew wasted no time devouring them. Rex was still grinning from ear to ear as the crew played the video, captured by the flybridge mounted GoPro, over and over on the TV. Seth printed a picture of the lit-up marlin, taken boat side with Freddy's digital camera, for Rex's refrigerator door.

"Now Rex, don't be broadcasting where you caught the big blue until the tournament is over. It's bad enough we're doing the scouting for Jock, too," said Seth with a smile.

"No worry Seth, I'm scheduled to fish in the Classic with Jock, so my lips are sealed too. Who else is coming down from Florida?"

"Captain Ramon Rodriquez and his boss are coming down from Palm Beach on his new Viking, *GET-A-LOT*, and Captain Toby Warner is making the trip on his newly acquired charter boat *SPELLBOUND*."

"I thought he retired from charter fishing," said Freddy.

"I think the honey-do list was getting too long at home. He bought an older 52 foot Hatteras, refurbed her, and put in two new Cummins," laughed Seth. "Toby definitely needed to get out of the house."

"Who's coming down with him?" asked Freddy.

"Ray 'Jingles' Jones chartered the trip. Billy Chandler and Robby Hamburger are the mates, with Dave 'Banty Rooster' Bender, Ricky Whirly, and Doug Clorey angling."

"Why do they call him Jingles?" asked Jock.

"Well, Ray wanted us to take a friend of his into our fishing club up in St. Pete. One of our members questioned whether his candidate possessed the financial wherewithal to travel to all the far-flung destinations where we fish. Ray stood up, put his hand in his pocket and rattled his change saying, 'Don't worry, he has the jingles.' Everybody laughed, and his buddy got in — but Ray had acquired a new nickname."

"We're expecting about 20 boats this year for the Classic, including five local boats. There are more boats coming through here every year on their way to the Dominican to fish the 'FADS' for marlin. From there they travel to Tortola in August for the big marlin bite on the north drop," said Jock.

"What's on the agenda for tonight?" asked Seth.

"We could go to Baci's for Italian food. Afterward, I wanted to take y'all to an island Junkanoo performance down at the Bight Beach Park. A friend of mine, David Bowen, was named Cultural Director of the Turks and Caicos a year ago and has been teaching our youth the heritage of these islands. He figures in the last twenty years it has been lost in the rapid tourist growth and the introduction of the internet and MTV. The Island's youth have opted for the North American culture since half our tourists are from the U.S."

"Sounds like fun to me, what do you think, guys?"

All of the crew thought it sounded like fun, so they called for 7:00 p.m. reservations at Baci's. Rex, still grinning ear to ear, left with Jock. The crew settled in for a little rest as the thunderstorm started to clear.

Seth grabbed his sat-phone and headed to the flybridge to call Lori. While up on the flybridge this morning, he and Jock discussed how much information to disclose concerning Kat's kidnapping. Jock agreed that Seth and John should tell Lori and Stacy about it, but preferred they minimize the seriousness of the situation. They would ask the two girls to keep it confidential since the whole episode was not common knowledge on the island. Seth called Lori, and she picked up immediately. "Hey Seth, I was hoping you would call ... how are you?"

"'I'm fine, just missing you ... I'm glad you'll be here in a week. Are you back in St. Pete?"

"Yes, I flew down yesterday. I can't wait to see you. How's the fishing been?"

"Pretty good, we caught two marlin this morning, one was easily 600 pounds."

"Wow! How's everything else, no boat troubles?"

"No, the boat's been running flawlessly ... but we did have a situation arise on the island."

"What happened?"

"Well ... Jock's wife was kidnapped ... to try and force him to sell some valuable land he owns here."

"Oh-My-Gosh! How terrible. Did the police get her back? Is she all right?"

"She's fine ... we actually didn't need the police, and Jock was warned, by the kidnappers, not to call them if he ever wanted to see her again. But it turned out they were pretty amateurish, and Kat used a second cell phone she'd hidden to let Jock know where they were holding her captive. After checking out the location, we surprised and overwhelmed them, and brought Kat home."

"Did you call the police then?"

"No, the kidnappers were Dominican, mostly illegals. One died when his car crashed while trying to get away, and the rest of them fled the island. The house where they held Kat burnt down. Jock's lawyer is handling the details."

"Was anybody else hurt?"

"We're all OK. You'll understand it better when you meet Jock. He played tackle in the NFL. He and Dino went in the back door, after we created a little diversion out front, to pull half the kidnappers outside. Dino and Jock had Kat out of there in under three minutes. You can tell Stacy, but Jock wants to keep the whole thing confidential — this is a very small island, and there's politics involved."

"I'm glad I didn't know about it before now. I would have been worried sick about that poor girl, and worried about you guys looking for her. Should we get a hotel room? She probably won't feel like having company."

"Actually, she told me she was looking forward to meeting you and Stacy, and having a week's holiday away from her rental business."

"So the Billfish Tournament is still on?"

"Oh yeah … because the kidnappers were illegals, and they're gone, the authorities are treating it as a non-event. I mean … it's a little more complicated, but that's basically it."

"Well, I'm looking forward to some island time, but I'm the most excited about the trip home on *TAR BABY* with you, John, and Stacy."

"You'll enjoy staying with Kat and Jock at their home on Blue Mountain … it's spectacular. She'll take you and Stacy shopping, diving, and sightseeing while we're fishing the tournament, and we'll all have cocktails and dinner together at a different venue each night."

"Well, it all sounds good to me. I love you, and can't wait to see you next Thursday."

"I love you too, Lori. John and I will pick you up at the airport. We'll be waiting for you outside of customs."

***

Baci's was crowded, the food was good, the service efficient, all orchestrated by the hardworking owner, John. Seth had the Lasagna Bolognese and treated the table to two bottles of Antinori Toscana. Everyone enjoyed their dinners and looked forward to returning there during the tournament, as it was one of the venues. They paid the check and filed out to the parking lot to drive down to the Bight Beach Children's Park for the Junkanoo program. It was only five minutes away, but the police cordoned off the parking lot, so they parked along the Lower Bight

Road with scores of other cars. They followed the crowd to the parking lot where a makeshift stage had been erected and lit up. An island rake n' scrape band was putting out some funky music. Islanders in native dress were dancing on the stage, and the mixed crowd of islanders swayed in the darkness to the infectious beat. Jock pointed out David Bowen as he took over the microphone. David was a handsome man with a short trimmed afro and jet black skin. He spoke with a clipped British accent and delivered some information to the crowd about the island youths' participation in relearning their heritage. He kept the intro short and blew a silver police whistle after he finished. The Junkanoo band started up somewhere in the shadows. Suddenly, the parking lot overhead lights came on, and the raucous Junkanoo band paraded down towards the stage lead by two colorfully costumed revelers on stilts. The music was loud and lively. Several members punctuated the beat by continually blowing their police whistles. The Junkanoo musicians danced and snaked their way amongst the crowd of two or three hundred delighted islanders. It was all over in 20 minutes, and the entertainers received a rousing round of applause as they made their noisy exit. Jock motioned the crew to follow him, and they wove their way through the crowd to the bandstand.

David Bowen spotted Jock and came down off the stage and greeted him. Jock introduced him all around, and David said, "Your friend Jock here is one of our program's staunchest supporters. He has this vision of adding native food, drinks, and handicrafts to the music and dancing. Then launching the Junkanoo band as the finale. He wants us to invite the tourists to participate with us one night a week so they can learn about our culture and don't think this island is just a tropical paradise with no soul. What do you think?"

Dino spoke up and said, "It would be a hoot, and I think the Islanders might look at the tourists as something more than a dollar bill once they got to know some of them."

"That's almost exactly what Jock said. We need to get more support from businessmen like Jock, and some help from the government for port-a-lets, crowd and parking control, and cleanup. It'll be a tough sell, but it could make this island even more unique."

They all chatted for a while, and the crowd started to melt away. The Geezers said their goodbyes and walked back to the green Suburban. After a nightcap at Aqua, they called it a night.

***

Early Thursday afternoon, a thunderstorm chased Peter off of Long Bay beach, so he drove over to Turtle Cove, parked out in front of the Inn, and made a dash for his room. As he dried off with a towel, he pushed back the drape and looked out the sliding glass door expecting to see an empty slip. But there was the Hatteras, all docked, with two marlin flags flapping in the near gale winds. There were lights on in the salon, but it was raining so hard he couldn't see inside. When the thunderstorm subsided the new crew member and Seth's big curly-haired friend departed. There wasn't much movement until just before 7:00 p.m. Then the big guy showed back up, and they all got in the green Suburban and drove a block to Baci's. Peter watched the parking lot from Bridge Rd. After dinner, they left there and drove to an island festival at a public beach a half a mile down the road. Peter followed and parked further down the road and followed them in. He carried his .38 in his pocket, along with a few jumbo zip-ties and a small roll of duct tape. A large local crowd was in attendance, listening and dancing to an island rake n' scrape band. There were a few tents where the locals were selling jerk chicken, fried fish, and Turk's Head Lager beer. Peter stationed himself in the shadows next to a row of green port-a-lets, hoping Seth might have to use one. Then maybe Peter could cut him out of the herd. The only police presence were a few uniformed officers at the entrance making sure no one used the parking lot. There were some dunes and scrub growth behind the port-a-lets. Soon there was a speech, a shrill whistle blew, and all hell broke loose. A Junkanoo band with musicians of all sizes and shapes came dancing out from behind a dune at the top of the parking lot, led by two whistle-blowing characters walking on six-foot stilts. Peter lost track of Seth's group in the confusion. An hour later, he spotted them as they left together when the music was over. He tracked them back to Aqua where they had one drink and then turned in. Peter was not discouraged, this was the start of the rest of his life, and he had a plan and the money to accomplish it. But in his warped mind, Seth represented all the bad luck and bad decisions he'd made in his life. By confronting and killing Seth, he would change his luck and leave nothing to chance. The start of the tournament was eight days away, and it ran for five days. If he stayed close, he knew would get his opportunity.

CHAPTER FOURTEEN

DAWN broke to a perfect morning in paradise. The wind subsided to 15 knots, and there wasn't a cloud in the sky. Seth pulled *TAR BABY* over to the fuel dock and tied up before any of the commercial boats got there. The crew started fueling her the minute the marina personnel opened the pumps. Freddy and John whipped up scrambled eggs and scrapple for breakfast, and the captain and crew drank their coffee and chowed down while they fueled. An hour later they were putting the spread out off of Fort George.

"I kind of miss not havin' Jock and Dino around today," said Gene.

"Well," said Seth. "Jock has to pick Kat up at the airport later this afternoon, and he needed to put in an appearance at the dive shop. It's a perfect morning for him to take Dino to his favorite dive sites and show him how his dive business operates. I don't think we'll fish all day either."

"Yeah, this is gonna be a busy day. We have Kat's celebration dinner tonight, and it's also rock n' roll live band night at the Tiki Hut. It'll probably be a late night — are you thinking about fishing up past the freighter wreck today?"

"That's the plan. We'll go further east today in this lighter wind until the swells start to build as we come out of the lee of the island. Early next week, I want to try this area in the late afternoon to see if there's a bite here then."

"I'll go back down and get on a rod."

TAR BABY trolled for the next three hours and had only a mysterious knockdown on the right long rigger to show for it. Seth worked up past the rusty freighter until they started to pound into the growing swells, and the salty air started to whistle through the outriggers. He finally steered into a trough and carefully turned down sea. Once he throttled back, they started the long downwind run towards the Northwest Point. Seth figured he'd gotten 75% of his marlin bites while trolling down sea or across drop-offs. He zig-zagged the Hatteras down sea as the crew adjusted the lures on the waves until they were all smoking and popping. About a half hour into that undulating run, he saw a marlin swim in through a large swell and nail the black and green wide range on the right long.

"Marlin on the right long!" yelled Seth. "Look at that bite!"

The crew saw the bite happen up above them, as the boat surfed down the huge swell into the trough.

"Unbelievable! It's like watching a bite on a 60-inch flat screen TV," said John. The reel screamed as the marlin disappeared into the deep blue, only to rocket airborne a few moments later. Gene pulled the rod out of the rocket launcher and settled into the fighting chair. He hooked the bucket harness clips to the reel as the marlin continued to peel line off the reel. The fish jumped a few more times then started a tug of war. Gene switched off the clicker and started to pump and reel. As Seth worked the boat out to port, the fish finally started to give up some line.

"She's somewhere around 250-300 pounds, Gene," shouted Seth. "She's swimming down sea now so we'll have to turn her back around, or it will take us twice as long to catch her. Keep her tight, as I turn the boat."

Seth eased to starboard and powered down the trough, then slowly completed the turn as the taut line swung back off the transom.

"She's swimming up-sea now Gene, let's get on her!"

Gene reeled as fast as he could, and Seth backed *TAR BABY* on the fish just fast enough not to get the cockpit swamped. The cool water of the Atlantic splashed over him as the top of the swells hit the transom. The Hatteras's generous scuppers kept the water in the cockpit about ankle deep.

"Double line," shouted John, as he pulled on the leather gloves. The Bimini Twist knot, used to join the ten feet of double line, soon came through the rod guides followed by the leader. John grabbed the 400-pound test leader and led the marlin along the starboard side of the cockpit where he and Freddy used the de-hooker to make a clean release. The crew high-fived all around and started putting the spread back out.

168

"Good job, guys, there are marlin up here, but they're certainly scattered. Let's fish on down to the Blue Hills and call it a day."

Seth worked the boat up and down the troughs for the next two hours, and only managed another mystery knockdown on the left long. They called it a day and ran a couple of miles to the blasted out channel leading through the reef to Turtle Cove. Gene fastened a blue marlin release flag onto the starboard outrigger halyard and hoisted it up for all to see.

Once at the dock, Seth and the crew made the boat fast and washed the crusty salt off her exterior. The smell of French fries and pulled pork wafted out of Aqua's kitchen, making their mouths water. When the boat was clean, they filed off *TAR BABY* and onto Aqua's upper deck for lunch. Dino called Freddy to inform him they were in from their dive, and he and Jock would walk over in a few minutes to join them for lunch.

"The diving was superb," said Dino as he arrived at the table. "The water is the clearest I've ever seen. The reefs and the fish are spectacular, and Jock's operation is first class all the way."

"Dino's more at home in the water than he is on land," laughed Jock. "How was the marlin fishing?"

"Gene caught one nice blue, and we got a couple of mystery bites. There's fish up there, but they're scattered."

"I think the marlin are starting to move through here now in some numbers," said Jock glancing at his watch. "I gotta get on my horse. Kat will be at the airport in a half an hour - we'll see you guys at Opus at 6:30 for cocktails."

Back on the boat after lunch, Freddy and John replaced a chafed outrigger halyard, while Dino filled them in on all the details of his morning dive. Once they replaced the halyard, the crew retired inside for a much-needed nap before showering and dressing for dinner that evening. The hot sun and salt air had taken their toll.

***

CAICOS CONSPIRACY

Peter Petcock watched Seth talking and laughing with his crew from his room's sliding glass door. They'd left very early that morning and returned just after noon with another marlin flag fluttering from the starboard outrigger. Peter slept fitfully after enduring another episode of his nightmare. He was almost at the point of hating to fall asleep in anticipation of having to submit to the Crips and listen to Seth laugh maniacally as he tried to ram the football up his butt. His anger and hate towards Seth began to boil over again, and his thoughts turned to the atrocities he planned to commit when he finally captured him. Peter hoped that fate would give him Seth tonight.

The crew was working on replacing an outrigger halyard and generally straightening up the boat, now that it was dry. Soon they all disappeared inside, so Peter pulled up a chair and settled into surveillance mode. He fought off sleep by getting up and marching around the small room every time he caught himself nodding off.

At 6:00 p.m. the crew ambled out of the salon door, dressed in Tommy Bahama style shirts and Bermuda shorts. They exited the boat and headed for the parking lot. Peter hurried out the door, hustled past the pool and hotel office, and slipped into *Bonehead*. Seth and his crew drove east out of the parking lot and headed down the Lower Bight Road towards Grace Bay. Peter followed them past Sandal's Beaches, the Seven Sea's Resort, and the Casablanca Casino. They finally turned into the Opus Restaurant lot across from the Provo Golf Club entrance. Seth parked the green Suburban near the front steps, and they all piled out and disappeared inside. Peter drove down the side road towards the beach, turned around, and parked a half a block north. He recognized, from the license plate number, Seth's big, curly-haired friend's white Land Rover SUV parked near the green Suburban.

At 8:50, "Pablo Escobar" walked out of the restaurant, followed by Seth and the rest of the crew. A tall, striking, blonde woman and the stocky, sandy-haired fisherman with the cooler walked out in front of "Big Curly". They were all chattering and laughing back and forth as they got into their cars, pulled out and headed back towards Grace Bay. They drove back through the tourist-clogged streets of the Grace Bay retail district. Both cars

170

passed by Aqua's parking lot then turned into the road to the Turtle Cove Marina's office and the Tiki Hut. The Tiki Hut's parking lot was full, so Peter pulled aside and stopped while Seth and the Land Rover were parking in the overflow lot back by the water. Seth and his companions followed the sound of the music into the Tiki Hut. Peter parked his white Tahoe on the other side of the entrance road in a small gravel lot that serviced the charter boats during the day. He crossed the entrance road and walked down through the overflow lot. Peter stayed in the shadows and skirted the dive shop's perimeter, walking behind an outbuilding with RESTROOM signs on it. He came out of the dark behind the Tiki Hut's bandstand and continued towards a grove of palm trees whose trunks were wrapped with rope lights. He stationed himself behind the trunks, which gave him a panoramic view of the open air restaurant and bar. Peter adjusted his fishing hat over his brown hair and swayed in time to the music while he scanned the restaurant for Seth.

Within a few minutes, Seth and his party were seated at a picnic table under the restaurant's thatched roof near the kitchen, on the other side of the bandstand. The band was loud, tight, and played music Peter remembered from the 70's.

***

Seth and the crew left Turtle Cove Marina through the Aqua Restaurant entrance to meet Jock, Kat, and Rex at Opus. They were in high spirits and all dressed up in their best tropical garb. Fifteen minutes later they arrived and met their hosts, who were already indulging, in the cocktail lounge.

"Ah, the Geezers have finally arrived," laughed Kat, as they sat down.

"Hey, I resemble that remark," said Jock smiling.

Jock shared his favorite French red table wine, J. Moreau and Fils, with Seth while the other crew members ordered the cocktails of their choice. Kat sipped a Rombauer Chardonnay from Carneros, California.

She stood up, raised her glass and said, "A toast to the brave men who saved me from El Bomba ... my husband Jock, Seth, Dino, John, Fred, and Gene. I am eternally grateful and blessed to have you as my friends."

The party moved from the air-conditioned lounge to the outside walled patio dining area under the trees. The fish ponds and floral displays were spectacular, and the outside ambiance and tableside service were both superb. The lobster and prime steaks were out of sight. The dinner conversation concentrated on questions about Jordan's ocean sailboat racing, the upcoming marlin tournament, and Hillary Clinton's chances of winning the United States presidential election in 2008.

Rex said, "By the way, I got wind of a rumor today that Keith Richards is at his house on Parrot Cay ... and is coming over to sit in with our island's rock band at the Tiki Hut tonight."

"Really?" said Seth, who was quite a "Stones" fan.

"He sat in a couple of years ago when he first moved his residence to the Turks and Caicos. He'll come over in his boat, with a couple of his mates, and just hang-out until the spirit moves him."

"Some old time rock n' roll sounds good to me, even if Keith doesn't show," said Seth with a grin.

"Well let's go then," said John. "It's been a great dinner — Jock and Kat, but the night's young and it's our turn to treat y'all to a few drinks."

Everyone thanked the Bafferts as they left Opus for the Tiki Hut. Predictably, the Tiki Hut was packed, and parking was difficult. Jock parked in the far reaches of the overflow lot and Seth followed suit. They walked together into the crowded front entrance that was lined with flaming tiki torches and fronted by a 650-pound fiberglass blue marlin hanging by its tail from a weigh scale.

The hostess recognized Jock and whisked his party to a reserved picnic table, under cover of the bamboo and thatch roof near the bandstand. When everyone took their seat, drinks were ordered, and the table traded musical memories as the band took a trip through the "seventies" and "eighties".

Jock leaned over to Seth and shouted in his ear, as the band played a spirited rendition of Joe Cocker's *Feelin' Alright*, "Look who just slipped in over by those palm trees."

"Holy Shit! It *is* Keith Richards and a bunch of his buddies."

"Not much to do up on Parrot Cay at night, except drink or puff on a doobie."

"He looks fit," said Rex, who was sitting across from Seth. "But his face is etched like a 90-year old's."

"A lot of drugs and not much sleep," laughed Jock.

Someone in the band spotted Keith and his party, and the band struck up, *Jumpin' Jack Flash*.

Seth leaned over to Jock and said, "I forget where the men's room is ... fore or aft?"

Jock pointed back past the kitchen. "It's through there and out back — they use my dive shop locker rooms."

"Thanks, I hope I get back before Keith sits in."

Seth got up and walked past the kitchen door. The smell of fried fish and French fries filled his nostrils. He continued out onto a dark patch of grass behind the restaurant. He could see the dimly lit locker room doors lettered **Men** and **Women**. Seth pulled open the men's room door just as two young board-shorted surfer types were exiting. He located a row of urinals across the room and zipped down his fly in anticipation. Seth picked the one with the least piss on the floor around it and sidled up. The rock band swung into *Brown Sugar*, as he heard the door open behind him. Seth concentrated on the job at hand and aimed his solid yellow stream onto a pink urinal cake languishing near the drain. He noticed, as the footsteps came nearer, their owner had an uneven gait. At that moment, his world went dark.

***

Peter watched Seth get up from the picnic table and walk towards the restaurant's kitchen. It looked like Seth was headed out towards the restrooms, alone. Peter quickly slipped back into the shadows and hurried around the back of the bandstand in time to see Seth walk past two surfers and into the men's room. Walking calmly towards the men's room door, he rechecked his pockets for the .38, tie-wraps, and bandana. There wasn't any incoming foot traffic behind him. Peter strode into the men's room and saw only Seth's back facing him as he stood at the urinals. He checked under the toilet cubicles and saw no feet, so he continued toward Seth. As he reached the urinal to the left of Seth, he pulled the pistol out of his pocket by the barrel and hit Seth behind the back of his right ear with the butt of the handle. Seth fell to the floor like he'd been shot, hitting his head on the tile floor. Peter quickly dragged him into one of the toilet stalls and closed the door. First, he cuffed Seth's hands in front of him with a zip-tie, then zipped his shorts back up, and gagged him with the bandana. He left an unconscious Seth sitting on the toilet seat while he checked outside for any traffic. The coast was clear, and the band was just starting into a spirited rendition of *Honky Tonk Women*. The crowd was jumping and cheering, and Peter could see the weird-looking dude who'd been standing next to him by the palm trees taking over the microphone on stage. After removing the gag, Peter half-dragged, half-carried, Seth out the door. He struggled across the overflow lot, ducking in and out of the shadows that covered parts of the lot. When he reached the entrance road, he looked both ways and saw no traffic. He stood Seth straight up and started slowly dragging him across to the gravel lot. They were almost across when someone called to Peter.

"Do you need a hand, mon?"

Peter almost jumped out of his skin. He peered back into the darkness at the marina's edge and saw a black man standing in the cockpit of a large sportfish that was tied up along the quay.

Peter smiled and said, "No, I got it, my buddy here had too much to drink and passed out. I'm going to take him back to the hotel. My car's right over there," said Peter, nodding towards the gravel lot.

"Good luck," laughed the Good Samaritan as he moved back into the shadow of the mezzanine.

When Peter reached *Bonehead*, he laid Seth across the front hood while he opened the rear hatch. He wrestled Seth off the hood, carried him to the open hatch, and stuffed him in the way-back. He quickly zip-tied his feet and retied the gag, before closing the hatch.

Grinning, he drove slowly out the marina entrance road, where he turned right on Lower Bight Road and drove up the hill to Suzie Turn. There he said to himself, *Drive Left-Yield Right* twice, before turning left on Leeward Highway towards Long Bay and the secret cave.

As big and strong as Peter Petcock was, Seth was still a heavy load for him to carry. He used a firemen's carry but he still had to rest every 200 feet or so. The night was dark and windy as usual, and he didn't want to chance a light. The brambles along the narrow path tore at his arms and legs and made the going even tougher. Finally, he stumbled out onto the rocky clearing and headed for the pile of brush covering the cave's overhead entrance. He laid Seth on the limestone slab and cleared the brush away from the fissure. Peter put the extension ladder down the hole and retrieved the safety rope. With the end of the rope tied around Seth's chest, he lowered him, feet-first, down into the pitch black cave. Once Seth was resting on the cave's floor, he went down the extension ladder and switched on one of the battery operated lanterns he'd stashed there. The bats hanging from the cave's ceiling stirred, and a few of them flew out of the expanded fissure. He switched on his tactical pocket flashlight and checked out the rest of the cave. The stalagmites and stalactites cast eerie shadows across the cave, and the pooling crystal-clear seawater sparkled green and blue in the artificial light. Peter walked to the far south end of the cave where it tunneled down to the base of the rock slide that blocked entry to the underwater passage. After climbing up the rock slide, he shined the flashlight down on his dive gear on the other side. It was a 20-foot drop, down the sheer precipice, to the water which tunneled towards the sea. He rechecked his rappelling gear and the polyester rope he'd bowlined around a limestone pillar that sprouted from the top of the rock slide. The rope would allow him to escape down the sheer drop if a hasty exit was ever needed. Peter climbed back down the rock slide and returned to the base of the ladder. Seth's breathing and pulse vitals were good, but his pupils were definitely dilated. He'd seen enough concussion symptoms in his football days to know Seth had sustained one of some magnitude from the gun butt or from hitting his head on the tile floor. Seth was still unconscious, but it didn't matter, Peter would wake him up when he'd trussed him up properly.

Peter stood Seth up against a stalagmite formation and uncuffed his wrists. He took Seth's Rolex off and put it on his wrist, replacing the dive watch he'd been using. *Now we're making some progress*, thought Peter as he admired it on his wrist. Next, he ripped off Seth's Tommy Bahama shirt, popping all the buttons, leaving him in a white t-shirt and dress shorts. He tied a piece of rope around each of Seth's wrists, then lashed them to a stalagmite on each side of him stretching him up and out. His ankles got the same treatment. Peter moved the lantern behind him, took Seth's gag out of his mouth, and retrieved a bottle of cold water from the cave's igloo cooler. He opened it and poured the cold water over Seth's head. Seth sputtered and shook his head awake. His eyes opened and Peter shined his flashlight into Seth's eyes, blinding him.

"Where the fuck am I?" growled Seth.

"You're in Hell, Seth, and it's worse than you ever imagined."

"My head is killing me, and everything is blurry."

"It'll all get better — before it gets way worse, Seth."

"Who are you?"

"I'm your worst nightmare. I'm here to pay you back for ruining my life."

"But ... who are you?"

"We'll talk about that in the morning — right now we both need some rest."

Peter walked around Seth and made him drink a bottle of water, then gagged him again with the bandana.

"I'll be back at daylight, but you'll be here in solitary confinement tonight. You're in a cave 30 feet below the ground. Bats are hanging from the ceiling, and hordes of giant land crabs live on the floor of this cave. I know you can smell the bat guano and crab dung. Both will be attracted to your bodily functions, and both love the taste of human flesh. You'll notice I relieved you of your shoes, it should only take the army of crabs in here a few minutes to find you. Sweet dreams, big guy!"

Without warning, Peter punched Seth twice, once in each kidney, with short, powerful blows as Seth screamed through the gag in pain. After dousing the lantern, he climbed the ladder, pulled the ladder and rope out of the hole, and replaced the brush over the opening. He hid the ladder and rope at the edge of the scrub jungle. Peter took off running, sprinting all the way back to *Bonehead*, to help shed some of the huge adrenaline rushes he was experiencing. By the time he got back to the beach house, he was yawning and getting drowsy. He wanted to sleep fast because he was anxious to start what he'd planned for Seth tomorrow.

CHAPTER FIFTEEN

JOCK went looking for Seth when he didn't return to the table after Keith Richards had finished his third song. He plowed through the exuberant crowd and checked the men's room, which was empty. Jock went back and enlisted the rest of his table to fan out and search, as the band's set ended. Keith departed the stage to applause and cries of *Encore*. The fortunate patrons cheered and applauded until his boat pulled away from the marina dock. Jock located Stephanie, the Tiki Hut's owner, and she called the police immediately. An hour later the Provo Police were provided a photo of Seth, fresh off the *TAR BABY'S* printer, and they put an APB out across the whole island chain. Jock, Rex, and Kat sat in the salon with Gene, John, Freddy, and Dino trying to make sense of it all.

"Maybe Alistair or the new boss of the Dominican gang snatched him?" said Jock.

"I think it would be too obvious for Alistair to be involved, and how would they know Seth anyhow?" said Rex. 'The new Dominican boss might be flexing his muscles, but more likely, he would have targeted Jock."

"Maybe guilt by association … but that's pretty far-fetched," added Gene.

"I'm just sick about it," said Kat shedding some tears.

"He wasn't fucked up, I mean he only had three glasses of wine," said Dino. "Maybe some desperate Haitian illegals grabbed him?"

"I think we have to follow every avenue here," said John. "But if nobody finds him by tomorrow, we have to call Jeb."

"I agree," said Jock. "Let's try to get some sleep and we'll meet here at 8:00 tomorrow morning and see what has developed."

"OK, my police contacts have instructions to call me immediately with any updates," said Rex. "I will be back here at 8:00 a.m., and I'll call John and Jock if I learn anymore tonight."

***

Jeb's cell phone rang on his way to the Boatworks early Saturday morning in St. Petersburg.

"Jeb, this is John Harvey."

"Hey, Dr. Harvey. Is everything all right? I was expecting to hear a fishing report from dad about this time."

"The fishing's been fine, Jeb, and please call me John. We've had an unexpected problem ... Your dad disappeared last night at a restaurant, during a trip to the men's room."

"Oh my God!! Do you have any idea what happened?"

"At this point, no. He just vanished. We called the police within the hour, and they're working on it. Your dad's friend, Jock, was in a difficult situation when we first got here, and we helped him solve it. But, we don't know if it's related to Seth's disappearance."

"What kind of a situation, Dr. ... I mean, John?"

"Some real estate people here kidnapped your dad's old college friend's wife ... to force him to sell some beach property. We got involved because he couldn't go to the authorities here or risk getting her killed."

"Oh, shit! Here comes another Geezer story."

"Well, we did get her back rather quickly, and, *yes*, there were some loose ends, but we all stayed incognito. We even fished some. I don't think they really knew who we were."

"Jesus, John. It's a little island — Of course, they know who you are."

"Well, I, ah ... just thought you should know."

"I'm sorry, John, please forgive me ... I just get upset that you guys get involved in all these situations when you ought to be having fun and enjoying your retirements. Listen, the more I think about it, I think I better get on the next plane and come down there and help y'all. Fill me in some more on the real estate kidnapping. "

John finished his short version of Kat's kidnapping and rescue, the Dominican gang's motives, and the corrupt political situation in Provo and said, "We'd all feel better if you were here. Jock and his lawyer are pulling every string they can, but there aren't any leads yet. Let me know when you're landing and I'll pick you up at the airport. We're in the Turtle Cove Marina, and there's plenty of room on the boat. In the meantime, we've asked Gene Johnson to work up a plan for us to try and find him. We love your dad, Jeb, and we're all going nuts just sitting around."

Jeb rode the rest of the way into the Boatworks with his mind on overload. By the time he got there, he'd envisioned a possible course of action. He discarded any thoughts, which recriminated the Geezers. What was done, was done. Jeb was more worried that some operatives from the decimated ranks of the Tampa Mafia might have picked Provo as a place Seth might be vulnerable to revenge. He parked his car and found the yard foreman before he went to his office. Jerry had the half day schedule in his hand, and Jeb informed him he would be busy up in the office for a while behind closed doors. He instructed his office manager, Jeff, to hold any calls coming in on the land line. Jeb sat down in Seth's office and unlocked the right-hand desk drawer and took out Seth's address book — the book that held Beau's cell phone number in Costa Rica. He looked up Robert J. Cornett and dialed it on his cell phone.

The phone rang four times before Beau answered, "*Hola?*"

"Uncle Beau ... it's Jeb."

"Well, Jeb, I hope this is a social call. Seth told me he filled you in on our situation."

"I wish it was, Uncle Beau. Dad has disappeared under mysterious circumstances in The Turks and Caicos."

Jeb explained the situation, including Seth and the Geezer's part in Jock's wife's kidnapping and rescue, but also told him he feared it might be the remnants of the Tampa Mafia who snatched him. Beau thought he better fly into Provo too, but cautioned that he would have to work alone and with Jeb only when he could get away from the crew.

180

"You'll probably get there before me, and you'll be staying on the boat. Rent your own car so you can move around at any time. I'll find a hotel a little off the beaten path, and we'll communicate mostly by text. I'll have to fly into Miami and then backtrack to Provo ... one of my neighbors here flies there every year to dive. I'll probably arrive Sunday morning."

"OK, *TAR BABY* is docked at the Turtle Cove Marina. I'm going to book the first flight out of Tampa or Orlando, stop home to pack, and try to get there late today."

"See you there, Jeb."

Jeb got on his computer and took a few minutes to write out a quick work and hauling schedule for the following week. Then he booked himself a one-way ticket. The earliest Tampa flight to Provo had a one-hour layover in Miami. It would put him in Provo at 4:00 p.m. The work schedule would help Jeff and Jerry stay focused while he was gone. He explained that Seth had a problem in Provo, and he was going there to help him. Jeff, who'd worked at the Boatworks for many years said, "Don't worry, we've got you covered here. Call me if I can help out in any way!"

Jeb called Lynne on his way home and explained that Seth needed help in Provo, and he was flying there today. He explained about Dr. Harvey calling to tell him Seth had disappeared, and how they needed his help to find him. He also told her to take Cullen and go to her mother's in Delray Beach until he called her from Provo.

"Is foul play suspected?" asked Lynne in a concerned voice.

"Nobody knows anything for sure, but it could have something to do with Uncle Beau's death in Key West. I don't think we are in any danger, but I don't want to take the chance. Your mom will appreciate the visit, and I apologize for the drama my Uncle Beau and father have caused."

"Just get your dad back, I love him too."

***

CAICOS CONSPIRACY

The Turtle Cove Inn was Peter's second stop early the next morning. His first stop was for coffee and some breakfast at the Caicos Café. As he wolfed down his breakfast, he wondered how Seth was doing in the dark dank cave fighting off the relentless army of land crabs with his bare feet.

Peter cleaned out his room, being careful to wipe his prints off all the furniture and surfaces he may have touched. He checked out at the front desk paying his bill in cash. The clerk tore up the Grant T. Morris Visa credit card imprint he'd taken at check-in.

"Flying out today, Mr. Morris?"

"Yeah, back to Miami."

"Well, I imagine it's probably just as hot there. Have a good flight and come back and see us."

"Maybe in January," said Peter with a smile as he walked out the door.

He steered the white Tahoe up the hill and stopped at the IGA for two bags of ice, a bunch of bananas, a broom, and a shrink-wrapped case of bottled water. He stopped and gassed up at a station up on Leeward. Gasoline was $6.75 a gallon on this island, *Fuckin'-A*, thought Peter. Fifteen minutes later he was moving the brush pile off the top of the cave entrance.

He shouted down into the cave in a booming voice, "SETH ... this is GOD. Do you know why you're down there? ... BECAUSE YOU PISS ME OFF!!!" He tied all the supply bags to the safety rope's end and lowered them down. After reinserting the extension ladder, he clambered down into the darkness.

Peter pointed the flashlight at Seth's face blinding him again, before lowering the flashlight to Seth's feet and ankles. They were scratched, cut, and bleeding almost up to his calves. The land crabs had probably worked him over most of the night. He looked strained, gaunt, and very tired, which was exactly what Peter wanted.

"Sleep well, Seth? Or did the crabs keep you busy all night."

Seth's cargo shorts showed some dark stains in the crotch area. Peter guessed they were bloody urine stains. I brought you some breakfast — if you're hungry and thirsty, shake your head *yes*."

Seth shook his head up and down to show him the answer was an emphatical yes.

182

"Before I feed you ... I'm gonna show you who I am. Then you'll know why you're here."

Peter moved towards the extension ladder and turned on the battery operated lantern, and walked slowly back in front of Seth, with his head down. He put his flashlight up under his chin and looked right at Seth.

"Do you recognize me now? Yeah, I know, I look like a horror flick monster in this light," said Peter laughing crazily. He moved the light away from his chin and shined it down and across his face. Seth blinked a couple of times, and then his eyes got as big as saucers and the blood drained out of his face.

"So you recognize me now, *don't ya*? You never thought you'd see ol' Peter again, *did ya*? Thought I was rottin' away in fuckin' prison, *didn't ya*? Well, I escaped and tracked your sorry ass down. Now you're going to experience what I've been through for the last few years while you've been livin' the good life. Feet hurt? It don't matter, cause you ain't leavin' this cave alive anyhow. Now, I'll take the gag out so I can feed you and give you some water. I'm not ready to kill you right yet, cause you need to experience some more of my pain. But don't talk, or I'll hit you like I did last night."

Peter peeled a banana, then took the gag out of Seth's mouth and fed him small pieces until the whole banana was gone. He forced Seth to drink a bottle of water and put the gag back into his mouth. He peeled another banana and rubbed the banana all over Seth's bleeding feet and ankles. He checked the tie-up on Seth's wrists and ankles.

"I'm going to go now ... you have a nice day hanging out here. *Ha-ha-ha-hah*! I want you to think about how you have ruined my life. First in high school, then in the Keys, after I recovered from the Feds shutting down my St. Pete bottom cleaning business. When I kill you, *Mr. Big Time Defensive Back*, I'll leave you hanging right where you are. The bats and crabs will pick your bones clean. I'm going to cut off your head and throw it into the blue hole in Chalk Sound — where nobody will ever find it."

Seth shook his head back and forth and tried to say something through the gag, but it was unintelligible.

"Your skeleton will stay here hanging from the ropes, and maybe someone will find it and maybe they won't. Maybe the limestone ceiling will fall in, like the slide behind you, and cover your bones forever. But I promise you this — before I finish with you in the next few days, you'll be begging me to kill you."

Peter went up the ladder, and again pulled the rope and extension ladder out of the cave and hid them both in the scrub next to the clearing. He replaced the pile of brush over the opening and walked back to the Tahoe whistling Johnny Cash's *Ring of Fire*. He would spend the rest of the day swimming and lounging at the beach cottage, before going back to the cave after dark to feed Seth and mete out some more physical and mental torture. The only thing that could make him feel any better than he felt right now would be a two-hour session riding Rikki.

***

Seth heard the noisy aluminum extension ladder scraping the limestone as Peter pulled it out of the hole in the cave's ceiling. He could see a narrow shaft of light out of the corner of his eye, but it quickly disappeared as Peter put something over the opening. Seth tried to organize his thoughts and put what was happening to him into some perspective. His vision was improving, and his splitting headache was down to a dull throb, so he must be recovering from his concussion. It still hurt to pee, but not as bad as the night before after Peter had punched his kidneys. He felt much better after eating the banana and drinking a bottle of water. As his head cleared, he became even more aware of the overpowering smell of bat guano. His wrists and shoulders hurt from bearing his weight when he dosed off. The tops of his feet and his ankles were bleeding and swollen, and Peter had rubbed banana all over them to attract the relentless land crabs further. If he could sleep more than a few minutes at a time, he would feel a little better. The crabs were a constant problem, but he'd come up with a plan for the crabs this morning. The bats swooped past his head a number of times, but they seemed more interested in working their way past whatever Peter put over the opening in the ceiling than in him. They flew in and out

184

at different times. He guessed he'd been in the cave, maybe 12 to 15 hours. He figured even if he could speak to Peter, he probably couldn't reason with him. Seth realized that Peter had gone absolutely, irrevocably, certifiably, mad. He needed to get free and gain some element of surprise over Peter to escape this cave and certain death. Even if he just got free, in his present weakened physical condition, Seth would be no match for him. Peter looked bigger and stronger than ever. He needed a weapon. He was working on shredding the polyester rope above his left wrist with his fingernails, thread by thread, but the going was slow.

The land crabs interrupted Seth's thoughts, and he put his plan into action. As two crabs climbed his right foot he raised it off the limestone and balanced on his left foot. When he felt a third crab under his right foot, he slammed his heel down shattering the crab's shell. The other crabs quickly cannibalized their squished brother. This allowed Seth more time to doze off. Slowly, he decimated the crabs' ranks while switching feet to rest his heels. If he lived through this nightmare, he promised himself he would eat a boiled giant blue land crab covered with remoulade sauce at his first opportunity. Seth continued to pick apart the line on the left side and started to work on his gag with his teeth, between quick naps and crab stomping.

***

The crew, plus Jock, ate lunch at Aqua after trying to put some kind of plan together to find Seth. Their only hope was for Rex to keep Seth's disappearance in front of the police. At this very moment, Rex was systematically moving from one precinct station to another trying to light a fire under them.

"You know, I think I'll go down to the Tiki Hut and check out the men's room and the parking lot area again," said Gene. "Maybe I missed some evidence when I checked it out this morning."

"I wish there were something I could do," said Freddy. "I know the police already have the airport and ferry boats on alert."

"I have an idea," said Dino, gesturing with his hands. "Why don't we blow up a picture of Seth on the computer and print a bunch of posters. Like … **MISSING**-*HAVE YOU SEEN THIS MAN?* $1000 *Reward if your information finds him* — with my phone number on the poster. We'll put them up in the IGA's, bars, restaurants, telephone poles, drug stores, everywhere. We've got the printer and paper right here on the boat."

"I'll help you set up the computer, Dino," said John. "I don't have to be at the airport until 4:00 this afternoon, Jeb just sent me a text."

"OK, let's print the posters, then Freddy, Jock, and I will start putting them up all over the island."

CHAPTER SIXTEEN

The 737 flew over Crooked Island in the lower Bahamas. As the captain identified it over the loudspeaker, Jeb looked down on it from his window seat. They'd be on the ground in less than a half an hour, right on time. He hoped Beau was on his way and would get to Miami tonight and Provo early tomorrow morning. When Beau got to Miami, he would text him. Jeb wondered to himself if he'd inherited the misadventure gene that Seth and Beau seemed to have. Wherever they went, shit happened. He knew Beau had always had that gene. Just listening to the stories his dad and his friends related, and watching his Uncle stumble through life while working with him at the Boatworks, told the tale. Talented, capable, fun-loving, but troubled and self-destructive. His dad came off as solid, athletic, serious, honest, and competitive. But in his later years, he seemed to be willing to mix it up with the ne'er-do-wells and criminals in the name of fair play and justice. Maybe when you've "been there and done that" your whole life, the element of danger is appealing. Jeb wasn't sure how this whole thing was going to play out. Obviously, throwing in with Beau could be dangerous, but he reckoned he probably would find out a whole lot about himself before it was over.

Thirty minutes later Jeb cleared customs in the little airport and walked back out in the sunshine looking for Dr. Harvey. He spotted him about 20 yards away talking to a short, muscular, dark complected man, dressed in black slacks, and a white guayabera shirt. The man had a wide smile on his pleasant face and wore a pair of Ray-Ban sunglasses. A bump at his waist tipped off Jeb he was "carrying". John saw him and motioned him to come over.

"Hey Jeb, meet Leon Lewis, he's the head of airport security, and also moonlights as chief of security for the Casablanca Casino near Grace Bay. Your dad's college friend, Jock Baffert, told me to look him up and have you meet him."

"I'm sorry about your dad. We've got departures on alert, and I took some missing person posters of your dad from John. My men are putting them up all around the airport."

'Thank you, Mr. Lewis, I appreciate anything you can do."

"I met your dad the last time he was down here fishing and tipped a few beers with him. We'll do everything we possibly can to find him."

"You sound like a busy man, Mr. Lewis."

"Please, call me Leon. I have two daughters in college in Atlanta right now, and I could use three jobs if I didn't have to sleep a little."

Jeb laughed and said, "Thanks for helping, Leon. I hope we find him soon."

"Me too."

John and Jeb walked across the entrance road to a small parking lot. Jeb put his carry-on bag in the back hatch of the little white Subaru.

John paid the parking toll, and Jeb asked, "Do we have another car?"

"Yeah, a Suburban."

"Why don't we stop at Hertz or Avis on our way out of here and I'll rent another car. It'll make us more mobile."

They stopped at Avis and Jeb rented a black Suzuki minivan.

Before he pulled out John reminded him, "They drive on the wrong side of the road here, there's no stoplights, just roundabouts. Remember, *Drive Left, Yield Right.*"

Jeb followed John down to Turtle Cove and the Aqua parking lot.

"You can park here if your slip is on this side of the marina. It looks like Dino and Freddy are out putting up reward posters. We can wait in the boat while Gene is looking for clues down at the Tiki Hut. That's where Seth disappeared while Keith Richards was sitting in with the band."

"How about I stow my bag on the boat, then we walk down there so I can see the scene and the surroundings. I brought this map of the island I got from Avis so I can get my bearings."

As they walked past the two-story Turtle Cove Inn's waterfront patios and balconies and the back of Scooter Bob's Rentals, John filled Jeb in on more details. They crossed the marina entrance road and walked through the open-air Tiki Hut Bar and Restaurant. They found Gene out behind the men's locker room.

"Hey, Jeb! I'm glad you're here."

"Thanks, Mr. Johnson, I don't know what to say."

"You've gotta start calling me Gene, I think you're talking to *my* father."

"OK, Gene."

"This is the overflow lot where we parked last night. I haven't found one clue. Talk about frustrating."

'This is a big place … maybe he left by water," said Jeb.

"That's entirely possible. The police haven't found anyone who saw anything."

"Jeb, why don't I give you a spin around the island so you can get your bearings," offered John. "I can show you most of it in a couple of hours, and by then Freddy and Dino should be back from hanging the first round of missing posters. Do you want to come along, Gene?"

"No, I'll stay here and go over the whole area again."

John and Jeb went back to the boat, grabbed a couple of bottles of water and started touring in the Subaru. John headed for Grace Bay to view the luxury beach hotels, gourmet IGA, and the upscale shopping and restaurant district. They drove on to the island's leeward end where a new floating marina and hotel were in the planning stages. After touring the Walkin Dock container area, John showed him the kite surfing beach at Long Bay, along with the Caicos' Marina and Shipyard, and the government docks down at the entrance to Juba Sound. Next, they drove west on Leeward Highway, and John pointed out the other IGA store as they neared downtown.

"I have to admit you're scaring the shit out of me going around these roundabouts, John."

"It takes some getting used to, but they have no stoplights to maintain."

189

John turned down into the Discovery Bay area and showed Jeb the soccer stadium, and high school sports complex. Next, he headed out Blue Hills Road towards the sparsely populated Northwest point, past the Boss Iguana, then circled back on Millennium Highway and drove through the original downtown near the airport, through Kewtown, and past Five Cays to Chalk Sound. He showed Jeb the Las Brisas restaurant parking lot, the site of Kat's kidnapping. They continued around Chalk Sound and drove out Silly Creek Road to the Emerald Cay mansion, where some workman were reconstructing the damaged swing bridge. Along the way, he pointed out some of the different neighborhoods and buildings that played a part in Kat's kidnapping and recovery. He was a matter of fact and didn't play into the drama, but gave Jeb an accurate account of the current political conditions and what had actually transpired.

"You guys never cease to amaze me with the situations you get yourself into, but I have to admit you're resourceful."

"Well, we couldn't just stand by and let the bastards get away with it. They might have killed her."

"I see your point, and I think Jock and his lawyer made a good decision to let it ride. When the country goes bankrupt, the Brits will prosecute the crooked ministers. It also kept you, dad, and the rest of the crew out of the spotlight, and let Jock and his lawyer issue a warning. But the jury's still out until we find him."

"Amen, Jeb."

"Look, there's another Seth poster on that telephone pole. The guys are putting them up everywhere."

John and Jeb drove back to the Hatteras and found Jock, Dino, Freddy, and Gene printing more posters.

"Hey, Jeb," said Fred. "You remember Dino?"

"Yeah, we met at the yard a couple of years ago before he moved to Key Largo."

"And this is Jock Baffert, your dad's old college buddy."

"Hey Jeb, I'm sorry we have to meet under these circumstances ... your dad and I played football together."

"I've heard a lot about you too, Mr. Baffert, my dad holds you in very high regard."

"He's very proud of you, Jeb. I hear you're doing a great job running the Boatworks."

"Thanks, Mr. Baffert."

"Please call me Jock. Listen, fellas, I better be getting home to Kat, I'll check in with you tomorrow morning about 9:00. When I get home, I'll call Rex and see what he accomplished with the police today." On the way out the door, he turned and said, "Call me if anything breaks. I can be here in five minutes."

Jock left, and Jeb turned to the crew and said, "Thanks for putting up the posters guys, you never know what might work."

"Probably the $1000 reward," said Gene. "As soon as the police would offer a reward in St. Petersburg, all the crazies started calling. But you've got to follow-up each one because you never know. Get ready, Dino."

"Well, we're out of the photographic paper, but we printed 50 more posters to hang tomorrow morning. That'll probably be enough."

"Jock's sticking to Kat pretty tight when the sun goes down," said John.

"You can't blame him when he can't even trust his own police force," said Gene.

"How was your tour of the island, Jeb?" asked Freddy.

"I was surprised at how small it is, and how much of it is still undeveloped. Parts of the immigrant neighborhoods look very poor, I mean ... I saw Haitians living out in the bush, but the rest of the island is way upscale. Hey, are you guys getting hungry? I haven't had much to eat today."

"How about some cracked conch at Da Conch Shack?" asked Gene.

The crew's vote was unanimous, so they all piled in the *Frigate* and drove out to the Blue Hills. During a fabulous dinner of fresh conch, Jeb got a text from Beau. He'd arrived in Miami and would land in Provo tomorrow morning, just before 10:00. Beau would be staying at the Ports of Call hotel just off Governor's Road near Grace Bay and would have a Hertz car waiting for him at the airport.

191

Jeb texted back, *Text me when you're checked in and we'll meet.* He looked up and saw the crew watching him text.

"I forgot to text my wife that I was here safely, so I'm in hot water … 800 miles away from home," laughed Jeb. "I guess I'll have another one of those Turk's Head Lagers."

When the crew got back to the *TAR BABY,* Jeb said, "I think I'll turn in fellas, the trip down and time change have worn me out. Wake me up if something happens tonight."

Jeb went into Seth's cabin, closed the door, and quietly locked it. After unpacking a few things from his duffel he stashed them in an empty drawer. He opened the hanging locker, laid Seth's clothes and jackets on the bunk, then grasped the two coat hooks and pulled off the false back wall. He quickly inventoried the rifles, shotguns, and pistols in his mind. *Dad brought quite an arsenal with him,* he thought. He removed a Smith and Wesson .38, a Glock 9mm, some extra rounds, two tactical flashlights, and two Kevlar body armor pullovers, hiding them under the queen mattress. Tomorrow he would transfer them to the under floor storage in his minivan. He had to laugh — he *was* becoming his father's son. Like his ol' granddaddy Robert E. would have said, 'Plan for the worst and hope for the best'.

***

Seth heard the extension ladder clatter through the hole in the cave's ceiling. There weren't any rays of light shining in from above, so it must be night time. Peter threw the safety rope back down and descended the ladder noisily. He shined his flashlight on Seth and walked over and checked his bonds. Crab shells crackled under his shoes, so he shined his flashlight down on Seth's feet.

"Got a war on crabs goin' while I was gone, huh? Well, I'll have to nip this in the bud."

He stomped on Seth's right foot and then his left. Seth howled in pain behind his gag.

"Good thing I only have boat shoes on, asshole. Maybe if I broke your ankles, you wouldn't try that again."

Peter turned on both lanterns and the cave lit up in spectacular shades of blue, greens, and dark yellows. After rummaging in a bag behind Seth, he faced him once again.

"This line should keep you from stomping anymore of our slow moving friends."

He tied Seth's left ankle to his right and cinched it tight. Then he tied another line to the middle of the new tether and tied it around a stalagmite ten feet in front of Seth at floor level.

"I'm going to feed you before I get mad and forget. I want you to suffer a few more days before I put you out of your misery. Remember, don't talk, or I'll hammer your kidneys again."

Peter removed Seth's gag and fed him a banana, and let him drink two bottles of water. As he prepped the gag to retie it, he noticed the chew marks on the frayed bandana.

"Well you fuckin' shithead, you just won't learn, will you? You're not going to escape — you still think you're smarter than me, don't you? This cave is way more secure than a fuckin' federal prison."

Peter walked back towards Seth and moved behind him.

"Let's try this duct tape over your mouth ... *There* — that should hold you. I was just tryin' to be nice to you, jack-off, usin' the bandana instead of duct tape."

Peter hauled off and punched Seth in the jaw, then kicked him squarely in the crotch. Seth writhed in pain and almost passed out. He hurt so bad he wished he would pass out.

"For your information, nobody but me knows about this cave. I swam over here with my scuba gear in an underground water passage that leads to the bay. I started in a sinkhole called The Hole, about a half mile upstream. I found a little opening up above in this cave and made it bigger. We're the only two humans that have ever been down here. Well — have a good evening, dick-wad. When I come back tomorrow I hope you've been better behaved," said Peter as he turned off the lights and headed up the ladder.

Seth barely heard him go up the ladder and pull it out of the opening. He was concentrating very hard not to throw up and lose the water and banana, which was keeping him alive.

The outside world was starting to take leave of Seth's mind. With his feet immobilized by the added ropes, he could no longer appeal to the crab's cannibalistic nature. It was a dark, dank, putrid existence, and there was no room in his head for anything but the constant pain and the hoard of crabs who constantly tore off tiny bits of his skin and mind. Seth entered a twilight where the dream world and reality collide — his body fought for consciousness, as his mind slowly slipped into fantasy. Until now, Seth was able to steel himself with thoughts of family. Reliving the good times with Beau, Jeb's mother Lisa, Jeb, and his family — and of course, Lori. Even his old lover Annie Hart slipped in, smiling up at him naked from *TAR BABY's* fighting chair. The optimism that filled his thoughts dissipated like a rain cloud dumping its load — letting Seth plummet to earth with a thud.

Seth peered into the darkness and saw his torturer, but it wasn't Peter. It was someone Seth had locked out of his consciousness many years before. Someone who made Peter Petcock look like a rank amateur.

Nicaragua, 1972; Seth was posing as a ship's cargo broker to gain the confidence of Nicaragua's wealthy cattle ranchers and produce farmers. His University of Virginia football teammate, Bobby Thompson, who was earning his chops in the CIA counter-espionage section, recruited Seth after his Vietnam hitch was up. Seth's first assignment was finding out who the Sandinista sympathizers were, in Nicaragua's upper class. Once identified, they disappeared into Somoza's prisons, and the U.S. backed Contras burned their ranches and farms.

"Reinhold, where the fuck have you been hiding?"

"I've been right here with you all along, *Kapitän,* just waiting for the right time. I especially enjoyed listening to you explain to your women the old scars I gave you — like they were football and fishing injuries. Are you ready to tell me why you're really in Nicaragua?"

"Why don't we drink some of that rum over there, instead of pouring it in my wounds, *Schwanzlutscher?*"

194

"Such harsh words from the prince of crabs, *Arschloch*. Do you remember the shapely nurse you used as a courier? She suffered a slow, agonizing death at my hands. The pain you feel now, is nothing like she felt. I took her apart, bit by bit, not allowing her to pass out, and forced her to watch the scalpel do its work. She gave up many useful names."

"It wasn't my fault …."

"It's all your fault, *Schwanz Atem*. You put everyone you know and love at risk as a result of your reckless actions. You deserve even more severe punishment."

Seth felt lightheaded, then nauseous, and started to dry heave.

"Go ahead you *feigling*, die. If you die before you give me the information I want, your family will suffer. Give it up and you all go free."

Seth's core need was to defend and protect his family and country. He would not quit, and he would fight to stay alive to make a difference. Seth felt resolve start to flood back into his body. Two tiny shafts of light suddenly shone down into the cave, interrupting the continuous darkness and signifying a new day.

"Thanks for the pep talk, Reinhold, go back to cleaning up the dog shit from the Hounds of Hell where you reside."

Seth took a deep breath and concentrated on the tiny shafts of light to hang on to reality. He hadn't thought about Nicaragua for many years now. Seth was young and patriotic back in those days. But an epiphany took place in that Nicaraguan torture chamber. Some lines started to blur in his mind, and he began to recognize that U.S. foreign policy might be serving special interests back home, rather than protecting the American people. Vietnam had benefitted the U.S. industrial/military complex, and Nicaragua was one of the U.S.'s foremost suppliers of beef and produce. He vowed to domesticate his career path if he got out of Nicaragua alive. Fortunately, Bobby Thompson led a daring nocturnal raid and freed him from the Sandinistas. Seth resigned from the CIA and went back to St. Petersburg to start working at the family Boatworks. He and Bobby Thompson, nonetheless, remained fast friends.

As thoughts of Nicaragua faded, Seth started steeling himself for Peter's inevitable return.

***

Beau slept during most of his flight from Miami to Provo. It had been a long night in the Miami airport. He spent most of it wrapped up in his foul weather jacket trying to get some sleep. He was amazed the terminal announcements were now in Spanish first and English second. Why would the government of the most successful social experiment the world had ever known, create a long range problem with such a short term solution? No matter, his own problems were pressing. The pressure in his ears woke him up, and he quickly realized the plane was losing altitude, and they would land soon.

After his flight taxied in, Beau deplaned and walked the 50 yards to the small terminal. The 20 or so private jets that were sitting at the FBO at the other end of the runway, spoke volumes about the foreign residents of this tropical paradise. He cleared customs quickly. When he spoke English, Beau had gotten in the habit of ending his sentences with the customary Canadian idiosyncrasy, *eh?* When he walked out the customs door, there was a small black man holding a Hertz sign for Robert J. Cornett. The driver took his carry-on suitcase and drove him just outside the airport to the Hertz office. Twenty minutes later Beau was following his Hertz map to the Ports of Call Resort in his dark blue Ford Taurus. He drove out Leeward Highway and chanted to himself at each roundabout, *Drive Left, Yield Right.* After a couple of close calls, he started to get the hang of it. Beau was glad Costa Rica drove on the right side of the road.

The Ports of Call was a block off the main drag in the fancy Grace Bay area. The neighborhoods around the airport were old and shabby, but the Grace Bay area was all uptown. Trendy shops and restaurants lined the streets, and Beau could see the tops of the seven and eight-story resorts dotting Grace Bay's shoreline. Beau's hotel was three stories high and built around a pool. The lobby bar opened onto the pool deck. Beau parked in the rear lot and checked into a poolside room that had a front and rear exit.

There were four exit points from the pool. He settled in his room and texted Jeb:

"Here at PoC, rm 113, how about lunch, I'm hungry. Front desk recommended Danny Buoys Pub — it's a block from here."

"Guys are out putting up Seth missing posters, just got back from meeting police with Jock and his lawyer, what a joke! I'll meet you at Danny Buoys Pub in 15 min."

"K"

***

Jeb found his black-bearded Uncle Beau in the very last booth in the pub. Beau jumped up and embraced him in a bear hug. Jeb felt a very different set of emotions than he did when his dad told him Beau was dead. He felt safe, relieved, joyful, and hopeful all at once. His Uncle was back from the dead when he needed him the most. They sat down facing each other — Beau offered his hand, and Jeb took it. Beau closed his other hand over Jeb's and looked deep into Jeb's eyes.

"I wish it were me, and not Seth. I deserve whatever the Mafia is doing to him. Seth is the finest brother anyone could ever have. This whole thing is my fault, Jeb."

'We don't know that yet, Uncle Beau. Dad was involved in rescuing Jock's wife. It might not be the Mafia — But, Hey! — It's good to see you alive. I never thought I'd see you again. I almost didn't recognize you, with the mustache and the beard."

"I got used to it during the trip to Costa Rica when it made me look like Ronald Santos' picture on his passport. I keep it trimmed short, and I don't think anyone would recognize me across a room or with just a glance. Man, I sure miss you and your ol' dad!"

"We miss you too, Uncle Beau."

"Did you have time to check out the Hatteras for weapons?" said Beau, getting down to business.

197

"I checked out the gun closet, and Dad has quite an arsenal. I brought you a 9mm Glock, a flashlight, and some lightweight Kevlar body armor. There are rifles and shotguns if we need them — even some Tasers."

"He's become quite the adventurer. But you know, he can't stand to see his friends get the short end of the stick."

"So it appears."

"Hey, there's my old Rolex, your dad told me he'd given it to you."

"Here, you can have it back."

"No, no, I picked up another one on the way to Costa Rica, I want you to have mine. He told me you were pretty broken up when you found out the sharks ate me in Key West."

"I'm really glad they didn't, Uncle Beau."

"Me too, they only got these two fingers," he said, holding up his left hand and laughing. "And the Rolex."

Jeb winced and said, "That had to hurt!!"

"You got to do, what you got to do," smiled Beau.

They both ordered a burger and a cold one After lunch, Jeb rode him around the island on the same route John had taken him the day before while filling him in on all he knew. After the tour, he dropped him off at the Ports of Call.

"Stay in contact, Jeb. I'm going to check out the Tiki Hut tonight. Keith Richards, Wow! — that must have been quite a surprise. After that, maybe I'll do some up-close reconnaissance at the Silly Creek Mansion you showed me, where the crooked minister lives. Thanks for the weapon, text me if any of you start to walk down to the Tiki Hut after dark."

CHAPTER SEVENTEEN

BEAU drove up Sandcastle Drive after a light dinner at the Provo Golf Club. It was just getting dark, and he figured he wouldn't run into Seth's crew at the golf club. Earlier, he purchased a pair of swim fins, a mask, dive knife, and a black Lycra lightweight wetsuit, along with a waterproof fanny pack to carry his pistol and Kevlar vest, at the dive shop near Danny Buoys. Now, he drove across the roundabout, turned right on Leeward Highway, and headed to Turtle Cove five minutes away. He turned into the marina entrance road and parked right next to the Tiki Hut restaurant. Before entering the Tiki Hut, Beau checked out the boats tied up along the quay. It was a mixed bag, some commercial dive boats, a couple of parasail boats, one high dollar 55 foot Viking sportfish, and a few small express sportfish boats. He looked down the canal and saw the same mix as far up the quay as he could see. Beau turned and walked back across the road, past the huge marlin hanging by his tail and into the Tiki Hut.

"Here for dinner, sir?" asked the attractive black hostess.

"Just going to sit at the bar, thanks. Where is the men's room?"

"It's past the bar and kitchen ... across the grass strip out back."

Beau checked out the men's room and was surprised at its remote location. Jock's dive shop and boats were just off to the right. The parking lot stretched out quite a ways to the left. He walked back in and sat at the first seat at the elliptical bar. If anybody he knew walked in, he could slip out the back way. After ordering a beer, he turned around to observe the seating and bandstand layout. The restaurant was two-thirds full, and people kept arriving. It was easy to see how Seth could have been coerced out of the men's room area by a couple of assailants and stuffed into a car

199

waiting at the edge of the parking lot. With the restaurant's patrons and employees concentrating on Keith Richards up on stage it was no wonder nobody saw anything suspicious. After finishing his beer, he ambled out through the back entrance the same way Seth would have gone to the men's room. It was pitch black once he left the restaurant, the only light came from the bulbs illuminating the restroom signs. He walked around the corner of the restaurant and proceeded up the gravel drive alongside the grass parking lot towards his car out front. As he approached the entrance road, he saw some movement in the big Viking's cockpit. There were also people coming out of the Tiki Hut, who were walking over to look at the boats before going to their cars.

Beau walked up to the Viking and said, "Sure is a handsome boat you have here, Captain."

"I'm not the captain, sir, I'm just a security guard," pointing to the Turtle Cove Marina logo embroidered on his dark blue polo shirt. "The owner of the marina, Mr. Beegs, he owns this boat, and he has me sit on it to keep the tourists off."

"You mean people just get on this boat without being invited, eh?"

'Sur'nuff, the damnedest thing I ever saw. They get coupla drinks in 'em and get on board in their street shoes to get a better look … tearin' up his teak cover board and cockpit sole."

"What's your name, eh?"

"Percy."

"I'm Robert. I guess they're not boating people, eh, Percy?"

"You got that right. Mr. Beegs has me come on from dark till midnight, every night, and later on Fridays because of the band. Then, I do rounds on the docks with Thomas until 6:00 in the morning."

"Did you see anything strange around here on this past Friday band night, Percy?"

"No … well, there was one thing … not really out of the ordinary, but this big white tourist comes out of the parkin' lot hauling another white guy along with him. I figured they was comin' up from the men's room. I asked him if he needed any help … He said his friend had passed out, and he was gonna put him to bed."

200

"Were they both drunk?"

"The big guy wasn't in too bad a shape. He kinda half lifted and half dragged the smaller guy up the road and into the little parking lot on this side. Left in one of Scooter Bob's cars."

"Scooter Bob, eh?"

"Yeah, he rents cars and scooters right over there," and he pointed over towards The Turtle Cove Inn. "Hey, are you a cop or somethin'? You ain't the right color to be a cop on this island."

Beau laughed and said, "No, no, I'm an insurance adjuster just running down some damage on a Hertz rental, eh? The renter claims the car was damaged while he was parked here for dinner last Friday night — Two drunks, eh? Maybe I should check Scooter Bob's car out for some bumper or fender damage — how did you know it was one of Scooter Bob's cars, eh?"

"Scooter puts a different name on the front hood of all his cars. That way the locals know they're his cars, and they don't mess with them — Scooter's a badass, and you wouldn't want to cross him. It was a white Tahoe named *Bonehead*."

"Thanks, Percy, probably be a blind alley, but I'll check it out, eh?"

Beau got in his rental car and drove out, turned left and pulled into Scooter Bob's lot. They were closed, but there were five or six cars in his well-lighted lot. Beau got out and saw an SUV named "*Arawak*" and three compacts named "*Conchgirl*", "*Gybe*", and "*Divebouy*", and a minivan called "*Leeward*". Tomorrow morning he'd come back with a concocted story and see if he could find out who had rented *Bonehead* and where they were staying. He headed back up to Leeward Highway and used his map to navigate to Chalk Sound and the Silly Creek area.

Beau turned out his lights as he coasted in behind the center island of the cul-de-sac and exited the car with his binoculars. There were only a few lights on in the mansion, but the landscape lights on the paths and walkways were visible. Beau stood in the stand of palm trees in the center island and swept the property with a pair of pocket binoculars, looking for movement. Ten minutes later he observed a guard with a rifle slung over his shoulder walking between the house and the tennis court. For about an hour, he watched the guard's movements, then moved his car back down the road and parked it near a pink house with its hurricane shutters rolled down. After changing into his Lycra dive suit, he pulled his Kevlar mesh vest on over it. He strapped his waterproof fanny pack around his waist and put the Glock, dive knife, car keys and his tactical flashlight in it. As Beau walked quickly back to the open swing-bridge, he glanced at his Rolex Submariner and visualized where the guard should be on his rounds. He climbed down the bridge's foundation and slipped quietly into the water. The water felt warm as he donned his mask and fins and then swam slowly up the sheer-sided canal towards the Caribbean. As he neared the sea, he followed the mansion's seawall into two large boat slips that were empty except for four jet skis on a ramp. Beau stowed his mask and fins behind a jet ski, checked his watch, and exited the water. Ten minutes later, the guard walked by the clump of croton bushes where he was hiding and headed west along the back of the mansion. Beau headed for the nearest lighted window. Sitting on a leather couch in a huge paneled living room, was a middle-aged black couple in casual clothes, watching a large television. He checked three other lit windows and saw a uniformed cook cleaning pots and pans, a teenaged girl in pajamas reading or studying, and a uniformed maid watching TV on a small screen portable. A watch check made him stay put until the guard went past again. The mansion had no outbuildings except for a few gazebos. Everything else was self-contained. Many of the larger rooms and corridors were two stories high with cathedral ceilings. Those windows were also wide and two stories high, to take advantage of the spectacular ocean and bay views around the entire 360^0 perimeter of the little island. Beau was able to look down the halls and into virtually all the rooms as he stealthily circled the house. He finally found the outside stairs leading up to an exterior portico that served the entrances of the second-floor rooms. There was only one window lit up there. He peeked into a gap in the curtained window and saw an older black man stretched out on a bed watching soccer on TV. A chauffer's livery hung on a coat rack, and a chauffer's cap sat on top of a small chest of drawers. Beau slinked down to ground level and re-entered the clump of crotons. Again, he waited for the guard before sliding silently into the water. Beau made his way to his car satisfied that Seth was not a prisoner at the mansion. Everything there seemed normal. If Seth were being held captive at the mansion, there would have been more security, and the Minister's family would not have been there.

Back in his room at the Ports of Call, Beau showered, then texted Jeb; "*Swam over and checked out the Silly Creek mansion … close-up. Don't believe Seth is there. Might have found a lead at the Tiki Hut, will follow-up in the a.m. If it pans out, I'll text.*"

***

Peter was in no hurry to see Seth in the cave. He wanted him to be as hungry and thirsty as Peter was in solitary when the guards were lazy or mean. First, he went for an early morning swim, showered, and had breakfast at the Seaside Café near Seven Seas. As he ate breakfast, he thought he might finish the game with Seth tomorrow night. He'd rough him up a little, then feed and water him in the early afternoon. It would give Seth a long stretch alone to think about his impending demise. Maybe he should call Rikki and see if she was up for a quickie … if there was such a thing possible with Rikki. He could fit her in this afternoon or tonight. He'd call her later this morning, from the beach cottage, after he booked his ticket to Australia.

Booking his ticket took longer than he planned. Peter finally went to a travel agency on Leeward Highway, TCI Reservations Ltd., and had them book an American Airline ticket through Miami, connecting to Los Angeles, then on to Sydney. It was too complicated to book it by phone. His flight left Provo Wednesday at 1:00 p.m. and he'd arrive in Australia, a day later. He would turn the Tahoe in at Scooter Bob's, and they would shuttle him over to the airport. He prepaid the beach cottage, so there were no loose ends there. Peter took his ticket and passport back to Long Bay and called Rikki.

"Guess who this is? Can you talk?"

"Well, hello stranger. I thought you were long gone, are you still here?"

"Yeah, but I have to leave in a couple of days. Can we hook-up before I go?"

"The doctor is still doing Mondays and Tuesdays at the Cockburn Town hospital. He won't be home until Tuesday night."

"How about tonight? I'll be busy packing and getting ready to leave Tuesday."

"Where do you want to meet?"

"I got a new place ... a cottage on the beach at Long Bay, very remote. We can go skinny dippin' tonight."

"Ohhh, baby! I'll roll myself in that sugar white sand and look like a chocolate jelly donut."

"You're whetting my appetite already, girl. I'll get a roasted chicken and some cole slaw at the IGA deli ... and a couple of bottles of the Chardonnay you like. The cottage is just before the turnaround at the east end of the Beach Drive — you'll see my white Tahoe down the driveway in front of the house."

"I'll be there right about dark."

Peter drove to the cave with a smile on his face. There hadn't been another reoccurrence of his nightmare since he captured Seth. It was a good sign his plan of retribution was working. Peter felt rested and fit, for the first time in ages. There was no traffic at the Man-O-War crossroads, so he pulled through the narrow opening in the foliage and turned quickly into the macheted space to hide the SUV from passersby. He strode quickly through the scrub jungle to the clearing, carrying a bag of ice he brought from the freezer in the cottage. He extended the ladder into the cave and dropped the safety line alongside it. Then he clattered down the ladder and turned his flashlight on Seth.

"Beautiful day outside, Seth ... if you didn't notice. I see you only stomped a few of my crabby friends since I left," said Peter, laughing at his own feeble joke. "I guess I won't have to hit you quite as hard today."

He turned on the two lanterns, then went over and carefully checked Seth's bonds. It certainly didn't smell any better in the cave — it was hard to breathe. He noticed Seth's feet and ankles were bleeding again. Peter put the ice in the cooler and took out a banana and a bottle of water. He walked up to Seth, who could barely keep his eyes open, and abruptly pulled the duct tape off his mouth, taking some of Seth's skin with it. Seth screamed in pain — while Peter laughed.

"I guess you're sorry you chewed up my bandana aren't you, asshole?"

Seth was still in enough control of himself not to answer and get punched again, but he knew he couldn't hang on much longer. Soon he wouldn't give a fuck. Peter fed him a banana and let him slowly drink the water.

"You won't have to tough it out too much longer, Seth. Judgment day is right around the corner. Do you want some more water? Just shake your head yes or no."

Seth shook his head *yes*, and Peter meted out the second bottle of water, slowly. He put a new piece of duct tape on Seth's mouth and stood back and looked at him.

"After I kill your sorry ass, I'm thinking about going back to St. Pete and grabbing your new girlfriend and taking her 50 miles offshore. I'll fuck her like a rag-doll, and throw her overboard when I'm through with her."

Seth lost his composure and started straining against his bonds and getting red in the face. Peter just stood there and laughed.

"See Seth, when you're in prison you can't do shit about anything. You're stuck in solitary, and the rest of the world just moves on."

He walked around behind Seth and picked up the house broom he'd left there, held it by the bristle end, and started to whack the back of Seth's legs and butt with the handle. After 15 or 20 whacks, and one for good measure, he dropped the broom, turned off the lanterns, and started up the ladder.

He stopped halfway up and said, "This is not the last time you'll feel that broom, Seth. See you tomorrow."

Peter pulled out of the scrub and headed for the Leeward IGA to get the roasted chicken and other dinner supplies. He'd already sprung a woody just thinking about Miss Rikki rollin' around in the sugar sand — she better be careful she didn't get sand in her *Schlitz*.

205

***

Beau was up at first light. He ate breakfast with the early tee time foursomes at the fashionable Provo Golf Club. The club wasn't private, but the Provo clubhouse had the air of an uptown country club. He took his time, as Scooter didn't open until 8:00 a.m. Beau drove over to Turtle Cove about 8:30. He pulled into Scooter's lot and saw an employee washing one of the rentals in a tent structure.

"Can you tell me where I can find Scooter Bob?"

"Inside the office. He has long surfer blond hair — he should be behind the front desk."

He walked in, and there was Scooter, tall, tanned, rawboned, with his blond hair under a hat with a maple leaf embroidered on the front.

Scooter smiled and said, "Can I help ya, eh?"

Beau decided to skip his Canadian accent, and said, "You must be Scooter."

"Right."

"Well, the other night I got shitfaced over at the Tiki Hut, threw up on myself, and passed out. I was told by the doorman at my hotel that a gentleman driving a Tahoe with the name *Bonehead* on it delivered me to my hotel. I vaguely remember sitting at the bar and talking to a very nice big guy, but I don't remember his name and the Tiki Hut bartender, Jack, didn't know him. The doorman told me you rented him the Tahoe. He said you named all of your rental cars."

"I do."

"Anyway, I would like to get in touch with this fella' if he's still on the island to say, 'thank you', and buy him dinner if he'll let me."

"He's still on the island ... *Bonehead's* not back yet, eh? You seem like a right kind of guy, wanting to say thanks and everything. He probably thinks you're a 'hoser', eh? Let me see what I got here ... he doesn't have a local phone, but his name is Grant Morris, from Miami, and he's stayin' at the Turtle Cove Inn — almost right next door, eh?"

206

"Thanks, Scooter, next time I vacation here I'll rent my car here, for sure."

"Just give me a call, eh?"

Beau drove a few doors down and pulled into the Turtle Cove Inn. He was elated to be following this lead. He walked to the front desk and asked the clerk for Grant Morris's room number.

The clerk checked the computer and said, "Mr. Morris checked out Saturday morning."

"Did he say where he was moving to?"

"He said he was going back to Miami."

"Well … I guess he didn't get my message, thanks."

Beau got back in his car and started to drive back to Ports of Call. The more he turned it over in his mind, the better he felt about it. Seth disappears Friday night. Grant Morris was in a hotel overlooking the marina. He checks out Saturday and tells the hotel clerk he's going back to Miami but doesn't turn his car in. Grant Morris is still on the island, and for some reason, he wants the clerk to think he was leaving for Florida. Purposeful misdirection? We need to find this Grant Morris, who is still on the island with *Bonehead*. Beau looked at his watch - it read 9:30. He pulled over and texted Jeb;

"The Tiki Hut lead has promise, meet me in the eastern corner of the Leeward IGA parking lot, next to the bookstore."

Forty minutes later Jeb pulled in next to Beau in his black minivan. Beau quickly filled him in on his conversations with the marina security guard the night before and with Scooter Bob this morning.

"So his name is Grant Morris, and he lives in Miami. We need to find *Bonehead* and make sure he didn't just abandon it and fly out."

"Right, I've been sitting here thinking about it while I was waiting for you. I think we should take two approaches. Almost everybody in Provo comes to this IGA at least twice a week. They need food, ice, water, beer, wine, drugstore items. It's twice as big as the tourist IGA in Grace Bay. I'll stake this one out 24/7. I can get deli food and coffee here, and they have restrooms. You can systematically check all the hotel, bar, and restaurant parking lots from downtown to the Leeward end of the island. I topped off my tank on the way over since they only put a half a tank in at Hertz. I want to run my air conditioning while I'm sitting here. Anyhow, they still have gas jockeys here and don't accept credit cards. You have to pay cash. So, stop at all the gas stations and ask if they've seen a white Tahoe named *Bonehead*. Can you figure an excuse to be out all day?"

"Well, Fred and John are running down the calls Dino is getting from the *Missing* posters. Dino and Gene are doing the same thing, they all decided it was safer if they worked in pairs since the calls have all been from the rougher parts of Provo."

"Any good leads?"

"No, mostly tourists somebody saw driving around, or the callers are crackpots. We give the ones with license plate numbers to the police, and they've turned out to be rental cars and innocent tourists. Rex set us up with the desk sergeants at the downtown police station next to the hospital."

"I'll take one of the posters and tell them I'm going to check the gas stations, bars, and restaurants personally."

"Like you said, check the airport parking lot first, to make sure Morris hasn't ditched *Bonehead* there and skipped town. Then work east — we'll stay in touch by phone. Let's check in at the top of each hour."

"OK, Uncle Beau."

CHAPTER EIGHTEEN

BEAU watched the cars, trucks, and shoppers come and go. The traffic through the IGA store was constant and prolific. People had to eat. One employee did nothing but collect shopping carts and push long lines of them back inside the store. In the first hour, Beau saw two white GMC Tahoe's, but neither one was *Bonehead*. Jeb called and said he was working his way through the Kewtown section of downtown, and the Tahoe was not at the airport. Another long hour went by before Jeb called again.

"I just left a Shell gas station near the power plant on Leeward, and the pump attendant remembered fueling up *Bonehead* two or three days ago. 'A big white guy', is all he remembers. He said he laughs every time he sees *Bonehead*."

"Keep looking — it sounds like we might be on the right track."

Beau found one FM station on the radio that played oldies and also reported local and world news every half hour. Jeb checked in from Grace Bay where the going was a lot slower, due to the number of hotel and retail parking lots. Beau took a quick bathroom break, bought an eight-pack of water, and a box of granola bars. When he came out of the IGA, he quickly surveyed the parking lot, but there was no white Tahoe to be seen. Jeb called again and was just starting into the Leeward neighborhoods at the eastern end of the island. Beau was grooving on Steely Dan's *Kid Charlemagne* when the white Tahoe went over the speed bump and drove past the front of the IGA. As he turned up a row, Beau could see black lettering on the front hood. A big white guy, with shaggy brown hair and a mustache, got out. He was tan, wore board shorts and a performance t-shirt, and walked with a limp into the IGA. Beau waited until he was sure he was inside the store, then hustled over and confirmed it was *Bonehead.* There was a Scooter Bob sticker on the front windshield and back hatch. He walked calmly back to his Taurus and dialed Jeb, excitedly.

"Good news! The Tahoe just pulled in with a big white guy in it. I'll follow him when he leaves, why don't you stand-by out there in Leeward somewhere?"

"Fantastic, Uncle Beau!! I'll standby on Governor's Road, call me! "

Fifteen minutes later the big guy came out with a couple of bags of groceries and drove out east on Leeward Highway. Beau followed him, two cars back, through two roundabouts, before the Tahoe turned in on Long Bay Highway. Beau took deep breaths to ease his excitement and slowed down considerably so he wouldn't end up right on his tail. When Beau turned right across the road, the Tahoe was easing around a bend. The Tahoe turned left on Lignumvitae Drive. There was a small sign with an arrow there stating, *Long Bay Beach.* Beau slowed way down again and saw the Tahoe turn left at the Bay. He drove down a gentle grade, turned left, and watched the Tahoe turn into a sand and gravel drive. There were several brightly colored kiteboard sails whizzing back and forth at the east end of the bay. When he went by, there was still dust hanging in the air from the Tahoe's entrance. The same scrub foliage, which covered the whole island, hid the house. Beau went another 250 yards to a gravel turnaround and parked, facing back west. Behind him were a few parked cars with roof racks, and a narrow, packed sand road leading to what appeared to be two multi-unit condos.

Beau settled in and called Jeb.

"Where are you?"

"According to my Hertz map, I'm up at the east end of Long Bay. The Tahoe pulled into a remote driveway leading to a beach house. There's lots of foliage, so I can't see it, but I'll check it out when it gets dark. I'm parked facing west in a turnaround at the end of Long Bay Drive. This end of the bay is full of kiteboarders. There are four or five of their empty cars parked here by me. Why don't you come down and get the lay of the land? But before you do, how about getting me some insect repellant up on the highway somewhere?"

"I'll see you shortly. Need anything else?"

'If you go back to the IGA, how about a sub-sandwich? I've got enough water to last me."

"Roger that."

Beau got out and stretched his legs, then walked out the sand path to the bay and stood on the small grass covered dunes. This was the windward side of the island. The wind was blowing 20 to 25 knots, and the kiteboarders were ripping and shredding the whitecaps. In the gusts, a couple went airborne for a second or two. The wind would help keep the bugs off him, but in close quarters in the scrub jungle, some of them would score if he lacked repellant. Unlike most places in the world, these islands were located in the trades and were more likely to have the wind increase in velocity at night rather than have it lay down. He made his way back to his car and listened to the radio while he waited for Jeb.

Twenty minutes later Jeb pulled into the turnaround and parked next to Beau.

"Here's your sub and a spray bottle of Off®," said Jeb, as he slid into Beau's passenger seat. "Who do you think sent Grant Morris to abduct dad?"

"I've been thinkin' about that, too. He's a big, muscular guy — maybe the Tampa Mafia hired him? They'd have to take Seth out of here on a private jet, or maybe Morris is interrogating him here? It obviously has nothing to do with what happened on this island."

"I just keep hopin' he hasn't already killed him."

"I don't think Morris would still be here if that was true, Jeb."

"I hope you're right."

"Why don't you go back to *TAR BABY?* Just be ready to come back with or without the crew."

"What do you mean?"

"It depends on what I find out during my surveillance tonight. If Morris has Seth in the house with him, I'll text you first and then call Dino's poster number with a tip. You and Jock can make sure the authorities surround this place and get him out safely. If he has him hidden somewhere else, I'll

211

follow him there. If Seth's alive, I'll want you to help me take this guy down if there's time. If he's killed Seth, I'll just kill him and disappear. But, I'll keep you in the loop all the way."

"I understand, good luck."

Jeb leaned over and gave Beau an awkward hug, and left with tears in his eyes. Beau thought Jeb had grown into a fine young man — he reminded him so much of Seth. Jeb was here, and Jeb was dealing with it, just like Seth would have.

As dusk fell, a dark blue seven series BMW sedan drove up Long Bay Drive and turned into the beach house's driveway. All Beau could see of the driver was her big hair. It wasn't long before the sun set back behind Long Bay Hills, and all the kiteboarders packed up and left in their cars. Beau cut off the overhead interior light and changed out of his shorts and t-shirt into his lightweight black Lycra dive-suit. It covered his arms and legs and had a tight hood that framed his face. He put on his fanny pack with the Glock 9 mm, flashlight, and other gear in it, adding the bottle of insect repellant and his car keys. He gave it another hour before he sprayed up and went down the kiteboarder's beach path. He cut in behind the dunes and worked his way west towards the beach house, along the scrub foliage border. When he got close to the house, he dropped down on all fours and crawled up the dunes and peered over. The moon was rising and was almost full. It shined a path of light on the choppy water illuminating the pure white beach sand. Beau spotted Morris romping in the surf with a voluptuous dark skinned female. Both of them were naked. They splashed, ran, and dove in the sparkling water like two happy children. There was a blanket, and a couple of beach towels spread out at the base of the dune in front of the small beach house. The woman laughed and shrieked as he tried to catch her. She ran towards the house, tripped, and rolled in the sand.

Morris laughed as he caught her and shouted, "You do look like a jelly donut!"

He scooped her up like she weighed nothing, and ran back into the water with her.

Beau thought they would occupy each other for a while, so he quickly approached the house. There were a few lights on, and the front door was open except for a screen door. Beau eased silently into the living room and checked the two small bedrooms down a narrow hall. They both were dark and empty. He backtracked and found a third bedroom off the dining room and kitchen area. It was lit, clothes were strewn all over the room, and the bedspread was pulled back and tousled. A huge leather purse with an MK logo sat on a chair. He spotted a well-worn Rolex Submariner watch on the nightstand, along with a wallet and some empty beer bottles. There was something familiar about the watch. Beau picked it up and turned it over. The inscription, he knew would be there, leaped out at him, *U.S. Yacht Club Champions 1987*. It was Seth's watch. Beau pulled open the nightstand drawer and found a plastic bag full of money, a U.S. passport, and a Smith and Wesson .38 revolver. As he opened *Grant T. Morris's* passport, an airline ticket voucher fell out. Beau quickly scanned the itinerary, final destination *Sydney, Australia.* Beau grabbed the gun and took the top and bottom shells out of the cylinder, and put them in his fanny pack. He closed the cylinder and returned the gun to the drawer, along with the passport and ticket voucher. He peeked out of the bedroom door, and the kitchen and dining room were clear. He slid quietly out of the kitchen door and checked the driveway leading back to the road. There were no outbuildings or garage, just their two cars. He re-entered the scrub jungle and worked his way slowly back to the dunes.

Beau turned it all over in his mind. *Seth was either dead or captive at another location. He suppressed a sudden urge to confront the amorous couple on the beach and torture the location out of them. But, the woman might be innocent, and then things would start to get messy. If Seth were imprisoned somewhere, Morris would go there soon, since his flight left Provo in two days. If Seth didn't turn up, Beau would make sure that Morris wouldn't be on that flight.*

When Beau got back to the dunes, he swept the surf and the beach but didn't see them. He zeroed in on the beach blanket location, and there they were. The moonlight glinted off the woman's shapely buttocks, as her pendulous breasts bounced up and down on Morris's chest. She held her right arm straight up in the night air and rode him like a Brahma Bull. Beau smiled inwardly, *no matter which way it went, this would definitely be Morris's last night playing Beach Blanket Bingo.*

Beau worked his way along the backside of the dunes and reentered his car. He texted Jeb;

"Seth's not at the beach house, Morris has female company, I'll text you and follow him whenever he moves. He has an AA ticket to leave Provo Wednesday at 1.00 p.m. He's our man, he has Seth's Rolex. Stay cool!"

"Do u think Dad's alive?"

"That's how I'm going to play it."

"K"

***

The dejected crew was sitting in TAR BABY'S salon, after a dinner at SharkBites, watching a baseball game on cable TV. It was getting hard to talk about the "elephant in the room".

Finally, John said to Jeb, "This is tough to say, but if we don't get a break in the investigation in the next couple of days, I'm going to call Stacy and have her cancel her trip down here with Lori this Friday. You'll probably have to break the news to Lori, or I'll do it if you want me to."

"I've thought about it, but I didn't want to alarm Lori unnecessarily. But I agree, let's give it a couple of days. If the situation doesn't change, I'll call her the same time you call your wife. I'll make arrangements to get the boat moved back to the states, too."

"Hey, I've blocked the time out already. Gene wants to help. We'll bring her back up to the Boatworks for you. I'm sure you need to get back there, or maybe stay here longer if you want."

"Well, I appreciate it, but I'm not giving up yet," replied Jeb.

"Neither are we," chorused the rest of the crew.

"Thanks, but I know we needed to talk about it, thanks, guys."

They went back to watching the baseball game. Two innings later Jeb's phone dinged, and he sent a text back. It dinged again, and he texted back.

"You look like you saw a ghost. Are you all right, Jeb?" asked Freddy.

"O, Oh yeah, I'm OK … I'm just tired. It was Lynne, she and Cullen are visiting her mother over in Delray — she knows dad's missing, but I asked her not to tell anyone. I had to tell her we didn't have any news yet. Now I know how helpless the parents of those kids who are snatched by the pedophiles and serial killers must feel. I think I'll try and get some sleep. See y'all in the morning."

***

Antonio Arroyo lounged *au natural* on a chaise next to the darkened pool and looked up at the full moon. It had been a busy week since he took over. His staffing move at the Club Capri was working out so far. Paco was doing fine as a greeter and bouncer, and Diego was already exhibiting some organizational talent. The Iguana and Zodiac managers were handed fatter paychecks and were all smiles. Sarita's mother and two kids would be coming in on the *CALAMAR GOTEO* from the Dominican in a couple of weeks when the working girls were changed out. Frederico seemed to be over his concussion and Chico became Antonio's *Capo*. He'd ordered a couple of Black Dodge Durango's from Mac Motors to replace the totaled Suburbans.

Antonio had finally talked to Alistair earlier in the day, and they concluded it would be business as usual. Chico would drop off his monthly cash stipend. Alistair told him there would be no retribution against Jock Baffert or his American friends. Apparently, there was some evidence incriminating Alistair, La Bomba, and several members of the Dominican gang, which would surface if any harm came to any of them. He was relieved to hear that Antonio and his men had nothing to do with the disappearance of one of Jock's American friends who went missing last Friday.

Probably got drunk and fell in the water, thought Antonio. Nobody had asked about Jacque Mehoff yet. But he was a strange one and a loner anyhow and went off by himself from time to time without even telling his secretary.

215

Sarita called to him softly from the swimming pool, "*La mamada, mi amor?*"

Antonio drained his glass of Barceló rum and took a long pull on his Fuentes *Hemingway Perfecto* cigar. He walked over and sat on the edge of the pool with his legs dangling in the cool water. It was time to get his whistle blown.

CHAPTER NINETEEN

AS BEAU watched the sun rise out of the Caribbean, vibrant shades of pastel pinks and blues colored the sky and the water. When the sun climbed higher, they gave way to clear skies and a blazing yellow sun. He got out of the Taurus and stretched his legs on the kiteboarders' path. His breakfast of bottled water and two granola bars was less than satisfying but better than nothing. By 10:00 he was running the engine and air conditioning, and four van loads of kiteboarders had headed to the beach. The wind held steady at 20 knots.

At 11:15 the blue BMW pulled out of the beach house's driveway and headed west. Beau could see the woman's big hair through the bimmer's rear window. She appeared to be alone.

Beau texted Jeb at 12:00 noon;

"*Lady-friend left at 11:15. He's got to move soon.*"

"*Can I bring u anything?*"

"*How about a sub, ice coffee, three 5 hour energy drinks, and more water.*"

"*K, 30 minutes.*"

Jeb pulled up next to the Taurus and got in.

"Thanks for the ice coffee, I didn't sleep much."

"I'm not sleepin' well, either. What do you think is goin' on?"

"I don't know — he's probably very hungover. They were havin' a wild time out on the beach last night when I was sneakin' around."

"You obviously got into the house to find the airplane ticket."

"Yeah, he's flyin' to Miami Wednesday at 1:00 in the afternoon, and on to Australia, through LAX."

"I don't get it … a professional hitman?"

217

"I don't know. If he doesn't come out soon, I guess I'll have to go in after him?"

"You look pretty stealthy in that Lycra dive suit, Uncle Beau."

"I noticed a couple of the kiteboarders were wearing them too, smart-ass."

"Hey look, the Tahoe just came out of the drive."

"Where's your gun and Kevlar?"

"I have a duffel."

"Get out slowly and get it, and get back in here. But don't look like you're in a hurry."

Jeb got the duffel and got back in the Taurus. Beau eased the car onto the road and started after the Tahoe.

"He didn't turn at Lignumvitae, where's he headed?"

"Looks like he's slowing down to turn. The roads at this end are all gravel, and the road dust makes it hard to see."

"I'll stop a minute, so I'm not too close, it's some distance up to the highway," said Beau.

Beau turned, but he didn't see the Tahoe up ahead.

"Where the fuck is he?"

"Maybe he turned up ahead … at the crossroad."

Beau drove up to the crossroad, but there was no Tahoe in either direction.

"There's no road dust up here, so he must have pulled off somewhere behind us. Do you think he made us?"

"No, not with all the road dust he was putting up," said Jeb.

"I'll park the car here, and we'll check the road on foot from the crossroads down. I didn't see any houses, just jungle. Take your gun and put on your Kevlar, *and* — by the way, I took the first and fourth bullets out of his .38 last night."

Sixty yards down the road, Jeb discovered the opening. They entered with their guns drawn and quickly found the hacked out space where Morris hid the Tahoe. Beau and Jeb followed the narrow macheted trail to the first clearing, seeing nothing unusual. They moved around the flat limestone clearing's perimeter and found the trail cut in the jungle on the other side.

Brambles and thorns slowed their progress, but they finally reached the jagged rock clearing. They started around its perimeter and stopped when Beau found the scrub tree with the cave's safety line tied to its trunk. They followed the line and saw the top couple of rungs of an aluminum ladder sticking out of an entrance hole. Beau tapped Jeb on the shoulder and put his finger to his lips to signal *no talking*.

Jeb nodded, and they both knelt at the hole and peered in. There was a dim light coming from below, and they could hear someone talking. Their eyes adjusted to the light below and they could see Seth further back in the cave, tied up spread eagle to the stalagmites. The cavern floor was 20 or 30 feet below them.

They could hear Morris talking from below, "I'm going to pull the tape off your mouth and give you some water, and you know the rules."

They watched him give Seth a few good pulls on the bottle and then put a new piece of tape over his mouth. "You won't need any food today because this is going to be your last hour. You've been in solitary for four days and nights now, so you have an idea what I went through. Now I'm going to cut off your shorts and stick this broom handle up your ass … so you'll know how I suffered when those animals attacked me in the prison shower. I was still too weak to defend myself because of the bullet wound in my right shoulder — *and* the broken ribs and cracked vertebrae you gave me with your *fucking grandstand tackle*. When I'm finished using the broomstick, I'm going to slit your ankles and wrists and watch you bleed out. After you're dead, I'm off to Australia to start a new life, and by the time I get there … the crabs and bats will have picked you clean."

Beau looked over at Jeb. Jeb's eyes were as big as saucers and full of tears after listening to that diatribe. They both knew it was Peter Petcock.

He motioned Jeb away from the opening and whispered in his ear, *"I'm going to slide down the rope, there's only room for one of us. When I start down, shine your flashlight on Peter and fire a shot at him if you can. Yell, Police! You're surrounded! Put up your hands!"*

Beau slipped the Glock in his belt and clenched his flashlight between his teeth. He grasped the rope, crossed his legs around it, nodded, and

219

disappeared down the hole. Jeb shined his flashlight on Peter and yelled, **"Police. You're surrounded. Put your hands up!"** and fired a shot over Peter's head to avoid hitting Seth. The shot ricocheted off the rock walls and startled Peter. Beau hit the floor and rolled up with his gun in hand and got a shot off that grazed Peter's left shoulder. Peter dropped the broom and ran towards the tidal pool and rock slide. Suddenly, he stopped, pulled his pistol, then turned and aimed at Seth. He pulled the trigger, but it just clicked. Beau shot and missed as Peter turned back and scrambled up the rockslide. Halfway up the rock slide, he turned to return fire. This time, his pistol fired, and the bullet whizzed past Beau's head. Beau shot again as Peter ducked behind a stalactite. It was hard to see in the pitch dark with just the light from a bouncing flashlight. Peter reached the top of the rock slide. Beau dove for cover, as Peter's next shot narrowly missed him. Peter shrugged into his rappelling harness and quickly clipped onto the friction hitch he had tied around the rope. Beau's flashlight caught him as he held the rope behind his waist and pushed off to rappel down to his scuba gear. On his second push, the pillar gave way. Peter crashed to the limestone floor below. Beau started up the rock pile but heard an ominous rumbling and cracking sound. He turned and ran for his life as that part of the cavern's ceiling turned itself into a sinkhole with a deafening crash. Peter was buried under a thousand tons of limestone. The noise subsided, and Beau fought his way through the choking dust. He saw some light ahead of him and put his hands in the air and yelled, **"Don't shoot Jeb, it's Beau."**

Jeb watched Beau emerge from the cloud of dust with his hands up. He was covered with limestone dust from head to toe. Jeb had climbed down the ladder, cut Seth down, and was cleaning him up with the remaining bottled water. He heard the ricocheting shots and then felt the ground move under him as the rock ceiling in the lower part of the cavern came crashing down.

"Let's get out of here, Beau, before this whole fucking thing collapses on us."

Beau tied the safety line around Seth's chest and climbed the ladder. He pulled Seth up the ladder from the top while Jeb guided him one rung at a time pushing up on his bare behind. They escaped the choking dust and moved Seth away from the opening.

"Holy Shit, am I glad to see you guys! I thought that crazy bastard was going to kill me for sure," said Seth weakly.

"Sounded like you were about to have an uplifting experience, Bro'," laughed Beau.

"What an understatement," whispered Seth through his cracked and raw lips. "How did you find me, and how did both of you get here?" Large tears of relief poured from his bloodshot eyes.

Tears welled up in Jeb and Beau's eyes as they hugged Seth and each other.

"Let's go to my hotel and get you a shower," said Beau. "I have a pair of shorts in the car … pull your t-shirt down, thru the neck hole, to your waist like a skirt until we get to the car. We'll recap this whole thing back there, and figure out how we want to play it out."

Beau, Jeb, and Seth walked away from Peter's hole. Seth's bare feet were too swollen to walk fast, so they took their time getting to Beau's car. Seth put on Beau's shorts and wiggled back into his stretched out soiled t-shirt. As they left to take Jeb back to his minivan, two trucks drove down to see what caused the huge dust cloud that was drifting towards Leeward Highway. Beau gave Seth a bottle of water and a handful of granola bars.

"This will hold you until we can get some real food."

They stopped at the Grace Bay IGA. Beau got a couple of six-packs of cold Turk's Head and three roast beef and ham sandwiches at the deli. Jeb dusted himself off and walked over to the drugstore. He bought hydrogen peroxide, iodine, antibiotic cream, cortisone cream, gauze, adhesive tape, and a bottle of Aleve. Beau said he carried a bottle of amoxicillin tablets in his Dopp kit for infections when he was traveling. The antibiotics would help Seth ward off any infections from the many cuts on his feet and ankles. Seth dozed off as he waited in the Taurus.

Seth and Jeb followed Beau into his hotel room through the back entrance near the rear parking lot. Seth hit the shower first, and Beau was right behind him. Afterward, Seth lay on one of the Queen-size beds in a clean pair of Beau's underwear, while Beau cleaned and dressed his wounds.

"Jesus, the back of your legs are all black and blue, and your lower back has some huge bruises."

"Peter took a lot of free shots at me while I was tied up. He literally was stark raving mad. He blamed me for all his bad luck and bad decisions. He must have been tracking me from the time he escaped from prison. Very creepy, man!"

"Here's the bottle of Amoxicillin; take three a day for ten days. It will keep you from getting an infection. Your feet and ankles have bat shit and crab dung in those cuts. Keep my shorts — and here's a clean t-shirt and a pair of flip flops. You won't be wearing boat shoes for a while."

"I'll take all of it."

Jeb cleaned up some but didn't want a change of clothes. It would help the story. The three of them ate their sandwiches and drank a cold one while they discussed their options.

"So this is how I think you guys should play it," said Beau. "Jeb was going to the IGA on Leeward around noon for a sandwich and passed Peter on his way to the front door. Luckily, Peter didn't see him. Jeb has known him for years — Peter cleaned *TAR BABY'S* bottom at the Boatworks every month for years."

"That's actually true, he also bought shaft and rudder zincs, from our ship's store, for the other boats he cleaned around St.Pete," said Jeb. "I would know him anywhere."

"The brown hair disguise didn't fool you. You followed Peter to Long Bay and the beach house, then followed him to the cave. You didn't call anyone because you figured Peter's been watching the Hatteras. He probably knew who was on the crew and what vehicles were involved. You didn't want to spook him."

"Sounds logical," added Seth. "When you got to the cave you overheard what Peter was planning for me. You had to act right away, or I was a dead man."

222

"Right," said Jeb. "I made believe I was the police, made a lot of noise, waved my flashlight, and fired some shots at Peter. His gun jammed and he took off running through the cave. That's when I slid down the ladder."

"Peter obviously knew of an escape route and took off, with you in hot pursuit. When he rappelled down the old cave-in to reach his scuba gear, the rock pillar holding the rope crumbled and the ceiling fell in on him. The rest of it is there for them to see," said Beau.

"The cops can find Peter if they want to move a thousand tons of limestone," laughed Seth.

"They'll find his fake passport at the beach house, along with a bag of money, and an airline ticket. *Bonehead* is still sitting by the cave, and his prints are all over the SUV," added Beau. "And ... his DNA is all over the beach house bedroom. Call the boat, and tell them you found Seth, and you're bringing him there now. When you get there, tell them you stopped at the drugstore to clean up his cuts."

"I'll just say I needed to clean up at the public beach house, where they have the Junkanoo. I didn't want anybody to see me the way Jeb found me. I'm grateful Jeb had a change of clothes in the minivan," said Seth.

"Good story, and it's a good thing we're all pretty much the same size," said Jeb.

"Have them call Jock from there too, Jeb — to have him get Rex to run interference for you with the local police. Everybody will be so glad to see Seth they'll believe anything."

"And guess what? ... The island has a new tourist attraction for free," laughed Seth, coughing and wheezing a bit.

They all cracked up laughing.

***

Jeb made the call to a depressed, disconsolate crew. When he told John he'd found Seth, John turned to the crew and said, "Seth's alive!! Jeb found him." Jeb could hear the crew celebrating in the background.

223

"Don't tell anybody else yet, John, but please call Jock and ask him to get Rex to handle the police. We'll be back at the boat in about 30 minutes, Seth's cleaning up some in the shower at the public beach."

"You got it," said John.

***

"Well, I guess we better shove off, Uncle Beau. I hope I get to see you again soon, but under better circumstances."

"It was good to see you, you know I miss both of you. We better do the fishing thing in Costa Rica this winter that we've been talking about — all three of us. I'm catching the next plane out of here!"

"I'm in for this winter," said Seth.

"Me too!" echoed Jeb.

They all hugged and as Seth and Jeb went out the back door, Beau smiled and said, "Seth, why don't you get a new hobby, like writin' novels or shootin' skeet, eh?"

***

Seth's homecoming back at *TAR BABY* was subdued until he got inside the main salon. Once the door closed, the pent-up emotions that the crew had bottled up over the past four days were unleashed. After a couple of rounds of hugging and high-fives, Jock and Rex walked in, and the celebration started again. Finally, over a round of cold ones, Jeb and Seth related their version of the saga.

Gene shook his head and said, "Fucking Peter Petcock. I'd have never guessed that. He must have had a pile of drug money stashed to try and pull this whole thing off and then disappear to Australia."

"What a freakin' nightmare," said Fred.

"It's a good thing this is such a small island," said Jock. "Sooner or later you <u>do</u> see *everybody* at the IGA."

"I thought it was retribution from the Dominicans," said John.

"Me too," said Dino.

224

"Rex's plan may have Alistair under control, but we trounced those Dominican bastards," chortled Jock.

"Do you want to blow off the marlin tournament, Seth? It might be too much for you at this point," asked John.

"You won't hurt Kat's or my feelings Seth, not after what you've been through," said Jock, chiming in.

"No way, I ain't no wussy … and that's why we came. I'll be fine in a day or two. Anyhow — all I do is sit up there and steer — you guys do all the work. I'm looking forward to the tournament, having Lori and Stacy here, and staying up at Jock's. I'm tired of bunking with you ol' Geezers and sleeping with crabs."

Everybody laughed and gave Seth another round of *Hoo-rahs*.

When the frivolity subsided, Rex stood up and said, "I've taken some notes, Seth. I think I can hold the police interview off until tomorrow. They may want to impound *Bonehead* and search the beach house the perp rented on Long Bay, before the interview. I'm sure they'll contact the Caribbean FBI attaché in Santo Domingo, and he will be interested in Mr. Petcock's whereabouts and demise since he escaped from one of your federal prisons."

"Right now, I'm exhausted," said Seth. "But, I want to thank all of you for never giving up on me. I know I'll feel better if I can get 12 hours of uninterrupted sleep. I'll see you guys tomorrow."

Seth retired to the forward cabin and closed the door.

Jeb asked John Harvey, "Truthfully, do you think he'll be all right, Dr. John?"

"Well, he doesn't look overly dehydrated, mostly it's sleep-deprivation and the crab wounds. He was fed a banana and a couple of bottles of water every day. You already have him on amoxicillin for any infections. I have some vitamins in my medical bag. I'll give him a couple of B-12 shots, and we'll put him on hi-protein smoothies for the next few days."

"They should perk him up," said Jeb.

"I'll also change those dressings on his feet and ankles every day to monitor for infection. We'll make sure he stays well hydrated and gets plenty of sleep. For a man his age, he's lucky he doesn't have any other health issues to complicate things. I think once he's over the sleep deprivation, he'll be fine."

Rex turned to Jeb and said, "That's good news. But, there may be some questions from the authorities concerning the gun you used to scare off Mr. Petcock. The Turks and Caicos have some very strict gun laws. Where will you tell them you got the gun?"

"It's the ship's weapon. I carried it for protection when I was checking the gas stations and local bars for leads."

"I may be able to get you a special permit for the gun. This kidnapping has been an embarrassment to the police force. Can you lock the gun up?"

"Yes, we have a strong box."

Rex left after cautioning everyone not to make any statements to anyone without him being present.

Dino and Fred made plans with Jock to dive the next day. John and Gene were happy just to hang out and relax with Seth.

***

Seth's cell phone rang at 10:00 the next morning — it was Rex.

"Good morning, Seth. I hope I didn't call too early, and I trust you are feeling better. You looked bloody awful last night."

"I feel much better. It's amazing what 12 hours of sleep can do for you. I've been up since 8:00 a.m. I'm drinking plenty of water, and I just ate a truck driver's breakfast."

"Sounds like you'll be fit by tournament time."

"I don't see a problem."

"I've been in touch with Police Commissioner Spencer Arnold. He has put Chief Inspector Gordon Hubert in charge of the Peter Petcock case. Gordon would like to interview you and Jeb, at 2:00 this afternoon at the downtown police station, if you're up to it. I have briefed him on the circumstances, and he understands your abduction stems from a three-year-old grudge held against you by Mr. Petcock resulting from his arrest for grand theft of a yacht, attempted murder, and cocaine smuggling. I informed him you solved that crime and helped the sheriff and his deputies apprehend him in Key West. I further explained that Mr. Petcock escaped from federal prison in Florida during May of this year and was still at large."

"Did they check out the beach house or his rental car yet?"

"Yes, I gave him those locations first thing this morning, and he called me back a few minutes ago. The forensic team found a counterfeit passport and a multi-destination airline ticket to Sydney, Australia. The car rental company had the same passport information, plus a bogus driver's license from Florida. He was using the name Grant T. Morris, and a Miami address. They're lifting fingerprints and DNA samples as we speak."

"He must have a big wad of cash stashed somewhere on this island?"

"It wasn't mentioned. Maybe he carried it with him, and it's under the rocks. There are no plans to excavate his body at this time."

"Anything else?"

"Yes, Commissioner Arnold has issued Jeb a special weapons permit retroactive to June 23rd. All he asks is for you mention how responsive the police were to your crew's report when you went missing — in any official or press interviews."

"No problem."

"Oh, the commissioner has alerted the FBI attaché in Santo Domingo that their investigation includes an escaped fugitive under U.S. federal jurisdiction. He is flying in and will take your deposition tomorrow. I will be with you and Jeb during all these interviews."

"I appreciate it, Rex … please send me a bill."

"Take me marlin fishing again and we're even."

"No problem."

"Cheerio mate! I'll pick you both up at 1:30 this afternoon."

***

Seth poured himself another cup of coffee. John and Gene were taking a walk around the marina. After a night on the salon couch, Jeb was checking into the Turtle Cove Inn at this very moment, but Seth knew he would want to fly back to St. Petersburg as soon as they were clear of the local police. He knew he should call Lori and fill her in, so he climbed up to the flybridge and dialed her on his sat-phone.

"Hey Lori, it's Seth."

"I wondered when you were going to call me, Seth Stone. I've already started to pack, and I have a hair appointment at 2:00 this afternoon."

"Well, I apologize ... I've been out of commission for a few days ... I had an unexpected run-in down here with Peter Petcock ... you know, the guy who stole Charley Blevins boat."

"Unbelievable, he's the one who just escaped from a prison near Orlando, right?

"Right."

"So, he held a grudge about that?"

"Well ... that and it kinda went all the way back to high school."

"Oooh ... One of those male things."

"I guess ... Anyway, he followed me down here somehow, hit me over the head, and hid me in a cave. John called Jeb when I went missing, and he flew down. To make a long story short, they found me, and I'm all right."

"Oh my God! ... Why didn't they call me?" said Lori sniffling and crying on the other end.

"Well, they didn't know what was going on, and they didn't want to worry you. Anyhow, calm down, Honey — I'm fine now, and I can't wait for you to get here."

"You certainly get yourself into some scrapes, Seth. Is this Peter Petcock character back in prison?" said Lori regaining her composure.

"No, he fell off a cliff trying to get away, and a bunch of big rocks fell on him ... He's not with us anymore."

"*Well!* That serves him right. I'm just glad *you're* OK. I love you, and miss you, and can't wait to see you ... Do you know of anyone else who is *that* pissed off at you?"

"Nobody who's alive, Honey."

"Well ... that's a relief!"

"I miss you too, Love. I'll be at the airport with John when you and Stacy fly in here Friday."

Women really <u>are</u> a different breed, thought Seth as he put his sat-phone back in its leather case.

CHAPTER TWENTY

SETH, Jeb, and Rex walked out of Police Headquarters, smiling. Their respective interrogations, closely monitored by Rex, had gone smoothly. They encountered a reporter from the TCI weekly newspaper waiting for them in the lobby. Rex made a statement regarding the abduction and rescue of Seth, along with a brief statement outlining Peter Petcock's prison escape in Florida, noting Seth's part in his incarceration and Peter's subsequent revenge motive. He also stressed that the TCI police have been extremely cooperative at every level and immediately mounted a task force to find Seth, well before Jeb spotted Peter exiting the IGA on Leeward.

As he drove them back to Turtle Cove Rex said, "It all couldn't have gone any better. You both are free to leave the island whenever you want. I think you should stay, as a courtesy, until you meet with the FBI agent who's coming in from Santo Domingo tonight. They scheduled the meeting for 9:00 tomorrow morning. Commissioner Arnold told me the agent has a 1:30 p.m. flight back to the Dominican. I will, of course, be with you at that meeting."

"I guess I'll book a flight out Thursday afternoon too, Dad. I need to get back to the yard. I'm sure the work is backing up some."

"I'm sure everybody in the yard wants their boat finished next week for the fourth of July."

"You got that right!"

"Why don't you book a flight for early Friday morning instead? Then you can fish with us tomorrow after our meeting — one-half day won't make *that* much difference. We'll leave the dock right after the FBI meeting. You're invited too, Rex."

"Alright, you twisted my arm," laughed Jeb.

"You don't have to twist my arm, mate," said Rex.

They were back on *TAR BABY* ten minutes later with John and Gene.

"How did it go?" asked Gene.

"It went fine. The story will probably hit the newspaper here next week. We're going to go fishing around noon tomorrow after our meeting with the FBI agent from the Dominican Republic. Rex is going to the meeting with us and then fishing too."

"Sounds good to me," said John. "I was starting to get island fever."

"With the girls coming in, we only have a couple of days before the tournament starts. Dino and Fred ought to be back from their wall dive soon. I think I'll take a little nap now. I'll see all you guys for a cold one about 5:30."

Seth laid out on his berth and looked up at the headliner. Taking a deep breath, he slowly closed his eyes. The reality of what almost happened came crashing down on him. He thought back to the long periods of time he had spent alone, with his own demons, down in the pitch black cave. Putting hunger, thirst, and pain on top of it all made it a fight for survival. Thinking about what really was important to him got him through it. He would have traded everything he owned to bounce his little grandson Cullen on his knee again, or just to sit out on his porch with his arm around Lori watching a sunset. He thought about relaxing with his buddies and drinking a cold one, just one more time. If he hadn't constantly been working with his fingernails to sever the line holding him, or stomping the crabs attacking him, he might have become as deranged as Peter. During his ordeal, he also suffered the consequences of ignoring Harvey Daniel's number one rule — *Never trust a fart*! However, being surrounded by at least a ton of bat guano had somewhat mitigated that experience. Seth knew, from this day on, he would cherish the little things he'd always taken for granted. As he was thanking his lucky stars for giving him another chance, he dozed off.

***

"Seth looks like he's bouncing back pretty fast," said John. "His ankles are starting to heal, and he's gotten a little bounce back in his step."

"Yeah, he'll probably be pretty much back to normal by tournament time. It's a good thing Peter didn't have him for more than four days," said Gene.

"I just hope he gets enough rest with Lori coming in and all," said Jeb.

"Well, the tournament dinners are always over early, and there's a lay day between the second and third fishing days. Jock will be ready to turn in early since he's fishing too," said John.

"I think it'll all work out ... Seth's a horse," added Gene.

During that exchange, Dino and Fred walked in.

"Hey, Freddy! How was the diving?"

"It was spectacular, clearest water I've ever seen. Lots of big fish along the wall near where we caught the big marlin."

"What about you, Dino?" asked John.

Freddy jumped in and said, "Oh, Dino's in love again. Tell them about Zoe, Dino."

"It was a great dive, and the dive master was gorgeous."

"How about her butt-floss bikini? You followed her around like a puppy dog with your nose up her butt all day."

"OK ... that would be her *spectacular* butt, Freddy."

"Did she look like Miss Stupentaket in Mexico?" laughed John.

"How did you guess?" said Freddy. "She's a tall blonde with high cheekbones, has an rear-end that would bring a tear to your eye, and to top it off she has a nice pair of natural slopers."

"Hey, hey! Her name is Zoe Fugazi, and she's worked for Jock for two years. She has a master's degree in marine biology from The University of Miami, is very intelligent, and we have a lot in common. I happen to have a dinner date with her tonight."

"Are you planning on introducing her to your red-necked friend?" asked John, chuckling.

"All in good time, Doctor, all in good time," said Dino smiling.

"How's Seth doing?" asked Freddy.

"Everything went as expected at the police station. He's in his cabin taking a nap now. Seth is looking better. He wants everybody to go fishing tomorrow — after he and Jeb meet with the FBI agent in the morning," said Gene.

"I'm up for fishing, but I think Jock's going to work tomorrow, and Dino is going diving again," said Freddy.

"I'll cancel if Seth really wants me to go," said Dino.

"It probably won't make any difference. Jeb's going, and Seth asked Rex to go too," said Gene.

"I'm going to hit the shower, but I'll have a beer with you guys before I leave for my date."

"I'm going to have a cold one now, who wants to join me?" asked Fred.

John, Jeb, and Gene raised their hands as Fred made his way to the fridge.

***

Seth, Jeb, and Rex sat in the downtown police station anteroom waiting for the FBI to arrive. They ate breakfast at Aqua, where Rex picked them up at 8:30 in his Jeep Cherokee. The trade winds were blowing 22 knots from the southeast, and the sky was clear. Jeb and Seth dressed in fresh Columbia fishing shirts and Aftco shorts. Rex wore a tropical beige suit, a white shirt, and a blue and white striped tie.

"I have my fishing togs in the back of my Jeep. I also brought lunch and some Turk's Head in my big cooler."

"You shouldn't have done that, Rex. This is supposed to be my treat."

"I'm just making damn sure you'll ask me again when you come back next year."

"You have nothing to worry about, Rex."

Inspector Gordon Hubert opened the door and walked in with a tall, muscular, light-skinned Latin, who looked to be about fifty years old.

"Gentlemen, this is Agent Ricardo Bannon, the FBI attaché from Santo Domingo. He has just been transferred there after eight years as the attaché in Panama. Ricardo, meet Seth Stone, his son Jeb, and their lawyer Rex Hodson."

233

Agent Bannon had a quick smile and a firm handshake. They all moved into Inspector Hubert's office and sat down.

Agent Bannon spoke first, "Inspector Hubert has briefed me on your abduction Mr. Stone, then being held captive in a previously unknown cave, and your fortunate rescue by your son Jeb … before Mr. Petcock could allegedly kill you. It all seems plausible given your actions in Key West and Mexico in 2004 when you helped recover your customer's stolen yacht and assisted the Monroe County Sheriff in putting Mr. Petcock's drug ring in prison. Sheriff Stodgins holds you in the highest regard. I wish there were more Americans like you, sir."

"Thank you, Agent Bannon."

"I do have a couple of questions, though. How certain are you that Mr. Petcock is buried beneath the thousands of tons of limestone that created the new sinkhole? The Inspector took me out early this morning to see both sinkholes in Long Bay Hills."

"Perhaps Jeb could answer the question, Agent Bannon."

"OK."

"I'm 100% certain, Agent Bannon. It all happened in a matter of seconds — no one could have escaped that cave-in."

"Mr. Stone, Mr. Petcock's profile states he is a strong swimmer and a scuba expert. Can you corroborate those facts?"

"Yes, Peter was an all-state swimmer in high school and a commercial diver for most of his life. You probably saw in my deposition he discovered the cave he held me in by swimming a half mile in a dark underground water passage from a nearby sinkhole called The Hole. He found it so he would have a place to hold me captive."

"It had to be very expensive for Mr. Petcock to follow you here for a revenge killing and also plan to flee to Australia. Do you think he has any accomplices?"

"No, other than the prison doctor who may have helped him escape. I think he had a significant amount of his illegal cocaine profits hidden somewhere in Florida."

"Based on everything I've learned here, I can recommend that the U.S. Government can safely close the book on Mr. Petcock. Thank you for your help, gentlemen."

***

Seth felt good to be behind the wheel of his Hatteras. The wind whipped through his hair and the salty smell in the air made him feel alive again. They ran up to Fort George and started trolling east towards Parrot Cay and the rusty wreck. Jeb and Rex reeled in a couple of 60+pound wahoos, and Fred added a nice 40-pound dolphin. They finally got a marlin bite on the downhill run two miles off "Leeward Going Through" passage. Gene got in the chair, but the small blue marlin pulled the hook after his first jump.

They trolled another two hours with no success. Seth zig-zagged the *TAR BABY* down the big swells pushing a little further offshore. Suddenly a marlin appeared out of the blue, chasing the left flybridge teaser.

"Left teaser, left teaser," yelled Seth. "Blue marlin!"

John reacted immediately in his quiet and graceful way, and effortlessly pitched a circle hook rigged horse ballyhoo smoothly in the water. He free spooled the bait back past the teaser as Seth wound the teaser out of the water. The marlin lit up and pounced on the ballyhoo and raced away with the bait in his mouth. John flipped on the clicker, then slowly eased up the drag lever until the circle hook found the corner of the marlin's mouth.

"He's hooked," said John as the fish came tight, and line screamed off the 50-wide reel. John retired to the fighting chair and engaged the marlin as he launched into a series of spectacular jumps. The rest of the crew reeled in the other lines and pulled out the dredge and remaining teasers.

"He looks about 250-300 pounds, John. I'm going to turn the boat and run after him. Get ready to reel."

Soon, Seth turned down-sea, and John reeled the marlin to about 50 yards off the stern. John put the pressure on the tiring fish as Seth backed down on him. Five minutes later Gene and Jeb cleanly released the fish at boat side. The crew whooped and hollered and let their emotions run free. Every victory out here moved Seth farther away from his ordeal with Peter.

An hour later, the crew was back at the dock, hosing down the boat, hoisting cold ones, and chatting about a good day of fishing. The blue marlin flag flew from the starboard rigger and signified that the Geezers were back. Rex went home with a cooler full of wahoo and the crew headed for the showers.

***

"Where do you want to go to dinner tonight, Dad?" asked Jeb, fresh from the shower at his hotel room.

"I'd like to go to the Tiki Hut."

"Really?"

"Yeah, really. See who else wants to go, I'll call Jock and see if he, Rex and Kat would like to join us."

The whole crew walked down the dock at 7:00 p.m. and met Jock and Kat at the Tiki Hut. Dino, smitten as he was, even brought Zoe to join the crowd. Rex showed up five minutes after they took their seats. The ten of them commanded a large table, and they were all in good spirits.

Seth sat next to Kat with Jeb on his other side.

"I'm looking forward to meeting your lady friend Lori and John's wife Stacy," said Kat. "I can't wait for you all to move into our big old empty house; we'll have such fun."

"I hope you don't mind keeping the girls occupied while we're out fishing the tournament," said Seth as he drained his beer.

"It will be fun. We'll hit the spas at the big resorts, do some shopping in Grace Bay, and go snorkeling with Zoe. Then I'll take them over to Cockburn Town on the Grand Turk Ferry for a day trip. Each night it'll be dinner at a different tournament venue with all you boys. They'll get to meet some of my girlfriends too."

"Maybe we can have a pool party on our lay day."

"A 'lay day' sounds like fun to me," said Kat with a wry smile.

Seth turned to Jeb and said, "I think I better take a leak."

236

"I'll go with you if you don't mind."

"No, it's something I've got to do by myself. You know … it will bring me full circle."

Seth walked past the kitchen door, across the dark strip of grass leading to the men's room, and went inside. There was no one at the urinals. He checked under the toilet stall doors and saw no feet. He zipped down and breathed a sigh of relief as he watched the solid yellow stream start. A hinge squeaked, and he turned to look behind him. Peter Petcock burst out of the second stall. Seth swiveled around and pissed all over the tile floor. Peter brandished a serrated dive knife in his right hand — his left arm flopped uselessly at his side. The left side of his face was unrecognizable. He lurched spastically towards Seth, uttering a low primordial scream. Peter slipped as he stepped into the spreading pool of urine. Seth seized that opening to duck under the flailing knife and bury his shoulder into Peter's solar plexus. He drove his aching legs like pistons, crashing Peter's head into an adjoining urinal. He heard Peter's neck snap and let him fall. Seth stood up straight, took a couple of steps, and picked up the dive knife. He edged closer to the urinal. Peter's unseeing eyes were glazed over like a dead mackerel's. Seth flushed the urinal twice, watching the water rush over Peter's disfigured face. He leaned down and felt Peter's neck for a pulse. Seth pulled his Rolex off Peter's limp wrist, smiled, and said out loud, "As Ol' Robert E. would have said, 'Peter Petcock has ridden in his last rodeo'!"

EPILOGUE

THE wind was steady at twenty-two knots, perfect for kiteboarding. Nick Kasaris was on his third run along the Long Bay beach, reaching speeds of more than 30 miles per hour while up on his foil. Suddenly, he saw something yellow floating in the water in front of him. Nick pulled hard on his control bar and went airborne — neatly jumping over the offending flotsam. He looked down as he cleared the object — it was a scuba tank and a yellow BC. Nick sailed his board to the beach, then swam out and retrieved the empty scuba tank and attached BC marked *Dive Provo*. He would return them both to their dive shop in the morning.

***

FBI Agent Ricardo Bannon flew back to Provo from Santo Domingo to positively identify escaped U.S. federal convict Peter Petcock. He viewed Mr. Petcock's body at the TCI Police Station morgue in downtown Provo. Agent Bannon fingerprinted and photographed him, and made further arrangements to ship the body stateside to the Federal Prison in Coleman, Florida for burial.

***

THE Calcutta bidding at the Caicos Classic Billfish Tournament kick-off dinner was brisk. The inimitable auctioneer Gabby Gaposis, Provo's answer to Don Rickles, Richard Quest, and Michael Strahan, deftly bid up all 20 boats, while thoroughly denigrating their respective owners. "It's all for charity, mates," whistled Gabby through his two front teeth. Ray "Jingles" Jones sported some deep pockets, when he paid a tournament Calcutta record of $7500, for team *SPELLBOUND*.

ON the 2007 Caicos Classic Billfish Tournament lay day, Jock and Kat Baffert hosted an authentic native Giant Blue Land Crab boil at the exclusive Meridian Club on Pine Cay in honor of their friend Seth Stone. The crews and significant others of *TAR BABY, SPELLBOUND, SEACOLT, PANOPLY*, and *AFTER FIVE* formed a flotilla to visit the remote Cay, a few miles east of Providenciales.

***

DEBAITABLE won the 2007 Caicos Classic, and the first daily, with four marlin releases. *NO EXCUSE* was second and won the second daily. *OUT O' BOUNDS* finished third, while *SPELLBOUND* took the third daily. *TAR BABY* won the largest wahoo at 93.3 lbs. *PANOPLY* caught the largest dolphin at 32.7 lbs. And *SEACOLT* weighed the largest tuna at 156 lbs.

***

THE two couples delivering *TAR BABY* back to Florida caught three blue marlin and two whites during their leisurely two-week cruise home, as they trolled up through the Bahamas and back across the Gulf Stream. Most nights they anchored in deserted coves, drank wine, and barbecued freshly caught dolphin or wahoo out in the fishing cockpit.

CAICOS CONSPIRACY

AFTERWORD

On June 13th, 2008, The United Kingdom, after years of complaints from concerned Turks and Caicos citizens and business interests, launched a Commission of Inquiry directed by Lord Justice Sir Robin Auld. His yearlong investigation yielded substantiated evidence of widespread, systemic, corruption throughout Prime Minister Michael Misick's administration. Bribery by overseas developers and other investors, illegal sale of Crown Land, misappropriation of public funds, and intimidation (climate of fear) of the country's citizens by government officials, were only a few of the crimes that Sir Robin uncovered. The country was essentially declared bankrupt, and the UK suspended parts of their constitution, installed an interim government, and appointed a Governor. The UK provided a $260 million dollar line of credit to keep the Turks and Caicos Islands financially afloat.

The following year, 13 suspects were indicted on numerous felony counts including the Prime Minister, four of his official cabinet ministers, five of his "kitchen" cabinet ministers, and three overseas developers. The Prime Minister, notorious for his "Hollywood" lifestyle, fled the island. At present (2016), he has been extradited from Brazil and is undergoing trial proceedings. The Governor suspended trial by jury, and a judge was appointed. Many former politicians never faced prosecution because of the complete lack of accurate government records and the absence of campaign fund laws.

The island is once again self-governed but is under the watchful eye of its UK appointed Governor. A new constitution with many new detailed laws defining campaign fund practices, revised Crown Land laws, belonger guidelines, and budgetary regulations, is in place. (Read report @GOV.uk)

***FEBRUARY, 26, 2016. LONDON, ENGLAND — In a written statement to the House of Commons, UK minister of state, Desmond Swayne, announced this Monday the Turks and Caicos Islands had repaid its $260 million line of credit guaranteed by Britain.